THE
PERFECT
NURSE

BOOKS BY DANIEL HURST

THE
PERFECT
NURSE

DANIEL HURST

bookouture

Published by Bookouture in 2024

An imprint of Storyfire Ltd.
Carmelite House
50 Victoria Embankment
London EC4Y 0DZ

www.bookouture.com

ISBN: 978-1-83525-609-1
eBook ISBN: 978-1-83525-608-4

PROLOGUE

I'm standing in front of the bathroom mirror, staring back at the reflection of me in my nurse's uniform, and wondering one thing.

Is the next uniform I see going to belong to a police officer?

The suffocating panic is causing me to grip the sink, and my hands are aching. They are the same hands I have used to treat countless patients, but currently they are not even capable of caring for their owner.

I can see blood on the knuckles of my right hand, an injury caused when I punched the glass photo frame in the hallway two minutes ago. That photo frame, the one that hangs on the wall by my staircase, contains my nursing degree. I worked hard for the qualification, but I don't deserve it anymore.

The blood isn't just on my knuckles. I can see blood on my uniform too. There is a dark red stain on my right sleeve, the crimson soaked into my blue tunic, grimly discolouring them. But this blood is different to that on my hand.

This blood is not mine.

I force myself away from the mirror now, leaving my bathroom and passing the broken photo frame as I head downstairs to the kitchen. In here, I find exactly what I am looking for. A box of matches, in the cupboard above my toaster, and I take the packet out, checking how many matchsticks are inside. I count five, which should be more than enough to get a decent-sized fire going.

Securing the five matchsticks inside a closed fist, I unlock my back door with my spare hand and step out into the backyard. It's summer, but it's the middle of the night so the air is cool, and the blue skies that have lingered over this city for the last six days are still a few hours away from showing themselves again. It's pitch-black out here, but it won't be for much longer.

I place the matchsticks down on my wooden patio table and get to work, quickly stripping off my uniform until I am standing in the cold in nothing but my underwear. After throwing the clothes I've just removed onto the grass in front of me, I pick up the first match and quickly swipe the head of it against the rough surface of the table. The match instantly ignites, but a breeze quickly snuffs out the flame and now this match is no good. I still have four more, so I try again, picking up a second match and repeating the action. The flame on this one burns a little longer but still not long enough. Another swirl of wind through my backyard does two things: it makes me shiver and quickly extinguishes the flame, meaning I'm now going to have to be more careful. I'm quickly running out of matches.

I am more considerate with the third one, very quickly putting one hand around the flame to protect it from the elements, shielding it from the wind, caring for it almost with as much attention as I used to give to my patients. My extra effort is rewarded because the flame doesn't die.

I wish the same could be said for everything else I touch.

Gingerly kneeling down, I guide the lit match towards the pile of clothing on the ground before dropping it onto my nurse's uniform, hoping to see the flame grow much bigger now.

It takes a moment until that happens, and I fear I might have been delayed again, but I see it. The flickering orange glow – but it's not coming from the match this time. It's coming from my pants, the ones I have worn for too long, the ones that mark me out as a nurse, along with the tunic that is now beginning to be affected by the flames.

Not wanting to let the wind blow out the fire while it's still in its earliest stages, I quickly use my two remaining matches to add more flames and, within a minute, my uniform is completely engulfed.

I step back and watch as a strand of smoke begins to rise up from the pile of burning clothes, and I'm almost feeling satisfied enough to stand here and watch the fire reach its inevitable conclusion. But then I remember that I am missing one thing, so I rush back into the house and desperately try to find it.

I locate it on the small table beside my sofa. It's sitting beside an empty wine glass and a bottle of sleeping pills. I scoop it up and run back out into the yard, praying that the fire is still burning brightly. I don't waste another second in tossing my ID badge onto the flames and, while it takes a few seconds, I see the plastic card slowly curling up and turning black as the heat rapidly overpowers it.

As my ID badge is destroyed, away goes the name alongside it and the name of the private nursing company I worked for, as well as the photo of me smiling in happier times. I had always wanted to be a nurse. It was my dream job. From a little girl role-playing at home, curing her parents' pretend ailments, to a grown woman, caring for real patients with deadly diseases, I had lived my dream.

But the dream turned into a nightmare.

I wait patiently until my uniform and ID badge are destroyed and then fetch a bowl of water from the kitchen, dousing the flames with the cooling liquid. The small fire goes out quickly and darkness returns to my backyard. I don't mind that. It's the darkness in my mind that I cannot stand, but that won't be as easy to escape.

Back inside my house, I lock my kitchen door and go upstairs, passing the broken photo frame one more time before entering my bedroom. Then I crawl underneath my sheets, my semi-naked body shivering as tears begin to roll down my cheeks.

I crave sleep, but I'm afraid of the nightmares I'll have. That's because I know I'll see them.

Him, the handsome man who led me astray.

And her, the pretty woman who is no longer alive.

In my troubled state, I cannot recall every single detail of what happened. But I do know one thing. That woman is dead because of me.

I let it happen. I didn't save her.

I broke my duty as her nurse.

The fire I set in the yard was to try and absolve me of all my guilt. But it hasn't worked. I still feel terrible.

Or maybe I simply know the truth, one that is even more frightening than death.

This isn't over yet.

NOW

ONE

It's not my alarm clock that wakes me, which makes sense because I totally forgot to set it last night. It's the loud knocking at my front door that stirs me from my slumber, causing me to glance at the time. I let out a loud groan that doesn't even begin to encapsulate the tiredness I feel.

I continue to lie in bed and make a wish that the knocking was nothing more than a figment of my imagination, a remnant of a dream I was having, perhaps, but then I hear it again.

It's the third knock that confirms I really have to get out of bed to go and answer it.

Reluctantly peeling back my sheets, I catch a glimpse of my slim body in my underwear in the mirror before I quickly grab the large sweatshirt lying on the carpet by my bed and pull that on. It's big enough to cover my top half and goes down to my knees. I get out of bed and place my bare feet on my bedroom floor. It's a floor that's littered with other items of my clothing, including a blue uniform that gives me a strange sense of unease when I spot it. But it's not as much as the unease I feel when I see the ID badge attached to the front of the tunic and the words that are printed on it.

Darcy Miller
Chestbrook Nursing

The woman in the photo beside the writing looks very different to the woman I see when I look in the mirror again, really studying my reflection this time. The person on the ID badge looks radiant, beaming widely, her brown hair tied neatly back, brown eyes full of light and her skin showing a healthy pink glow. But the woman in my mirror looks dishevelled, the same hair hanging loosely down to my shoulders, desperately needing a wash, while my eyes are dull, and my skin is red and blotchy. Most of all, there is no sign of the warm smile. But I know I am that same woman. It's just that this is a different day. Time has passed since that ID photo was taken. Things have happened.

But what are those things?

My foggy head makes it hard to have the energy to recall them all this early in the morning, and as I accidentally stumble over a bottle of sleeping pills on the floor, I guess the medication did its job in knocking me out last night, to get some rest. But I hardly feel refreshed as I put the pills on my bedside table so that I'll be able to easily locate them later.

I slept.

But I still had nightmares.

I hear the knocking again, and it's almost a good thing – it stops me dwelling on what I saw in my bad dreams. Instead, it forces me to leave my messy bedroom and head for the staircase. As I do, I see a couple of photo frames on the wall, hanging on white wallpaper, the colours inside them standing out starkly in this otherwise blandly decorated hallway. One of the frames shows a photo of a group of six nurses, all in scrubs and all with their arms around each other, smiling for the camera in a hospital operating room. I see myself in the middle of these women, smiling again, yet it feels so foreign to me because I cannot imagine being that happy now.

My eyes move across to the second frame and this one contains a medical certificate. I see my name printed on the qualification, the words *Darcy Miller* just above *University of Michigan*; and the university logo is proudly emblazoned alongside the writing, a large yellow *M* that adds even more colour to my drab surroundings.

My head is thumping as I wearily put one foot in front of the other, and I'm barely halfway down the stairs when I hear another knock.

'I'm coming,' I say, though it's barely audible, nowhere near loud enough for the person at my door to hear it. My throat is so dry, and I'm desperate for water, but I first need to answer this knocking. The noise is giving me even more of a headache than I've woken up with.

Reaching my door, I fumble for the key hanging from it. As I turn it and twist the handle, I feel a rush of cool air seeping into my chilly home.

'Here she is! Rise and shine! It's looking like it's going to be another lovely day!'

I grimace at the loud voice coming from the woman on my doorstep as I notice her dark hair tied back, her warm smile and the uniform she is wearing. It's the same colour uniform as the one upstairs on my bedroom floor, and pinned to it is an ID badge also very similar to mine.

PIPPA SIMPSON
CHESTBROOK NURSING

'Come on, sleepy head, you better go and get dressed. We need to get to work!'

Pippa seems amused at my lack of preparedness as she steps into my house, even though I don't remember inviting her in.

But she's comfortable here and she proves it with what she says next.

'I'll make us a coffee while you get ready,' she tells me as she heads for my kitchen. 'I'm guessing you'll need an extra strong one today.'

I watch as Pippa disappears into my kitchen before I close the front door to stop any more of the cold creeping in. Pippa was right, it does look like it will be a nice day today, but it's early and the sun is nowhere near at its highest point yet, so we're yet to feel the comforting benefits of the heat that's on the way.

I hear Pippa moving around in my kitchen and detect the sound of my coffee machine whirring to life, that useful household appliance waking up more efficiently than I have today.

'I don't feel well,' I admit to her, hoping this will disrupt my colleague's momentum and make her realise that I'm not in a fit state to go to work today. But surprisingly, Pippa seems to have been expecting that – she simply tells me that I'll feel better when I get out of the house.

'I know you're not a morning person, but I know you're a damn good nurse, so get your uniform on and let's get going,' Pippa says as the machine spits out our drinks. 'One cup of caffeine coming right up!'

Pippa's energy is in stark contrast to my own; but there's something infectious about it and I have to admit I do feel better for her being here. If not, I'd still be lying in bed having those nightmares – or worse, I'd be awake and alone and it's always better to have company, even for someone who is definitely not a morning person.

'Be right back,' I say as I leave the kitchen and go upstairs to get myself ready, more motivated than I was a few moments ago now that there is the promise of a coffee on the way. I need it – I'm feeling very groggy. As I return to my bedroom, I see the sleeping pills again and wonder if this is a side effect from them.

Sure, they helped me sleep, but if it means I wake up like a zombie, is it worth it?

I don't have time to dwell on that because I have to go to work, so I quickly pick up my crumpled uniform and start putting it on. It's clear that I should have hung it in my wardrobe as it's badly creased, and I desperately try and smooth out some of the wrinkles before giving up and hoping that they aren't noticeable enough for anybody else to see them and judge me. Time is of the essence, so once I'm dressed, I go to my dressing table and quickly apply some concealer, grab a hair tie and make my dark locks look a little more presentable. Then all that's left to do is adjust my ID badge on my chest so that it's straight rather than wonky and I guess I'm good to go.

I pick up my phone and check for any messages, though there are none, so I rush downstairs to find my shoes. Pippa is already by the front door waiting for me, a cup of coffee in each hand and an expression on her face that tells me she is used to having to wait for me in the mornings.

'Well, I guess you look more alive now,' she says with a laugh before handing me a cup of hot coffee. 'I have flasks in the car that we can pour our coffee into. But we better drink while we're on the road. We're already late.'

Pippa opens the front door and heads for her car, which is parked at the top of my driveway. It's a stylish vehicle, not particularly large, but trendy; it's not enough to make me feel like driving myself. There's no car on my driveway and that's because I never feel the urge to get behind the wheel. It means I'm less likely to be involved in a traffic accident, I suppose, as well as saving plenty of money that would otherwise go on insurance premiums and gas refills, so that's a bonus. But it does make getting around trickier, though I have no problems with Pippa here to transport me.

I think about putting on a coat but figure it will be warm enough soon, so I leave my house and lock the front door behind me. Then I join Pippa in her blue car – the perfect colour for a nurse as it almost matches our uniforms – taking my spot in the passenger seat as she hands me an empty flask.

'Pour your coffee into here. And be careful not to spill on the seats. I only had this cleaned at the weekend.'

I do as I'm told, carefully pouring the coffee from the cup into the flask and then placing the empty cup into the holder in between us. My first sip of my drink works wonders for my mood. As the caffeine instantly gets to work on waking me up further, Pippa starts the engine.

'Did you sleep well last night?' she asks me as we move down my street, passing numerous other properties that look just like mine. All modest duplexes, twin homes that are reasonably sized and all with cars parked in the driveways. I see a few of my neighbours as they leave their homes to begin their day too, including a mother who shouts after her two children as they race to their car, satchels on their backs and looks of mischief on their faces.

'I know you're never chatty in the mornings, so while I wait for that coffee to work its magic, let me tell you about where we're going today,' Pippa says as she steers us off my avenue and onto the main street. 'We've got a new patient. Their notes are on the backseat if you want to take a look. It's the part where it lists their address that caught my eye, though. They live in Sherwood Crescent. Yep, one of the most exclusive streets in Chicago.'

Pippa seems very excited to get to where we're going, and as I turn and reach onto the backseat to grab the notes, I might not be quite as excited as she is, but I am intrigued.

A new patient in an exclusive part of town?

I guess I better wake up soon, because it sounds like it's going to be a busy day.

TWO

The houses we're passing by are gradually getting bigger, the lawns in front of them greener and more maintained, and the vehicles on the driveways more expensive and stylish, but we're not quite at our destination yet.

Looking from the window back down to the notes on my lap, I see the patient's name as well as her address.

Scarlett Hoffman
1 Sherwood Crescent
Winnetka
Chicago, IL 60093

'I wonder if we'll pass the *Home Alone* house,' Pippa says breezily as we come to a stop at a red light. 'It's somewhere in Winnetka, right?'

I'm not sure, but I'm more interested in the patient's medical history. I find it quickly.

Scarlett first presented at the emergency room at Chicago General last summer with a head injury she said was caused by an accident at home (kitchen fall). A scan revealed intracranial hemorrhage, and she was operated on to release pressure in her skull. Scarlett recovered well from the operation and left hospital after two weeks to return home. She reported short-term memory loss issues – misplacing items, forgetting familiar faces, important dates – and underwent tests at Clearbridge Medical Center. An MRI scan revealed mild cognitive impairment; patient is to be monitored.

My eyes glance over several numbers that reveal the results of various memory tests as Pippa gets us moving on.

Symptoms worsened and another scan revealed further cognitive impairment, and signs of infection. Patient was scheduled for an immediate craniotomy where the infection was treated. However, patient's cognitive functions continued to decline and long-term memory loss became prominent.

Pippa says something about an annoying driver in front of us, cursing at one point, but I ignore her and keep reading, picking up other important details that will help me when I get to the patient.

- *Therapy*
- *Rehabilitation*
- *Confusion*
- *More scans*

These notes are painting a bleak tale, but it's the final part of them that is the worst.

Further tests showed a continual deterioration in the prefrontal cortex and patient requiring more assistance. Daily assistance with care required. Potential around-the-clock care recommended. Patient's husband requested patient remain at home, and private nursing sought to help as care becomes more necessary.

It's an awful medical history, but I feel even worse when I look at the patient's age and see fifty-eight typed in the box. Shaking my head and feeling an overwhelming sadness, I think about how this woman is not elderly. She's not yet sixty and is only twenty years older than me, yet her life is now one that involves nurses visiting her home to help her with the most basic of daily tasks.

'Are you okay?' Pippa asks me when she realises I've not spoken for a while.

'She's so young,' I say sadly, glancing at my colleague, and Pippa nods solemnly.

'Yeah, it's a real shame. Our patients are usually much older.'

'This was all caused by a fall in her kitchen?' I ask, looking back at the beginning of the notes, troubled by the apparent randomness of what has caused her condition.

'Yeah, she slipped and banged her head. It's one of those fancy kitchens with marble countertops and a tiled floor. Looks nice, and costs a lot, but it's an absolute hazard when the floor is wet. I believe she had just finished mopping the floor when it happened.'

'That's awful,' I say, though, of course, there's no type of brain damage that is good news. 'Imagine your whole life changing in a split second while doing an everyday thing.'

'I know. It's frightening, isn't it?' Pippa replies, shaking her head, and I feel slightly bad for bringing the mood down in the car, so I decide to steer the conversation onto less troubling grounds and recall the details Pippa just gave about the kitchen where this accident took place.

'You've already been to the house?' I ask.

'Yeah, the boss sent me last week to do a survey. The house is huge. Seriously, the biggest one I've ever been in, and that's saying something, because we've been in some big ones over the years, haven't we? But there's a sad atmosphere in there now, which is understandable.'

'What's the husband like?' I enquire, caring less about the property and more about the people who live in it, because that's all that matters.

'Adrian? He's nice, I suppose. Very polite. He seems to be holding up well considering what he's going through.'

Pippa steers us onto a wide street. Here the front lawns are so big and the houses beyond them set so far back that the front yards could almost double as parks.

'Imagine being a delivery driver here,' Pippa says with a chuckle. 'It must take five minutes just to get to the front doors.'

It's barely an exaggeration and I think about what the people who live here must do for work. Then it's as if Pippa reads my mind with what she says next.

'I'm guessing none of these properties belong to nurses,' she says with a self-deprecating smirk. 'They're clearly far too clever to have gone into our line of work, or they wouldn't be living in these mansions, that's for sure.'

Pippa looks at me and rolls her eyes, and I smile, though strangely I don't feel like I care about the reality behind the joke my colleague just made. Things like a high salary and owning a big house don't feel important to me, which might make me slightly unusual, but I guess it means I went into this profession for the right reasons, rather than chasing dollars in something more lucrative but far less rewarding.

I look back down at the notes again for anything else that might help me before we get to the patient's home, but there's nothing more, other than some blood test results and baseline recordings for things like blood pressure and heart rate. Of course, notes can only take a nurse so far, and there is no substitute for time spent with the patient, observing them at close quarters, so I know that I'll learn much more when we are with Scarlett herself. But the closer we get, the more I start to feel a knot twisting in my stomach. I don't know why I feel nervous, just that I do, and I wonder if it's another side effect of my sleeping pills. They might cause anxiety, or maybe I'm still waking up, so I quickly chug down the last of the coffee in my flask in the hopes that it perks me up and brings me up to Pippa's level sooner rather than later.

'Here we are,' my colleague says as the sign for Sherwood Crescent comes into view, and Pippa reduces her speed right down to no more than five miles per hour as we turn onto the exclusive street. There are two big homes on each side of the crescent, but it's the huge house in between them, immediately opposite us, that really draws my eye. As Pippa keeps going, I realise this is the property we are aiming for.

'Oh my gosh, it's massive,' I say as I marvel at the three-storey Georgian-style home, as well as the weeping willow that stands proudly in the front yard, a space that – in total, after counting the sides and back too – is probably half the size of a football field and must keep a gardener occupied for several days a month.

'Told you it was cool,' Pippa says as our car's wheels leave the blacktop and roll onto the curved driveway that leads all the way up to a double garage, outside of which sits a vintage vehicle that could be a passion project for the owner.

'What do the Hoffmans do for work?' I ask, still marvelling at this place.

'I think he was some fancy director at a big hospital,' Pippa says.

'Really?'

'Yeah, and that's not all. Scarlett was a nurse. Ironic, isn't it?

They've spent their lives caring for others and now they need people to care for them.'

It is ironic. It's also a shame that, even with all their medical knowledge, they haven't been able to improve their situation, which shows that there mustn't be anything that can be done to make it better, only more tolerable.

As impressive as this all is, I still feel anxious – the closer we get, the more uncomfortable I become. I put the flask back to my lips but it's empty, and fearing that the caffeine hasn't quite worked, I lower the passenger window to get some air inside the car.

'Are you okay?' Pippa asks me, looking genuinely concerned for a moment.

'Yeah,' I mumble as I feel a breeze blowing onto my face, but it's still not enough to calm the sense of unease I feel. As Pippa parks, I'm wishing that I could go back home. But I don't want to go back to bed because I'm still sleepy and feeling lazy, nor do I want to leave because these patient notes make it sound like this is not going to be a pleasant job.

I want to go home because something feels very wrong about this place.

'Let's go in,' Pippa says as she opens her door and gets out, moving with a stoic energy that shows she is used to working hard and knows it's better to get on with it and get it over with rather than hesitate and prolong the issue. But I remain in my seat for a few more seconds, looking at the front of the house and glancing back at the patient notes that are still in my lap.

Why do I feel like this? This is just another patient and just another job. One more day in my life as a nurse. Sure, this house is huge and the patient inside it needs our care, but there's nothing special about that to have me feeling like this.

Is there something in the notes that's troubling me?

I quickly reread them, wondering if something written here has triggered a memory of a former patient I treated and I'm getting déjà vu, or whether there is something new that I need to worry about. But it seems like a perfectly normal case, sadly, in that a person has a medical condition caused by something outside of their control and now they require our attention.

Pippa knocks on the passenger-side window, making me jump and causing me to drop the notes into the footwell.

'Come on,' I see her mouthing, so I quickly gather up the notes by my feet before getting out of the car to join my colleague.

'Looks like I should have made you a stronger coffee,' Pippa says, rolling her eyes at my pace of work. She opens the trunk and takes out the medical bag inside. As she locks the car, I glance back at the house but don't see anybody at the windows. Adrian, the husband, is surely expecting us, but I guess he's waiting for us to knock. Then I remember the condition his poor wife is in and feel bad for thinking he should have come out to greet us – he's obviously got his hands full inside the house, caring for his stricken spouse.

'Time to get to work,' Pippa says as she strides towards the front door, and I follow her, though very slowly and only because I have to, not because I want to.

Maybe I need to go easier on those sleeping pills, I think to myself as I see Pippa walking up the three stone steps that lead to the black front door. *It's surely not healthy to be feeling this tired and anxious at any time of the day, never mind before a busy day. Especially in my line of work.*

Snapping myself into action, I catch Pippa up and, as she knocks on the front door, I tell myself to get my head in the game, because there is a reason that two of us have been sent here today instead of just one. It's clearly a two-person job, and Pippa is going to need me as much as I need her over these next several hours while we are caring for Scarlett, so I will endeavour to do my best.

As the pair of us wait for the front door to open, I take a

deep breath and ready myself for the challenges to come. As always in nursing, it's going to be as much about a positive attitude as it is about medical expertise and training.

I can do this.

I am good at this.

So why am I so nervous?

THREE

'Hi, thank you for coming. Please come in.'

My first impression of Adrian, the man currently welcoming us into his home, is that he is incredibly well groomed as well as very polite. He looks to be in his late fifties, which I had already assumed considering his wife is in her fifties too, though he wears his age well. He moves with an easy confidence, not so much worn down by over five decades of life, but seemingly at ease with how his body has changed over the years. I could be forgiven for assuming he might look exhausted or depressed considering what is happening to the woman he loves, but if he is devasted by it then he is doing a very good job of covering it up.

He is a tall man, easily over six feet, and has broad shoulders too, which makes me wonder if he currently exercises a lot or has retained a lot of muscle mass from a more active life in his youth. He's wearing a smart green sweater and dark jeans, and the glint from the gold watch on his wrist catches my eye, making me wonder how much that particular timepiece cost.

Not nearly as much as this house, I'm sure.

'Thank you,' Pippa says as Adrian holds the door open for

us while we step inside, and as I pass him my nostrils detect the scent of his aftershave. It's not that it's an unpleasant smell, it's far from it, but it gives me a strange sense of unease again and I'm wondering what it is about this particular place and this homeowner that's making me feel on edge.

'How was the traffic on the way over? It can be a bit of a nightmare at this time of day,' Adrian says as I notice him locking the door behind us. This doesn't seem like a dangerous neighbourhood, but then it's probably a prime target for criminals – anyone who lives here is clearly a multimillionaire – so I suppose it makes sense for him to be cautious.

'The traffic was no trouble,' Pippa replies cheerily, and I notice she has neglected to mention the fact that she cursed at a careless driver on the way here, which is probably for the best. I'm not sure this man would appreciate it if he knew one of the women tasked with caring for his ailing wife was prone to losing her temper when driving.

'Can I get either of you a drink?' Adrian asks now as I look around at the spacious hallway we stand in. A large staircase rises up in front of us, the steps flanked on both sides by a curving wooden bannister, and all along the wall by the stairs are paintings in gold frames, works of art that I don't recognise but look impressive. To my left is a doorway and I can see a plush white sofa and a large fireplace beyond that, while to my right is an open door through which I can see a wall-to-ceiling bookcase full of hardback books, which all look very highbrow.

'I wouldn't say no to a coffee,' Pippa replies. 'And I'm sure Darcy will have one too. Right, Darcy?'

I realise I've lost myself in gazing around this home and quickly try to make it look like I wasn't gawking at the stunning interior that surrounds us.

'Coffee? Yeah, sure. That would be great, thank you.'

'No trouble at all. I'll be right back. You can take a seat in the living room while you wait. It's just through there.'

I already know where the lounge is because I spotted the sofa a few moments ago, but I pretend as if I needed the directions and smile at Adrian as he heads away to the kitchen.

The kitchen where his poor wife had her accident.

'Wakey wakey,' Pippa says to me, clearly amused by how dopey I have been so far this morning. She enters the lounge, and I quickly follow her in.

'Wow, would you look at this place,' Pippa says quietly, not wanting Adrian to overhear how blown away she is by his house. 'This room is almost as big as my entire home.'

'It's incredible,' I agree, noting the stylish coffee table by the sofas as well as the large bay window that looks out onto the backyard.

I approach the window, look outside and spot a bench out there as well as several well-maintained flowerbeds. It makes me wonder if Scarlett and Adrian spend a lot of time outside enjoying their garden. Perhaps they sit on that bench together and relax in nature. Or maybe those days are over, at least for Scarlett anyway.

Where is the patient? I assume she must be in bed upstairs, but I guess we'll be introduced to her soon enough.

'What do you think? Could you live in a place like this?' Pippa asks me as she runs her hand along the top of the stone fireplace.

'I wish,' I reply, taking a seat on one of the sofas and nervously clasping my hands together. I still feel very awkward.

Pippa sits down beside me as we wait for Adrian to return with our drinks, but as we do I suddenly realise we've forgotten something.

'The notes are in the car. I better go and get them,' I say, feeling foolish for not bringing them in with us, but Pippa stops me.

'Don't worry about them. Notes are only so good. It's quality time with the patient that counts, and we'll get that soon enough. We'll learn far more from that than from any notes.'

Pippa seems to be talking from experience and it makes me wonder why I don't seem to be drawing on my own experience to ease my time here. For some reason, I feel as jittery as if this was my first day on the job, even though it's obviously not, and the more I think about it, the more I think I need to pay attention to my own health issues as well as other people's. Maybe I need anxiety meds or perhaps I should come off the sleeping pills if they're making me feel this zoned out, even if they're the only way I can sleep lately. But I'm not the priority here, Scarlett is, and as Adrian returns, I refocus my attention to the task at hand.

'Thank you very much,' I say as I accept my coffee, and once Pippa has hers and Adrian has taken a seat in the armchair by the fireplace, I decide to prove to Pippa that I'm not going to be totally useless today by leading the first part of our conversation with this man who is paying for us to be here.

'First of all, I just wanted to say how sorry I am to learn about what happened with your wife. It sounds like it was a tragic accident and it's such a shame, but I want you to know that we are here to help and make things easier for both her and for you.'

Adrian seems to appreciate my sentiment and, when I glance at Pippa, I see she seems impressed too. I guess I'm not totally useless at this time of the morning, after all.

'Thank you,' Adrian replies as he sits back in his seat and crosses his legs, looking even more relaxed than he already has done since we arrived. 'Your services come highly recommended, and I know I've made the right decision hiring you. I certainly do need the extra help. Things haven't been easy.'

'Where is Scarlett now?' I ask, noting a photo on the wall by the door, which I missed when I walked in. It's an image of Adrian and who I presume to be his wife, smiling in a restau-

rant, a couple of glasses of red wine in front of them, and they
look totally at ease. I stare at the image of the woman, noting her
jet-black hair and her smart red blouse, and I wonder when it
was taken – probably a few years ago because Adrian looks a
little younger in it than he does now. That means it was before
Scarlett's accident, during a time when they probably felt they
had so many happy years together left to enjoy. There would
have been years that seemed to stretch out endlessly ahead of
them until fate cruelly intervened, and left them requiring two
nurses to become a part of their daily life.

'She's in our bedroom. I find she's most comfortable there,'
Adrian replies as I look away from the photo and back at him.
'It's rather a lot of work to get her downstairs now and I find she
becomes more confused that way, so she tends to stay upstairs.
There's a television in there for her, plus all her favourite books,
not that she can concentrate on them for too long anymore. I've
tried to make her as comfortable as I can but...' Adrian's voice
trails off and he looks upset. But he's staring at me, and I feel the
urge to say something, anything, that might make him feel better
in this moment, so I say the first thing that comes to my mind.

'You're doing the best you can, but you're not superman,
which is why we're here to help. So let us support you both,
okay?'

Adrian is still staring at me, and I see him wipe a tear from
his eyes before he nods and smiles.

'Thank you,' he says. 'Sorry, I'm very tired. It's been a long
process. There was the shock of the accident and then the after-
math. It's been brutal. Memory loss is an awful thing. I just
wish she would get better.'

'No need to apologise at all,' I say, and I notice a box of
tissues on the table in between us so I quickly pass them to the
homeowner. 'Of course this is going to be hard, and it's important that you acknowledge it rather than let it build up inside
you.'

Adrian takes a tissue and wipes his eyes as I look to Pippa to see if she has anything to add.

'Why don't you tell us a little about Scarlett before we go and see her?' she suggests, and that sounds like a good idea. 'Anything that might help us as we care for her. What was her normal personality like? What are her hobbies, passions?'

Adrian's face lights up then for a moment.

'Oh, she was wonderful. Very chatty. So funny too, though she never seemed to realise it. But she always made me laugh. She still does now, occasionally. She was always a very active person. She used to swim a lot. And she got involved in amateur dramatics. She kept very busy.'

'I believe you both worked in medicine?' I say, hoping it's not a bad thing that I recall what Pippa told me in the car.

'That's right. We met working in a hospital. I eventually became a director, but back in the day I was a pimply faced doctor starting out, and I know it's probably a cliché for a man to say my head was turned by a pretty nurse, but that's what Scarlett was. She was a damn good one too. We both shared the same passion for medicine and caring for others, and it was a pleasure to fall in love as our careers blossomed. But we both took early retirement at fifty. Our jobs were fulfilling, but tiring. We'd earned enough and we had lots of plans together. We wanted to see more of the world and spend more time with our grandson and any other potential grandkids that came along.'

'You have children?' I ask, and I'm a little surprised because I haven't seen any family photos around the place yet, although it turns out there is a good reason for that.

'Yes. Two daughters. Both grown. And a grandson. He's a beautiful little boy.'

'Do they visit much?' I ask, curious as to how the family have managed Scarlett's condition.

'They used to, but it's harder now,' Adrian replies, shaking his head sadly. 'Scarlett gets very confused and very distressed.

It's why there's no photos around here. It was upsetting her when I tried to tell her who people were. She gets so mixed up now. It's why we don't take her out anymore either. She'd see random women in the street and think one of them was her daughter. It's all very difficult. She also occasionally remembers caring for people with memory loss when she was a nurse and she saw what happened to them, so that doesn't make it any easier.'

'I understand,' I say, not wanting to make this poor man need another tissue when we've barely been in his house for ten minutes. I also don't want Pippa asking anything else in case it upsets him again, so I decide that now is the right time to get to work.

'I think it's time we meet Scarlett,' I say with a smile, forcing this situation to become more positive.

Adrian agrees, so we all quickly finish our drinks and stand up. But, as we leave the room and head for the stairs, I also feel like I'm forcing myself to be more positive too. Despite how lovely Adrian seems, I'm still getting the sense there is something not quite right about all of this.

I guess I won't know for sure until I meet the patient.

It's time to say hello to Scarlett.

FOUR

'Scarlett, dear? The nurses are here to see you. We're coming in.'

Adrian has called through the closed bedroom door and now he is very tentatively opening it, allowing the three of us lurking in the hallway to see inside.

The bedroom is dark as we enter but, as more light filters in, I see the shape of somebody in the bed across the room. As we step in, I get my first proper look at my new patient.

Scarlett is sitting up in the bed and watching a movie on the TV that sits on top of a dressing table beside a large wardrobe. Her dark hair hangs listlessly down by her shoulders, and she looks pale. She grimaces slightly at the extra light as we walk in. Without make-up and in a shabby set of pyjamas, this woman doesn't look particularly glamorous but, of course, that is not her fault. My priority now is to make her comfortable, and that begins with putting the patient at ease as quickly as possible.

'Hi, Scarlett,' I say as I approach the bed, and Pippa gives her own greeting too.

'These are the nurses we spoke about,' Adrian says tentatively. I guess that is because he isn't sure if his wife is going to recall him telling her that nurses were going to be visiting. But Scarlett looks at Pippa and me and then smiles, which is a relief, because I guess she does remember.

As I pass the television, I glance at the screen and see the movie playing, though I'm not sure what it is. The grainy footage suggests it's old, so I've probably never seen it, but there's something comforting about the actress on screen. I guess it might be making Scarlett feel the same way.

'I'm Pippa and this is Darcy,' my colleague says as we reach the bedside, still smiling at Scarlett to show her that we are friendly and to be trusted. 'How are you feeling today, Scarlett?'

'I'm okay,' she replies, though it's not very convincing.

'You can be honest with them,' Adrian chips in. 'You don't need to pretend if you aren't okay.'

'I'm splendid!' she snaps back, I'm guessing sarcastically, and he immediately goes quiet.

There's a slightly awkward silence and Pippa and I laugh to break the ice.

'Don't worry, I snap at my husband all the time too,' Pippa says, rolling her eyes at Adrian as if men are always the ones to blame, and he shrugs his shoulders as if he can't disagree there.

I glance at Pippa's left hand now because I hadn't noticed a ring there earlier and, sure enough, there isn't one, which makes me wonder what the current state of her marriage is. I don't recall her mentioning she was having problems, but the fact her ring is off, plus the joke she made that might not actually have been in complete jest, makes me wonder if there is trouble in her personal life. But there's no time for me to ask questions – we're busy here.

'How about we do a couple of routine checks, just to get started?' Pippa suggests, placing her medical bag down on a chair, unzipping it and rummaging inside. As she takes out a blood pressure monitor, I notice Scarlett is watching me, and I smile. Then I realise that I'm blocking her view of the TV, so I step to the side in case I've been annoying her. But her eyes don't go onto the TV. Instead, they stay squarely focused on me, and it's slightly unsettling.

'Okay, let's check your blood pressure,' Pippa says. 'Can I have your arm, please?'

Scarlett seems to come out of whatever trance she was in because she looks to Pippa before raising her right arm. Pippa wraps the cuff around the patient's limb and switches the device on, allowing the cuff to inflate. As she waits for the readings, I look between the machine and the patient, wondering if Scarlett seems to be finding this distressing or if she is used to it by now. I expect she's been subjected to a myriad of tests at various hospitals and specialist clinics, so this must be quite normal for her now – it seems that way. Pippa takes the readings and jots them down in a notebook before unstrapping the cuff and putting the machine to one side.

'May I check your heart rate?' she asks next. She gently takes Scarlett's wrist, placing two fingers on her skin and feeling for the pulse while scrunching up her nose in concentration. She smiles to indicate that everything is normal there.

I notice Scarlett is watching me again and, when I look back to the bottom of the bed, Adrian is too, so I smile awkwardly, but without anybody talking it seems a bit strange. I'm starting to feel like a bit of a spare part with my colleague doing all the work, but then Pippa hands me a penlight.

'Can you check Scarlett's pupils?' she asks.

'Erm, yeah, sure,' I say, relieved to have the chance to busy myself, and I click the light on before bringing it closer to Scarlett's face.

I had already noticed the patient had dark eyes, but as I examine them more closely, I see they are almost black. The only light in them seems to be coming from the instrument I'm using, because Scarlett is certainly not in any way energetic or excited, which is understandable given her position.

'Everything okay?' Pippa asks me, her pen poised above the pages of her notebook.

'Erm, yeah, fine,' I reply, shutting off the light and handing it back to her.

I feel bad for Scarlett for having to put up with two women entering her bedroom and essentially poking and prodding her while she's trying to watch a movie. She's gone back to looking at the television before Pippa can move on to the next test.

'Why don't you have a chat with Adrian while I finish up with the checks?' Pippa suggests, probably sensing that I'm not quite on top of my game at this moment in time, and Adrian says that sounds like a good idea.

I feel bad for leaving Pippa to conduct the checks alone, but it also feels like a relief to have the chance to get out of this dark bedroom, so I follow Adrian back out into the brightly lit hallway without saying another word.

'Let's take a walk,' he says to me after closing the door behind us, and I follow him back down the stairs, hoping Pippa is managing okay without me, but figuring there are things Adrian needs to say that are best said when not in the presence of his wife.

'Would you like another drink?' he asks me as we enter the kitchen, but I politely decline because I've already had two coffees – any more will give me more of a headache than I've already got. Besides, the caffeine doesn't seem to have had much of an effect on me today, so there's no point consuming extra.

'I wish it was later or I'd have something a little stronger,' Adrian says as he prepares to make himself a drink, and I feel for him because I'm certain he's not joking.

'Have you been using alcohol to cope?' I ask him, speaking without properly thinking it through, but I guess that's my nurturing side coming out.

'For a short while, but I quickly got on top of that,' Adrian replies as he grabs a bag of coffee beans from a cupboard. 'Things are hard enough without adding hangovers to the equation.'

As he turns his back to me to work the coffee machine, I look around the impressive kitchen. In the centre of the room is a marble breakfast bar, a perfect place to meal-prep, while on both sides of it are two long countertops filled with all sorts of fancy appliances alongside the coffee machine, like a touch-screen toaster, a water filtration unit and a blender that looks like it could make very light work of anything tossed inside it. The fridge is enormous, easily four times the size of the one I have at home, while there are enough cupboards here to house a similar number of utensils as any of the aisles in my local Home Depot store. But it's the tiled floor that I find myself staring at the longest, for one very sad reason.

'So this is where it happened?' I ask Adrian, and he stops what he's doing and turns back around.

'Sorry?'

'Scarlett's accident. She slipped and banged her head here?'

'Oh, right. Yeah. She'd just mopped the floor. It was all wet and I guess she lost her footing.'

'You guess? You weren't with her at the time?'

'Me? No, I wasn't.'

'Where were you?'

Adrian frowns. 'Does it matter? I don't see how it would have made any difference.'

I note that Adrian seems to be getting a little defensive on this subject, but maybe I'm being harsh – it's obviously always going to be a very sore topic for him.

'Sorry, I'm trying to paint a picture of what happened, that's all,' I say gently.

'I was upstairs taking a shower. When I got out, I called out to Scarlett but got no answer, so came down and I found her lying here, unconscious. I called nine-one-one and they were here within ten minutes. Anything else you need to know?'

I shake my head, but Adrian must sense that I picked up on how edgy he became – he fills the silence quickly.

'Of course I regret not being with her. Maybe I could have caught her before she hit her head, or got her medical attention sooner, but I wasn't present. It was a stupid accident and now all our lives have been changed forever.'

He looks on the verge of tears again and I feel awful for bringing him to this point, so I rush towards him and put a reassuring hand on his shoulder.

'It's going to be okay,' I tell him. 'Things will get easier now we're here to help each day.'

'I really hope so,' he says as he wipes his eyes, but he still looks very upset, so I push things a little further than I perhaps should.

'Come here,' I say, wrapping my arms around him and hoping that a friendly hug will lift his spirits, and while I'm initially not sure if he is going to accept it, he quickly does and gives me a tight squeeze.

He clearly needs a shoulder to cry on and I don't mind being that for him, at least while his children and network of friends aren't here. I suppose as a nurse it's never just the patient we're caring for but the patient's loved ones as well. As we embrace, I feel like I'm doing the best I can in this given moment, and when we separate he turns back to the coffee machine to finish making his drink.

I take a seat on one of the stools at the breakfast bar as I wait for him to join me. We have lots to talk about as I create a care plan to help Scarlett, but we will also have to figure out a way for Adrian to get whatever support he needs too. While I wait for him to sit down opposite me, I look down at the hard floor beneath my stool for a second and a troubling thought crosses my mind, because of Adrian's defensive behaviour when I first mentioned his wife's incident in here.

Did Scarlett really slip accidentally in this kitchen?

Or is there more to this couple's story than meets the eye?

FIVE

I have been sitting with Adrian and listening to him talk about his wife's condition and what it means for their daily life for the last twenty minutes. In all that time, I've been wrestling with the sense that something is not quite as it seems here. Rather than ask any questions that could get me in trouble if I'm wrong, I have chosen to simply stay quiet and let this man speak, though I have been taking notes as these could be helpful in future.

'Sometimes she needs help eating a meal or washing herself, help that I'm more than happy to give, except sometimes she doesn't recognise who I am,' Adrian says, staring vacantly at me when I look up from my notes. 'One day she knows that I'm her husband and she says she loves me and, the next, she shouts at me to get out of her bedroom. It's just so unpredictable.'

'I understand,' I say, though thankfully I cannot even begin to imagine the true reality of living like that, because there's only so much you can learn by being a nurse. It must be very different to actually live with memory loss and not recognise the faces of your loved ones. I can see why it is so upsetting for Adrian when that occurs.

'It's exhausting,' Adrian says sadly. 'Waking up every day and having to essentially convince someone I love of who I am and why I'm with them. I just wish her memory would come back but, so far, nothing. I've tried everything. There's literally nothing I wouldn't try at this point.'

The longer he speaks, the more I feel bad for doubting this man's story about the incident that caused his wife's memory loss, because he isn't sounding like somebody with a secret to hide. If Scarlett's slip was no accident, he wouldn't want her memory to return – but he does sound like a man eager for his wife's brain to heal, even if the prognosis is not great on that front.

'Being retired means I'm here to keep an eye on her, but I can't trust myself to do all the medical checks with how tired and worried I've been,' Adrian says after taking another sip of his coffee. 'She's not a patient to me, she's my wife and I'm far too close to the subject. That's where you and Pippa come in. It'll give me peace of mind to know you're caring for her without all the emotional baggage that I'm carrying for Scarlett.'

'Absolutely,' I say, nodding. 'I understand.'

'I guess, going forward, we'll have to keep assessing things and see if and when she needs more around-the-clock care,' Adrian goes on, and I am in agreement with that too.

'How about I give you a little tour of the house?' Adrian suggests once he's finished his drink. 'I can show you some of Scarlett's favourite places around here and, you never know, she might be feeling well enough one day for you to take her out of her room.'

'That sounds good to me,' I say as we leave our seats and Adrian leads me to the backyard.

'Scarlett used to love it out here,' Adrian says as I take in the wide, open space that is full of colourful flowers, tall and healthy trees, and a lawn cut so short and precisely that a professional golfer would be happy to putt a few balls on it.

'She spent a lot of time in this backyard?' I ask, and Adrian nods.

'Ever since we bought this house, whenever it was a dry day, she would come out here,' he explains. 'She would be out here all summer with our girls during the school holidays, playing on the grass, having pretend tea parties, running around playing silly games.'

I try to imagine this backyard filled with the sound of children's laughter and Scarlett's too, the happy mother chasing her children around without a care in the world, with no idea of the horror that was to come many years down the line.

'Were you close to your mother growing up?' Adrian asks me, shifting gears slightly, and the question throws me off.

'My mother? Erm, yeah, I suppose so,' I say, but I always find it harder to talk about myself than I do my patients, so I quickly steer the conversation back onto the right topic.

'Did you personally spend a lot of time with Scarlett out here too?' I ask Adrian as I notice a white butterfly fluttering over one of the flowerbeds.

'Yeah, we hosted a lot of barbecues out here,' he says fondly. 'We'd have friends and work colleagues over, sometimes their kids would come and they'd all play together. It was great fun.'

I'm now imagining this backyard packed full of people, the adults standing around with wine glasses in hand while their offspring run around at their waists, playing tag while smoke billows from the barbecue and the smell of cooked meat makes everybody's tastebuds tingle.

'I'll try and get Scarlett out here,' I say. 'I'm sure it'll help her.'

'Thank you,' Adrian says. He leads me back into the house, and he's about to show me somewhere else – where Scarlett liked to spend time before her accident – when we both hear shouting from upstairs.

'Get away from me!'

It's Scarlett's voice, and Adrian quickly runs to the staircase, taking the steps two at a time to ascend them as quickly as possible. I follow behind and, when I catch up to him, he has entered Scarlett's room, where we both find the patient looking very distressed while Pippa stands awkwardly by the bed, looking a little shaken.

'It's okay, darling. She's here to help you,' Adrian says, quickly slipping back into the role of his wife's carer. 'She's a nurse, remember? I told you about her.'

'I don't know who she is,' Scarlett says as she scowls at Pippa. Her eyes land on me. 'And who's that? Why is *she* here?'

Scarlett points at me now, and I feel my stomach churn as I fear this is going to be a much harder task than I first thought.

'This is Darcy, she's a nurse too,' Adrian explains, but I decide to give him some help, so I step forward towards the bed with a smile on my face.

'Hi, Scarlett. It's okay. Don't worry. I get confused sometimes. I often wake up after a big night's sleep and can't remember where I am or who anybody is for a few moments. Especially after a few glasses of wine the night before,' I say with a chuckle to let everyone know I'm joking, although only I know that my reality is not exactly far from that. 'But we are here to help.'

'You're a nurse?' Scarlett asks, still unsure, but looking like she is calming a little.

'That's right,' I say, reaching the bed. 'But not just a nurse. I'm a friend too. We can be friends, right?'

Scarlett thinks about it and looks to Adrian, before turning back to me and nodding her head.

'May I take a seat?' I ask, and Scarlett nods again, so I perch on the edge of the mattress and keep smiling at Scarlett who is half-covered by the comforter I'm on. 'Why don't you tell me a little about yourself?'

Scarlett looks to Adrian again before answering, which

could possibly mean two things: either she needs the reassurance of his familiar face during difficult times like this, or...

I shouldn't really think it, but I still do – it's a niggling thought that I've had a couple of times since I've been here.

She needs his permission because she's living in fear of him.

I could be wrong and allowing my tired mind to create something that doesn't actually exist, but I don't want her to feel like she has to have Adrian around for reassurance or permission all the time, so I speak again to draw her focus back on me.

'You're a mother, that's right, isn't it?' I ask, nodding, and Scarlett nods along with me. 'Why don't you tell me about your daughters? What are they like? Are they different or similar?'

Scarlett doesn't look to Adrian this time, but maintains eye contact with me, and I take that as progress.

'They're lovely. Beautiful girls. I'm so lucky.'

'We're both lucky,' Adrian chips in.

'Do you have any photos of them anywhere?' I ask, but I suddenly get the feeling I've just put my foot in my mouth, because Scarlett looks confused while Adrian grimaces.

'We have some photos in an album and I bring them out every now and again, but it's difficult,' Adrian says as he stares at his wife, who is still watching me. 'She gets more upset if she doesn't recognise them, so sometimes it's better to not show her every day.'

I make a mental note to try and show Scarlett the photos myself one day, to see if I can make any progress there, but as for now it seems the patient has had enough.

'How about you take a nap?' I suggest, and Scarlett smiles at that idea.

'I am tired,' she says. I expect her to snuggle down but, before she does, she reaches out and takes one of my hands. 'Thank you for coming back, darling. I've missed you.'

I'm not sure what Scarlett means, but Adrian does.

'She thinks you're one of our daughters,' he says sadly.

'Oh,' I say, feeling bad, but not wanting to correct Scarlett or let her hand go if it's making her feel better. I look to Pippa and she's watching me closely, which makes me wonder if she is testing me to see what I will do in this situation. Am I going to correct Scarlett or wait for Adrian to do it for me? In the end, neither of those things happen, because Scarlett starts crying before speaking again.

'Just call me Mom,' she urges me, gripping my hand tighter now. 'Say Mom.'

This is very awkward but now I can't even let go if I wanted to – Scarlett is really squeezing my hand.

'Say it,' she says again. 'Why won't you call me Mom?'

Now I'm the one getting upset, and I look to Pippa, but she seems as surprised by this as I am.

'Darling, let go of the nurse's hand,' Adrian says now, thankfully trying to intervene, and he attempts to separate our two hands. But Scarlett won't let go.

'Just say it!' she shouts, and the volume coming from this diminutive woman is frightening.

Fortunately, Adrian is able to get his wife to let go of my hand, and I stand up and step away from the bed, feeling flustered, which Pippa recognises because she suggests I take a break outside. I do just that, rushing for the bedroom door, but as I go I hear Scarlett still calling out to me.

'Where are you going? Come back!' she calls, but that makes me feel worse. It's a relief to get out of the room and close the door.

I take deep breaths as I lean against the top of the stairs, telling myself that I did nothing wrong and the patient got confused, which is to be expected. But I can still feel Scarlett squeezing my hand and glaring at me, and it's left me with a sinking feeling in my stomach.

I feel nervous to see her, because what if that happens again?

Or maybe my nerves are a sign of something else, something much bigger.

Maybe I'm no longer cut out to be a nurse.

SIX

It's been a very long day and it's a huge relief when it comes to an end and Pippa tells me it's time to go. We've spent the last several hours with Scarlett while Adrian had some respite. Now our shift is at an end, and I can't wait to get out of this house. The sense of unease I've had all day has lingered and was made worse by Scarlett mistaking me for her daughter. I've never felt more eager to get back to my own home, even if it is a poor comparison to this one.

'We'll be back at the same time tomorrow,' Pippa tells Adrian as she heads for the front door with the med-bag in hand, and I follow.

'Thank you so much for your help today. You've been great,' Adrian tells us as he shows us out. 'And I'm sorry for earlier, I hope you're okay?'

I realise he is talking to me, so I force a smile onto my face to try and show that I'm unaffected by it, but really I just want to be in the car driving away from here now.

'Have a good evening,' Pippa says as we step outside.

As I get into the car, I notice Adrian is still in the open doorway, waving us off. He could go back inside but I see him in my wing mirror, watching as Pippa drives us away. He finally fades from view when we leave his driveway and reach the end of his street.

'Well, that was fun,' Pippa says, looking to me with her eyebrows raised. 'Are you okay?'

'Yep, tip-top,' I reply, hoping that she won't ask me much more about how I'm feeling – I don't want to get into a deep conversation. I want to go home and crawl into bed.

'You did great back there,' Pippa goes on as she indicates left. 'All day, I mean, but especially when Scarlett got confused. You didn't get too flustered. It's never easy when something like that happens, but you did well.'

'Really? I had to leave the room.'

'So what? You came back in again and you got on with the rest of the job. It's normal for certain patients to get confused. If I had a dollar for every time I had a patient think I was their daughter or their sister or even their mother, then let's just say that I wouldn't still be doing this for a living.'

I appreciate my colleague trying to put me at ease, but I still feel weird, and it's not just about what happened with Scarlett.

'What do you think about the husband?' I ask, wondering if my concerns might be shared.

'Adrian? What about him?'

'Do you think he's genuine? Honest, I mean.'

'Honest? Why, do you not?'

'I didn't say that. I'm just wondering what your opinion is of him.'

'He seems like a nice guy. Struggling to come to terms with things, but nice. And rich as hell, obviously, but money can't buy happiness, not after what happened to his wife.'

'It's what happened to his wife that's bothering me,' I say, trying to lead Pippa to my wavelength.

'What do you mean?' she asks, still not getting it.

'Never mind.'

'No, go on. What are you thinking?' she asks, glancing at me before looking back at the road ahead, which is full of other commuters making their way home after a day of work.

'Well, it's just, the whole story of her mopping the floor and then slipping over. Do you think that's what really happened?'

'Well, yeah, I guess so. That's what was reported.'

'But is it what actually happened?'

'What do you think happened?'

'I don't know. It seems so random, her slipping. What if there's more to it? What if she fell? Or was pushed?'

'Pushed? By who?'

She looks at me again, and I stare at her, waiting for her to realise what I'm getting at.

'Adrian?' she cries, looking shocked. 'You think he pushed his wife?'

'I don't know. Maybe. It's a possibility, isn't it?'

'Why would he do that?'

'I don't know. They could have had an argument. He might have gone for her or maybe she was trying to get away from him. Anything could have happened in that kitchen, but if Scarlett can't remember it, we only have her husband's word to go on.'

Pippa is quiet as she thinks it all through, but then she shakes her head.

'No. No way. He's such a nice guy. I can't imagine him hurting his wife. You've seen how much he loves her. How desperate he is for her to get better.'

'Maybe, or maybe it's all an act,' I say. 'Or a guilty conscience. Who knows? Not us, we're just a couple of nurses looking after a patient. We only have a few notes to go off. But notes don't tell the full story, do they?'

Pippa seems worried by my train of thought, because she stops talking about that couple and returns the topic to me.

'Are you sure you're okay? You've been acting weird all day.'

'Weird, how?'

'I don't know. You seemed awkward at the house. What was that about?'

'I'm tired.'

'Well, make sure you get a good night's sleep tonight. We've got another busy day tomorrow.'

I hardly need Pippa to remind me that we're due back at that house tomorrow for another long day of work, nor do I need her to act like my mother and tell me to get some rest. It might be easy for her to say, but I have a feeling sleep is going to be hard to achieve for me. I fear I'll wake up tomorrow feeling more exhausted than I did today.

I wonder if this might be a good time to mention to Pippa that I'm having some doubts about my career and whether or not nursing is really for me anymore, but decide against it. It was already a mistake to tell her that I think there might be more to Adrian and Scarlett's story than meets the eye, so no need to overshare again and potentially make things worse. That's why I stay quiet for the remainder of the journey, the only noise between Pippa and me being the music on the radio, which she turned on after she realised I was done with chatting for the day.

By the time she stops the car and I'm getting out, I'm more than ready to take this uniform off and get into something more comfortable. So I thank Pippa for driving and then rush inside, already hoping that time is going to slow down so tomorrow morning comes less quickly.

Entering my home, I go straight upstairs and take off my uniform, throwing it down on the carpet in the same place I picked it up from this morning. Then I take a shower, washing off the day's stresses; but I'm not feeling much better when I get out and put on some clothes that don't remind me of work. Maybe that's because I have this entire house to myself, and while it's only a fraction of the size of the one that Adrian and Scarlett reside in, it still feels far too big for just me to occupy it.

A sense of loneliness seems to reverberate off every wall of each room I pass through, and nothing I do seems to distract me from it. I make a meal, eat it and watch television, but none of that works. I find myself staring at the unoccupied chairs at my kitchen table, or the spaces on my sofa beside me. As I do, I wonder if this is all worth it.

What if I tell Pippa that I'm not going back to that house tomorrow, and what if I stop wearing my uniform? Better yet, I could hand it back to my employer and tell them I quit – then at least I'll be free. I could reassess my life then, make a fresh start, try a new challenge, maybe even move. It might seem risky, but what would I be losing if this is all I currently have to show for my accomplishments so far?

I know there's wine in the fridge, but I tell myself that will only make me feel worse, so I consider going to bed and popping a few sleeping pills. The trouble with that is it's only eight o'clock, so it seems a little early to be going to bed, and something tells me I'll struggle to sleep anyway, even with pills. That's why I decide that I need to get out of here and get some fresh air, so I put on my shoes and leave the house.

I'm not heading anywhere in particular, just walking to try and clear my mind, and soon find myself on a busy sidewalk lined with late-night stores and a few small restaurants. I see a few couples in the windows of the restaurants, two happy people sitting opposite each other, dining and talking, enjoying their time together, seemingly at ease with one another and having a lovely evening. I wonder how many meals Adrian and Scarlett went for together, how many times they sat across a white linen tablecloth and smiled at each other as they sipped wine and savoured various delicacies. I doubt they ever ate around here, these restaurants aren't classy enough for them, but there's no doubt they would have enjoyed many meals with one another, as well as holidays and all sorts of other fun activities.

But no more.

I push that couple from my mind as I walk on. I'm not at work, so they're not my problem now, nor will they be if I choose not to go back there tomorrow. I reach the end of the street and turn, figuring I've come far enough and don't want too long a walk back. But as I'm heading in the direction of home again, a man comes out of a convenience store, and when he sees me he stops dead and stares right at me.

It's eerie because it's as if he has just stopped in his tracks. His mouth opens slightly and the shopping bag in his left hand is hanging limply beside him. Why is he looking at me? Why is it as if I am the most fascinating person on this busy street?

I turn away from him and keep walking, figuring that maybe he thinks I'm cute; but I'm not in the mood for entertaining any poor pickup lines, so I'll get going before he can try any of them on me. But when I look over my shoulder, I see that he is walking the same way that I am, and even when I reach the next street he's still behind me.

He's not closing the gap, merely maintaining it. The further we go, the more I get the uneasy feeling that I'm being followed, so I quicken my pace, hoping to lose him as I turn a few more street corners. I do consider hiding and hoping he walks right past me, but stopping might be risky if he spots me, so I'll try and get home as quickly as I can.

But he's still behind me when I reach my street, and now I'm certain that he's followed me. I don't want him to see where I live, but he will if I carry on to my door.

Who the hell is he and what does he want?

I turn to find out, deciding that this has gone far enough and it would be better for me to know than go inside my house with so many unanswered questions. As I stop, I see that he has stopped too, and he's staring at me again.

'What do you want?' I ask him, my voice loud on this otherwise silent street.

He doesn't answer me. He holds my gaze for several very long seconds before turning and walking away. I don't walk away though. I run, taking off as quickly as I can, and getting inside my house before whoever that was can change his mind and follow me again.

Once I'm inside, I peer nervously through the gap in my curtains to see if he is out there somewhere.

But there's no sign of him.

That was frightening.

I thought a walk would help me achieve sleep tonight.

But now I'll definitely need to take something to forget about him.

SEVEN

My head is pounding almost as much as the pounding I can hear on my front door. As I roll over on my pillow and glance at the bedside table, I let out a groan. Seeing the bottle beside me, I know why I feel so rough. I took sleeping pills again, but slightly more than the recommended dose, which is never a good idea. As a result, I'm feeling far worse than I did before I even got into bed, although my night was also ruined by the fear that I might have been followed last night.

Maybe I was overthinking it, though. It could have been nothing.

I hope so.

More banging at my front door forces me to wearily get to my feet. I step over my crumpled uniform and name badge. Leaving my bedroom, rubbing my bleary eyes with one hand as I go, my other runs along the side of the hallway wall so I don't lose my balance as I very slowly come around. I open my door and find my fellow nurse on the doorstep, sporting a big smile, a name badge and a coffee flask, although that's all I see before I squint my eyes and try to block out the bright light from another sunny morning.

'Rise and shine!' Pippa says, but the fact that I wince gives her a clear indication that she needs to lower her voice, or even better, shut up completely.

'I'll make you a coffee while you get ready,' she says, stepping inside and heading for my kitchen, which gives me a sense of déjà vu. I rub my throbbing forehead and take a few moments to figure out what my next move is here.

Shall I tell Pippa to go away? Shall I say that I'm not going to work today? If I do that, I could get back into bed and rest until I'm hopefully feeling a little bit better, and right now, that feels like my best course of action.

'I'm not feeling well. I think I need to take the day off,' I say as I reach the kitchen doorway and find Pippa unscrewing the lid off the flask. But any sympathy I hoped to garner does not materialise.

'Come on, you know we've talked about this. You always feel better once you've been to work. That's why I'm here, to make sure you go. So get ready.'

Pippa hasn't skipped a beat as she carries on making my coffee, but I find that weird because it's as if she doesn't mind that she has to come and drag me out of bed to face the day.

'Why are you helping me?' I ask as I slump down into a chair. 'You must have enough to do in the morning without coming to pick me up.'

'Damn right I do,' Pippa says breezily, as if I've just stated the obvious. 'But I'm a super mom, which is why I'm able to get my son ready and out for preschool before I come here to help you. Let me tell you, it's easier to get a four-year-old ready and out of the house than it is to get you going in the mornings.'

Pippa laughs as she turns on the coffee machine, but even the noise of that makes my head hurt.

'Campbell says hi, by the way,' Pippa tells me. 'He likes you, you know, so I was wondering, maybe I could bring him around soon? We could go out for the afternoon, what do you say? Unless you have any plans when we're not at work?'

I can think of absolutely no plans I have outside of work other than lying in bed, so I shake my head.

'Great, Campbell will be thrilled,' Pippa says, smiling as the machine grinds the coffee beans. 'Now, go and get ready or we're going to be late, and I won't be able to cover for you at work again with the boss if you fail to show up. I almost got in trouble last time.'

I don't want Pippa to get in trouble, not with how much she is clearly helping me, so I'm about to leave but, before I do, there is one burning question.

'You weren't wearing your wedding ring yesterday,' I say, suddenly remembering this, and Pippa stops in her tracks.

'What?'

'It's just that I noticed it while we were working and wondered if everything is okay? At home?'

'Everything is normal at home.'

Normal doesn't necessarily mean okay if the normal situation is bad.

'Are you sure?' I pry.

'Yes. I've just started taking my ring off when I work. I don't want to scratch it or lose it.'

That seems fair enough, even though I suspect there might be more to it, but I go upstairs and get dressed. By the time I see my colleague again I'm in full uniform, and she has a full flask in her hand.

'Off we go,' she says as she hands me my coffee via her ring-less hand and heads outside, and I follow her to her car, wondering what I did to deserve a friend like this one. It's clear that without her I'd probably have lost my job by now and, if I lose that, I'll lose this house at some point too. And then I really would be in trouble.

'I can't wait for the weekend,' Pippa says as she starts

driving. 'I can wear something more comfortable than this uniform in this heat.'

She turns up the A/C to get some cool air in but, as she does, the medical notes lying by my feet start flapping from the force of the vents, so I quickly pick them up to prevent them getting on the driver's nerves.

I have a read through them as we drive across town. By the time we reach our destination, my mind is full of thoughts about the patient we are here to see.

'Good morning, Adrian,' Pippa says once the door is opened and we are welcomed into the grand house. I smile politely at him as I step inside, and he greets us with a good morning.

'Pippa and Darcy are back again,' Adrian says as we follow him into the bedroom, where we find the patient sitting up in bed and looking reasonably well considering her condition. 'They're just going to make a few checks again and give me a little break. Is that okay?'

Scarlett looks at me and Pippa, then she smiles, and that simple expression puts me at ease – it's far preferable to her asking us who we are or, worse, telling us to get out. Pippa makes a start on the checks, taking Scarlett's blood pressure first, while I sit beside the patient and show her a smile of my own.

'It's a beautiful morning,' I say to her, still smiling. 'How about once we're done here, we try and go out back? Would you like some fresh air?'

Scarlett nods, so I tell her it's a plan and, while Pippa finishes the checks, I see Adrian smiling at me, which makes me feel better. I also realise that Pippa is right when she says that I always do feel better once I've got out of my house and got to work. I see the value in her banging on my door every morning and forcing me to get dressed, even if I'm sure she would prefer it if it didn't take quite as much effort.

'All good,' Pippa says cheerily once the last of the checks have been made, and then the two of us gently help Scarlett out of bed, where she slides her bare feet into a pair of fluffy slippers. We lead her to the bedroom door, one arm on each side interlinked with hers.

We make sure to take our time as we guide Scarlett downstairs. As we pass Adrian in his kitchen on the way to the back door, I see him watching us a little warily, no doubt worried if this might be too much for his wife. But she seems okay, and she certainly seems much happier once we're in the backyard with the warm sun on our skin and a gentle breeze blowing through our hair.

'This is much nicer than that stuffy bedroom, isn't it?' I say to Scarlett, and she agrees that it is as we reach the bench and I help her take a seat. But there's only really space for two on here, so I suggest Pippa takes a break while I keep our patient company.

'Are you sure?' she asks me, but I tell her I'm great, so she heads back into the house while I chat to Scarlett, who is busy looking at her beautiful flowerbeds.

'The garden is really pretty,' I tell her. 'I wish mine was like this.'

'You're welcome to spend as much time out here as you like,' Scarlett tells me, and that's very kind of her. She's clearly having a good day, but my mind is on her notes and the head injury she suffered, which meant she needed me and Pippa rather than living a normal life without supervision or support. More specifically, my mind is on what caused that head injury. I feel uneasy as I glance back at the house to see if Adrian is nearby, so I decide to enquire about it – particularly because it seems like Scarlett might be in a good state to discuss it.

'Did you find it hard walking through the kitchen then?' I ask tentatively. 'You know, with what happened there in the past?'

Scarlett's smile fades and I fear I've already said too much, but then she answers.

'No. I don't,' she says simply. But I'm not sure if that is her being very brave and letting me know that she is strong enough to be around the scene of her accident, or if she can't actually remember what happened, so has totally missed the point of my question.

'Do you remember anything about what happened?' I ask, putting it to the test and, as I do, I notice Scarlett look back at the house. *Is she checking to see if Adrian is listening?*

'It's okay. It's just me and you. You can tell me anything,' I say in case she needs that extra reassurance.

'I don't remember,' she tells me quietly.

But is that the truth?

'Nothing at all? Do you remember what you were doing before you fell?' I ask, purposely using the word 'fell' rather than 'slipped', in case that lets Scarlett know I would believe her if she was to tell me that her husband played a part in it.

'I don't know,' Scarlett says, and she frowns. I fear that I'm going to ruin what might be a period of lucidity that she is enjoying, so I consider leaving it there. But then she speaks again.

'What do you think of my husband?' Scarlett asks me, and now it's my turn to glance at the house to make sure he isn't eavesdropping.

'Adrian? Erm, I don't know. I mean, I don't know him very well. But he seems nice.'

Scarlett looks sad, and I wonder if it means I've misread him.

'Why? What is it? Is there something I need to know about him?' I ask, and I'm almost wishing I hadn't sent Pippa away, because maybe it would be good if she was to hear this conversation after all. Although perhaps Scarlett wouldn't be opening up to me if we had company, so I have to see how this plays out.

I notice Scarlett's eyes watering and wonder what's causing her tears.

'What is it? You can tell me,' I urge her, certain there is more than meets the eye with her husband now, but unable to fully understand it unless she gives me something more.

'How are we doing out here?'

Both Scarlett and I turn around when we hear Adrian's voice, and I see him coming towards us, carrying two glasses of fruit juice and beaming in the bright sunshine.

Scarlett has shelled up and she quickly wipes her eyes before he reaches us and offers us a drink each.

'I thought you might need some refreshments,' Adrian says as he offers me a glass, and I take it, but only to make it seem like everything is okay here. But it's clearly not, although I've obviously lost my best shot at finding out what Scarlett was going to tell me about her husband now that he's joined us. I get confirmation of that a moment later when Scarlett drops her drink and the glass rolls onto the lawn, not shattering but spilling its contents all over the blades of grass.

'Oh dear,' Adrian says as he picks up the glass. 'Maybe it's a little too hot for you out here. What do you say we get you back inside in the shade?'

He takes his wife's hand before she's even had a chance to answer him and, as she gets up off the bench, I see he is clearly eager to get her back into the house. Is it because he's genuinely worried about the heat, or is it because he doesn't like the fact that we were having a private conversation? He must have noticed that she had tears in her eyes. Does he know that I was prying? Does he think that it's a bad idea having me around without his supervision?

As he leads Scarlett back into the house, I watch Adrian and wish I knew what he was thinking. But I don't – no one is a mind reader, least of all me, a person who struggles to read my own mind at times.

But one thing is for sure.

I need to get Pippa to help me figure out what is going on here.

I need to know if Scarlett is still in danger in this house.

If she is, it might mean my fellow nurse and I are in danger too.

EIGHT

I've tried to get a private moment with Pippa ever since the uncomfortable experience in the backyard with Adrian and Scarlett, but it's not been possible. That's because Adrian has been keeping a close eye on the pair of us throughout the rest of our shift – not just when we've been with his wife but when we've gone for a break too. I had expected that I'd be able to tell Pippa during our lunch break about what had happened, how Scarlett had asked me what I thought of her husband before getting upset and then going very quiet when he came out to see us. But I was denied that chance when Adrian had inexplicably decided to sit with us while we took our break and chat to us about our personal lives.

'Do you have families of your own?' he had asked me and Pippa as we'd tucked into the salads that my colleague had brought for the pair of us. I'd found the question rather intrusive and not entirely appropriate. What did our personal lives matter to him? Was it any of his business? Surely the only thing that mattered was that we were suitable carers for his stricken partner, and he already knew we were because he had engaged our employer and they had sent us to him. But he had pried all the same, denying me the opportunity to chat to Pippa about my concerns.

'Yes, I'm married and have a son,' she had told Adrian, who had seemed interested in her answer.

'Wonderful. What are their names?' he had asked then, pressing further. I had studied Pippa to see if she was deeming this to be beyond her duties as a nurse here. We surely didn't have to share private information with our patients' families, but Pippa had humoured him and answered anyway.

'My husband's called Karl, and my son is called Campbell,' she had told him as I'd chewed my salad nervously. 'He's four.'

'Ah, what a lovely age,' Adrian had said then, clasping his hands together and smiling.

Pippa had smiled to be polite, while I had stared at my salad. Adrian had continued.

'How long have you been married?'

'Seven years,' Pippa had replied.

'Did you marry here in Chicago or elsewhere?'

'It was in Florida, actually.'

'Wonderful! Much warmer, I imagine. Was it a beach wedding?'

'Kind of. We actually went out on a boat with our family and friends.'

'Wow, how amazing.'

Pippa had smiled awkwardly then, stabbing at a lettuce leaf with her fork, while I had wondered how long it was going to be before Adrian directed some of his questions at me. It turned out it wasn't long at all.

'And what about you, Darcy?' he had asked, despite my trying to avoid his gaze by staring at my lunch. 'Are you married?'

I really hadn't seen what any of it had to do with him, but as Pippa had already answered her questions, it would have felt very rude if I'd ignored them.

'No,' I'd replied, keeping my answer short and sweet.

'Any boyfriend on the scene?' Adrian had gone on, so I shook my head, expecting him to drop it there. But he didn't.

'What about family? Are you from Chicago or have you moved here?'

I don't know whether it was the constant barrage of personal questions, the fact I was doubting the version of events that had led to his wife's accident, or simply that I was tired and stressed, but I didn't react to that third and final question very well.

'Can we change the subject?' I'd asked him then, making it clear I wanted him to stop pestering me. Thankfully he stopped his questions there, though not before he had looked surprised. Pippa had looked surprised too, but I carried on eating my lunch, feeling justified that I was entitled to keep my personal life personal here, even if I didn't have much of one to speak of.

The rest of our shift had passed mundanely enough, Pippa and I spending time with Scarlett, watching one of her favourite movies with her and asking questions about it to try and test her memory. Adrian came in and out with drinks and snacks and never left us alone for long enough for me to find out any more about Scarlett's marriage.

I'm feeling frustrated as another day comes to an end and I head to Pippa's car, but at least I'll get the chance to talk freely to my colleague once we're on the road – Adrian won't be able to eavesdrop then. However, Adrian is chatting to Pippa, delaying her joining me in the car, and I wonder what he's talking to her about. But it does provide me with the opportunity to do something I've been thinking about all day, and that is secretly take Scarlett's patient notes from Pippa's car and hide them underneath my uniform so I can have a look at them when I get home shortly. I know I probably shouldn't keep confidential information about patients in my house, but I want to go through these notes in more detail in my spare time to see if there's anything here that I can potentially use against Adrian if I continue to fear that he isn't trustworthy. I also have the few notes I've already made myself, which I can add to if necessary. Depending on how things go, maybe I'll be taking all of this to the police – if I eventually decide without doubt that Adrian did hurt Scarlett and caused her memory loss, that is.

By the time Pippa gets in behind the wheel, the notes are discreetly hidden on my person, and I doubt my colleague will notice that they're missing as she starts driving. They've been lying in the footwell, and she has a separate notebook for all the medical checks she made on the patient today. Now that we're on the move, I can finally talk freely.

'Something's going on with Adrian,' I tell Pippa as she steers us away from the house. 'When we were outside I was asking Scarlett about the accident, and when he interrupted us she tried to cover up her tears.'

'You were asking her about the accident? Of course that's going to be upsetting for her!' Pippa cries, not taking this how I want her to.

'I'm trying to let her know that she can tell me if Adrian has something to hide,' I reply, defending myself.

'Something to hide? What are you talking about? He doesn't have anything to hide!'

'Doesn't he? I think he does. He barely left us alone after I spoke to Scarlett, almost as if he doesn't want me asking her any more questions. And what's the deal with him asking us so many things? Why did he want to know about our personal lives?'

'He was just being polite,' Pippa says, but she's not convincing me, or even herself judging by how little conviction she said that with. Before I can say anything more, my colleague stops me short.

'How are you feeling?' she asks me, catching me off-guard.

'Me?'

'Yeah. I'm worried about you. Are you okay?'

'I'm fine.'

'We both know that's a lie. Forget me having to come and get you every morning, or your fantastical theories about Adrian. How are you feeling in yourself? Are you sad, anxious, upset?'

'Why do you care?'

'Of course I care!'

'Just leave it. There's nothing wrong with me,' I say, feeling far less comfortable talking about myself than I am about Adrian and whatever he may or may not be hiding.

Pippa tries to probe at the subject a few more times, but I stay silent until she stops the car and I'm free to get out and go inside. She says she'll see me tomorrow, but I say nothing as I rush to my front door.

Once I'm in, I quickly lock my front door and sit down at my kitchen table. There, I take out the notes and pore over them, reading and rereading in case there's anything I might have missed. There doesn't seem to be, but before I put them away, I find a pen and start making a few notes of my own.

Husband acting suspiciously. Patient gets upset then tries to cover it up when he's around. Could he be hurting her? Need to monitor them more, get closer to the patient, potentially observe the husband when he isn't aware of it.

Once I've finished my notes, I go upstairs to get out of my uniform, feeling like ridding myself of it will help rid me of my worries too. I take a shower and then decide to have an early night, and despite picking up the sleeping tablets and anxiety pills, I put them back down without taking any this evening. I'll try and keep a clear head around Scarlett and Adrian, at least until I have a few more answers.

Turning off the light, it takes me a long time to fall asleep, but I keep resisting the urge to take anything that might help me. It's tough, and I spend a long time lying awake and wondering if the main reason I can't sleep now is not just because I've refused pills, but because I've taken so many that I'm now withdrawing from them. I don't know, but I keep my eyes shut, as well as my mouth. I also spend time thinking about that man who seemed to be following me, though that is hardly likely to help.

Eventually, I achieve rest without anything to aid me. It doesn't last for long though because something wakes me up and, when I check the time on my bedside clock, I see that it's three in the morning.

What woke me? I'm not sure and, at first, I wonder if I just had a bad dream that stirred me from my slumber. Then I hear something, and I realise that waking was a result of the noises that are currently occurring in my home.

There should be no sounds here other than me snoring, but I can definitely hear something. Frighteningly, it's not something I want to hear in the dead of night, or any other time for that matter.

It sounds like somebody else is in my house.

I hold my breath and grip my sheet as I keep listening, but all that happens is that I get confirmation that something awful is happening here. Someone has broken in and they are downstairs. I can hear their footsteps in my kitchen, as well as them opening and closing cupboard doors. I can tell they are trying to be quiet – they're not exactly crashing around down there, but now I'm awake I can hear the tiniest of noises, and they are making plenty.

Am I being robbed? What do they think they'll find here?

More importantly, are they dangerous? And what will they do if they realise I'm awake?

I debate staying in bed and pretending like I don't know that they're here. With a bit of luck, they might stay downstairs, and they'll never know I was in or that I heard them. I presume they saw there was no car parked outside and figured this place was currently unoccupied. But it's not, and staying up here pretending like it is carries great risk, because what if they come upstairs and they panic when they find me here? They must think they're alone but they're not; maybe I should make that clear so they have the chance to run away.

As I peel back my sheets and place my bare feet on the carpet, I am shaking.

I am also clear on what I'm going to do.

I am going to defend my home, whatever it takes.

NINE

Opening my bedroom door as quietly as I can, I thank my lucky stars when it doesn't creak and alert the intruder downstairs. I also take great care to not make the slightest sound as I creep to the top of my stairs. Without a noisy floorboard giving me away, I am able to look down into the darkness.

When I do, my heart rate only increases.

That's because I see the shape of somebody by the front door.

'Get out!' I cry, forcing myself to make my presence known before they can come up towards me.

While I still can't see who it is because of the lack of light, I see the figure is startled, and they turn and run. Diving for the switch on the wall I hit the lights, but the intruder is out of sight as they scurry away into my house. When I run downstairs, I see that the back door is open. It's obvious which way they came in and went out, but I have no idea how they were able to gain access.

I thought this door was locked.

Unless...

Maybe I forgot to lock it earlier? I was so distracted with Scarlett's notes when I got home that it could easily have slipped my mind. But did I even lock it before I went to work? Or was it open all day?

It's not for me to figure out how the intruder got in. That is a job for the police, and they're the people I will call as soon as I'm certain that I am alone and safe. But am I?

Every cell in my body is screaming at me to close and lock the back door, in case the intruder is no longer spooked and tries to come back in. But if I do that, I won't have a chance at seeing who they are. So, against my better judgement, I poke my head out and try to get a better look. But it's dark and they moved fast and it seems like they're long gone, so I give my nerves a rest and close the door quickly and turn the key.

After that drama, it takes over half an hour for my 911 call to get a response. Eventually, I open my door to two officers wearing bulletproof vests over light blue shirts, guns in their holsters and serious looks on their faces. But in case they're still in any doubt, I'm willing to remind them just how serious this is, because as far as I'm concerned, they have taken far too long to get here.

'Someone was in my house!' I cry before they've had a chance to speak. 'They came in through the back! I don't how, but they got inside and if I hadn't woken up I don't know what they would have done! You have to find out who it was and catch them, please! What if they come back?'

That's rather a lot of information to throw at two people I've just met and, understandably, my frenzied state is met by a couple of blank stares.

'Please, try and calm down, ma'am,' the first officer brave enough to speak says. 'We're here now and you're safe. My partner here will take a look around, while we take a seat and you can run me through exactly what happened and what you saw.'

'I saw someone in my house!' I cry, frustrated that it's already been so long since I called for help – whoever was in here will surely be a long way away by now. 'What else do you want me to say? You need to be out there looking for them, not in here talking to me!'

'Please, I understand you've had a fright, but try and calm down,' the second officer says, but that only makes me angrier.

'A fright? I woke up and heard a stranger moving around inside my home. I think you'd have a fright too!'

I know I shouldn't be shouting at these cops, because it's not their fault that my home has been targeted tonight, and my reaction is out of character, but I'm scared and angry and probably a little bit in shock. However, I eventually realise that this is not getting me anywhere fast, so I finally do what I'm told and take a seat. Then I explain to the officer what happened while his colleague examines my home, which is essentially now a crime scene.

'Is anything missing?' one of the officers asks, but I shake my head.

'I don't think so. I don't know, maybe. It's hard to tell. But I can't see that anything has gone. I obviously spooked them, and they ran away.'

'What could they have been here for? Do you have any valuables on the premises?'

'Valuables? Erm, no, nothing expensive. But everything here is valuable to me. It's my home!'

'I understand,' the officer says. He looks to the open doorway, presumably hoping his colleague will return to help him out here. But he's not back yet and I wonder what he's checking. The back door? The perimeter? My bedroom? I don't like the idea of anybody snooping around in my personal belongings, but rather a police officer than a random intruder.

'Can you think of anybody who might have wanted to target you?' is the next question I have to face at this late hour of the night, or early hour of the morning, depending on which way I want to look at it. *Neither one is particularly appealing.*

'Target me? No, why would anybody target me?' I ask, sending a question back at the man in uniform.

'No ex? Anyone who might know you were alone? No enemies?'

'No. And judging by how fast they ran when I called out to them, I'm guessing they either didn't know I was here or did not expect me to wake up.'

I think that's a perfectly good answer, but then I suddenly remember what happened the other night and my body turns cold.

'Somebody was following me,' I say when I recall the man who seemed to tail me home after I spotted him during my evening walk after work. 'I'd gone out and I noticed somebody seemed to be paying me a lot of attention. I headed for home, but they were behind me the whole way.'

'You don't know who they were?'

'No, I'd never seen them before.'

'Could you describe them?'

'Erm...' I think back, trying to recall the details of that man. But it was dark, and I've barely slept properly since then, not to mention the shock I've had, so the details are a little foggy.

'I think he was tall. Maybe thirties, or forties, perhaps,' I say vaguely.

'Eye colour? Hair colour?'

I draw a blank. 'Like I said, it was dark and there was a bit of a distance between us, so I couldn't really see.'

'How can you be certain he was following you then?'

'He definitely was!' I insist, getting annoyed that I have to justify the anxiety I felt at the time. But him questioning what I thought I saw is now making me wonder if I had been slightly imagining it, although considering what has just happened tonight, surely I was not.

'It must be connected, right? Somebody following me and then somebody breaking in? It must be the same person,' I suggest, but the cop doesn't look like the kind of person who makes a habit of jumping to conclusions, unlike me, which I suppose is why we're grating against each other.

'Has anything like this happened before?' comes the next question.

'Has anyone broken into my house, you mean? No, never.'

'There's been the odd report of similar incidents in this neighbourhood over the years. This isn't a dangerous area, but crime seeps into all parts of the city, I'm afraid.'

'I'm not disputing that. I want to know what you're going to do about it,' I say, growing even more frustrated with this conversation. 'Maybe I have a stalker or something?'

'Have you had a stalker before?'

'No, but that doesn't mean—'

It's perhaps a fortunate thing that the second officer returns now, and when he does he gestures for his colleague to come and join him in the hallway. I realise I'm about to be left alone, but before I am I fire a few more questions at them.

'What's going on? Have you got anything?' I want to know, aware that I'm desperate, but how else am I supposed to be?

'Please, give us a couple of minutes,' the second officer says, and once they've both left me I have little choice but to do just that.

Holding my head in my hands, I try not to think about how scary tonight has been or how I'm not going to get any more sleep now before sunrise, and while I'm wallowing in both shock and self-pity, I overhear the whispers of the cops in my hallway.

'I can't see anything out of the ordinary here. What do you make of her?'

'I don't know. She seems a bit strange. Groggy even. She might have been drinking last night.'

'I thought that too. Found a load of sleeping pills by her bed as well. Not sure if we can really trust what she's said. There certainly doesn't look like there's been any crime here.'

'Yeah. What will we do then?'

I'm furious that I seem to not be being believed, and I'm about to rush out into the hallway and tell these rude officers that I've overheard their whispered conversation when they both return.

'What's going on? Are you going to help me or what?' I ask them, already fearing what the answer is going to be.

Both officers share a look – one of them sighs.

'There is no sign of forced entry, and nothing appears to be missing. I'm not sure what we can do.'

'I'll tell you what you can do – you can take this seriously! Somebody broke in here. I don't know how but—'

'Maybe you left the back door open?'

That assumption causes me to pause and, while I do, the officers take the opportunity to speak again.

'Lock your doors, make sure the house is secure and try to get some sleep,' I'm told. 'We'll sit outside in our car for a while and make sure nobody is hanging around here, but everything seems to be okay now. If you'd like to come to the station later and speak to somebody there, you can do, but, for now, I think we can leave.'

They turn to go, and I follow them out into the hallway. I don't know what else I'm supposed to do.

'Make sure you lock this door behind us,' I'm told as the officers leave, and while I fully intend to lock my front door and also check the back one before I go to bed again, I am still unsettled about all of this.

'You'll make sure there's nobody hanging around in the area?' I double-check as they walk to their car, and they assure me that they will. So with that I go to close my door, figuring I'll have to go to the station at some point and see if that gets me anywhere further. But before I can close the door, I hear one of the officers whispering something to his colleague that makes my blood boil.

'Dumb chick probably brought some guy back from the bar and then forgot he was there,' he says with a snigger. 'Chased him out of the house while he was probably looking for a snack, the poor guy. I bet he wishes he hadn't bothered.'

'Hey! I've not been drinking!' I shout in the officers' direction, furious that they are judging me, and they both turn around and look sheepish that I heard them. I'm so angry at them that I have nothing more to say, so I slam the door shut and lock it before rushing to the back door and checking that it's locked too.

There's no way anybody can get back in here now, certainly not without breaking something this time. With the officers supposedly sitting outside for a while to keep an eye on the place, I guess it's safe for me to go back to bed and try and get some rest. I doubt rest is achievable, at least not unless I take some pills, although judging by the cops' reaction to me, I'm already groggy enough. I decide to get a glass of water instead and, once I've downed that, I refill my glass. Before I go back upstairs, I catch sight of the notes on the table, the ones that refer to Scarlett and her condition, as well as a few scribbled notes about my opinion on her husband and what might have caused her to need care.

I wonder if the cop who was searching around read them. I hope not. It's hardly relevant. But if I am to go the police station in the morning and talk about this, it would mean missing a day at work, and do I really want to do that? Not if I think Scarlett might be in danger. That's why I decide that I won't try and go back to sleep, especially when the night is almost over with – the sun will be up soon. Nor will I worry about going to the police station straight away, especially if the officers there are likely to be as useless as the ones who came here tonight. It'll likely be a complete waste of time. What I am going to do is pick up these notes and take them to bed with me, so I can read them through a little more while I have the time. Then I'm going to get dressed at sunrise and prepare for another day at work, because at least that will get me out of here and take my mind off what just happened.

For once, Pippa isn't going to have to bang on my door to drag me out of bed.

This time, I'll be ready for her.

She might think I'm sleepy or depressed or even hungover, like those officers thought I was, but I'll show her and them. I'll show everyone that I'm not useless. While I might have my problems, I'm not deluded or confused.

I'll prove it.

I'll prove it by finding out if Adrian has anything to hide.

I'll keep Scarlett safe.

And, in the meantime, I'll be the perfect nurse.

TEN

'Good morning!' I say with a smile as I open my front door unprompted, surprising the woman standing on the other side of it with both my facial expression and the enthusiastic nature of my greeting.

'Oh, good morning. You're up?' Pippa says, recalibrating her next few movements because I've caught her off-guard – instead of her having to bang on my door to force me out of bed, I've come to her.

'Yep, and, even better, I've already made coffee,' I say, handing a full flask to my colleague.

'Is everything okay?' Pippa asks sceptically as she takes the hot flask, and the look of concern on her face is telling. Have I been that bad lately that simply being awake and active in the morning is enough to trigger concern?

'Not exactly, but it's a long story. Anyway, I'm up and ready, so how about we get going?'

I step outside and close my front door, making sure to double-check that it's definitely locked after I've turned the key. Without the need for Pippa to come in and wait for me to get dressed, we're already well ahead of schedule. My uniform is on and there's already caffeine in my bloodstream, though I haven't told Pippa yet why that is. To do so would mean having to tell her about the intruder who was in my house last night, as well as the visit from the police officers before sunrise. I've decided that I'm not going to tell her about what happened, because if I do she might suggest that I take the day off, or worse, insist that I do. I don't want that to happen though – no good will come from me being here where all the drama took place only a few hours ago. At best, I'll be cooped up at home growing more anxious and, at worst, I'll miss out on another opportunity to observe Adrian and Scarlett and figure out if they are hiding anything. So I won't give Pippa the chance to tell me to stay here. I'm going to work, even in this sleep-deprived and anxious state, because it gives me the excuse to get out of the house, if nothing else. But I'll make sure to do my best to mask my current state of mind and appear more positive, because that's what a good nurse should do.

'Are you sure everything is okay?' Pippa asks me again as we walk to her car. I wonder if I'm not doing as good of a job as I thought of making it seem like I'm fine. I'm deliberately trying to appear positive, but because that's in such contrast to my usual demeanour, maybe I'm overdoing it slightly and should try and tone it down a little.

'Yeah, I just woke up early today, so thought I'd get ready for a change,' I reply, getting into the car. That answer conveniently skips out all the dramatic parts of my night, and neglects to mention the fact that I have spent the past thirty minutes rereading Scarlett's notes as well as the ones I added in my own notebook yesterday. I'm hoping Pippa hasn't realised that the official notes aren't still in the car. As we set off, I'm guessing I've gotten away with it. I'll sneak the notes back in at some point, but for now I'd like to have them at home, where I can refer to them if need be.

'I've been thinking,' Pippa says, after we've been making

chit-chat about the taste of our coffees and how wonderful caffeine is for the first few minutes of our journey, 'how about you try and have a talk with Adrian today? Get to know him a little better? It might help with all your theories about him.'

'You think I might be right and he's hiding something?' I say, feeling excited that I might not be alone in my thinking after all.

'No, that's not what I said,' Pippa corrects me. 'I was suggesting it more along the lines of you getting to know him better so hopefully you can see that he is not the kind of guy who hurt his wife and then covered it up.'

'Get to know him? What do you mean?'

'I don't know. Just talk to him like you talk to Scarlett. Try and get him to open up. It could help us with how we deal with her treatment too. You were right in something you said yesterday. He is the one always asking us questions, so let's see if we can get him to answer a few. Want to try it?'

'Definitely,' I say, thrilled at the task I have been assigned and, even with the worries of what happened last night playing on my mind, I'm glad to have another purpose to distract me today.

We reach the house. When we go inside and I see Adrian, it feels like my stomach is doing a few flips, which is always an unsettling feeling. But I tell myself that it's because I'm wary of him and also because I need to try and talk to him quietly today, so hopefully I'll be feeling better about things by the time we leave here.

Or, depending on what I learn, maybe I'll have to go and speak to the police again.

The morning starts with the usual checks on Scarlett. I assist Pippa with those, though it's not easy because the patient is having a bad day today. I have to explain to her three times that I am her nurse, not her daughter. At one point, even Adrian has to convince his wife of who he is. It's upsetting watching a husband try and remind his wife who he is and how they met, but the stoicism with which both Adrian and Pippa deal with it forces me to be the same way. We soldier on, even getting a few lighter moments just before lunch. That comes when Scarlett, in a lucid moment, starts talking about her wedding to Adrian – she tells us how nervous her husband was on the big day. That makes him blush a little, but at least it's a good sign that she does have some memories still stored away in her head from before her accident. But I'm still sceptical about him, and with Pippa's suggestion in mind, I take the opportunity to leave Scarlett and my colleague behind in the bedroom and go downstairs to see Adrian while he's alone in the kitchen, making lunch for us all.

'How are you coping?' I ask him as I enter, and he seems surprised that I've followed him downstairs.

'Not so bad, thank you for asking,' he says, turning back to the drinks.

'Are you sure? You can talk to me. We're here to help both of you, not just your wife,' I tell him, hoping to get him to open up a little, but he still seems closed off, so I change tack.

'I hope you don't mind me asking... Did the police ever ask any questions about your wife's accident?' I say now, going for the jugular. When I ask my question, Adrian drops the teaspoon he is using, and it clatters loudly on the marble countertop.

'Excuse me?'

'I was wondering, was there an actual investigation into what happened in here? I mean, I know it was an accident, but did you have to convince the police that it was?'

Adrian still has his back to me, and I watch him as he picks up the spoon. His shoulders are a little hunched. Is he tense? Nervous? Wondering why I'm asking him such a thing? It's hard to tell when I can't see his face.

'I mean, yes, of course, the police wanted to know what

happened,' he says, finally turning around and looking at me. 'But they weren't very interested when they got the truth. People slipping over at home is hardly at the top of their list of things to solve.'

'I suppose,' I say as I maintain eye contact, because I almost want him to know that, while he might have fooled everyone else, I am not going to blindly believe whatever he tells me.

'Why do you ask?' Adrian says, turning back to the cups on the counter.

'I was talking to Scarlett about the accident yesterday and she started to get upset,' I tell him, wondering what Pippa would say if she knew I was saying this, because this surely wasn't what she had in mind when she told me to have a private word with this man.

'Of course she would have got upset,' Adrian says, replying quickly and looking more than a little cross. 'That accident has changed her life. It's changed all of our lives. She's hardly going to be cheerful about it.'

I guess Adrian has a point, but it's not the point that I'm alluding to. I get my answer when he stops what he's doing and walks to the door.

'Let me show you something,' he says, and I have no idea what he's talking about, but I follow him out of the kitchen and into what looks like a study. I see bookcases as well as a huge desk that is littered with paperwork, and Adrian picks up a few of those papers now to show me.

'I don't know what you think happened, but all I can show you is this,' he says, handing me one of the pieces of paperwork.

I look down at it and see that it's an invoice for a medical company downtown.

'What's this?' I ask him, unsure what he's showing me.

'That's how much I was paying for private brain scans,' he says. 'And I've got dozens more invoices just like it all around here. Then there's the rehab fees, not to mention work with a psychologist. Then that's all before the expenses I've incurred for more unusual methods of trying to overcome memory loss, from homeopathic remedies to more spiritualistic concepts, I've tried them all. Here, look, you can see all the bills I've got, as well as all the articles I've read about all this stuff, and the statistical chances of any of it working.'

He scoops up a load of paperwork and seems to offer it to me, or possibly even be on the verge of throwing it all at me. In that moment, I feel terrible because I know why he's doing this. He's showing me how hard he's been working to try and help his wife get her memory back, or at least how much money he's been paying various doctors and specialists to try and help her, and I can see that it's a lot. I guess this is his way of shutting down any suspicions I might have of my own about what happened, because if he did have something to hide, would he be going to all this trouble to make his wife remember again?

'I'm sorry,' I say, aware that a load of medical bills addressed to him from various hospitals and private practices don't necessarily make him innocent, but it does make him look like a guy desperate to save his wife.

'I don't want you to be sorry. I just want you to do your job,' Adrian says as he slumps down into his office chair, running a hand over his tired face, which makes me feel even worse.

'I am doing my job,' I try, but it's a feeble argument when I'm in here having this conversation with him rather than upstairs tending to Scarlett.

'Do you know what it's like, caring for a loved one with memory loss?' he asks me now. 'I mean, what it's *really* like? It's nothing like what you've read about in your medical books, or even what it's like when you visit a patient and ask their family members how they are coping. They never give truly honest answers. That's because the truly honest answer is that it is sheer hell. There's no other way to describe what it feels like to look into the eyes of someone who should know you better than anyone, yet realise that they have absolutely no clue as to who you are.'

It's Adrian who now looks on the verge of tears, and I don't know whether to try and comfort him or apologise for getting him to this point. Fortunately for me, he speaks first.

'What I'm saying is don't confuse my behaviour for a man who isn't broken inside,' he tells me sadly. 'I might not wander around here crying or looking inconsolable, but I'm struggling, and while it's nice that you are showing concern for my wife, please don't insinuate anything about me or her accident ever again, or I'll have to ask that you are transferred somewhere else.'

Adrian has left me in no doubt as to what will happen if I continue to harbour suspicions about him. As he gets up and walks out of the office, I decide to get back to work before he can call my employer and tell them that I'm no good. But just before I go upstairs, I find Adrian in the kitchen again, and I have something to say.

'I didn't mean to make you feel uncomfortable,' I say, watching him closely. 'I'm sorry,' I add, hoping he accepts it.

'Thank you,' is all Adrian says in reply; he cuts a stack of sandwiches in half. He smiles. 'Now, let's eat and then get back to the patient, shall we?'

Most people's mood improves when around food, but I'm feeling even worse than I was before I came downstairs and saw what Adrian was doing in the kitchen. That's because I'm unsure of myself again. Adrian is very convincing, which might be the sign of a good liar, but possibly it's simply because he's telling the truth. If he is, how could I be getting this so wrong?

I really need to figure out what I do next.

Trust this man?

Or trust my instincts?

ELEVEN

I spent the rest of the day trying to make up for my possible blunder with Adrian by being the best nurse that I could be, engaging with Scarlett and trying to cheer the patient up, even forgoing my full lunch break to watch another movie with her. It helped to go some way to ease some of the guilt I was feeling for doubting Adrian and the true nature of the accident. I've decided that I was wrong about him and I have less doubts about him now. Having seen how many ways he had tried to get his wife help, it was clear he was desperate for her memory to return, so that didn't seem like the actions of a man with something to hide. As I watched him sit there in his office with tears in his eyes, I saw a man who was probably used to paying for his problems to go away, but this was one that even money couldn't find a cure for.

I even brought up Scarlett being a nurse in the past to see how much of that she remembered. She spoke fondly when I first mentioned it, but quickly changed her mind, saying it was a tiring profession and she didn't envy the nurses of today, which I had to agree with.

By the time Pippa and I left their house, I hoped I had

redeemed myself and wasn't going to be told that my services were no longer required there. I guess everything is okay because Pippa didn't say anything to me about it on the way home, nor have I received any notice that I'm in trouble with my boss. Therefore, I expect to be back with Scarlett and Adrian tomorrow, and that's a relief – with everything else going wrong for me at home, I need my work life to be better. With that in mind, I am going to try and do a little more to hopefully help them – and show that I am the right nurse for them.

The first thing I did when I got home was check the locks and the windows for any possible signs of damage or forced entry. Paranoia was rife until I felt assured everything was as it should be, though it was no fun at all to be walking around my home and wondering if somebody was going to jump out at me. But once I knew everything was fine, I refocused my mind back on to the patient.

I don't exactly have an office at home that rivals the one in Adrian's house, but I do have a bookshelf full of medical litera-ture. It's those books that I'm reading now as I recline on my sofa, trying to find something that might help Scarlett, which potentially Adrian hasn't considered yet. I know it's a long shot because he's already paid for the best and brightest minds in Chicago to try and help his wife, but maybe there is something here he hasn't tried. Some form of therapy or treatment or an idea that might spark something in the future. But I've been reading all the sections in these books that deal with the brain, and more specifically memory loss and head trauma, and there's nothing new jumping out at me. Everything that is suggested here is probably something that's already been looked at and invoiced to Adrian, every modern way of trying to heal a patient like Scarlett already having been explored and billed to the desperate husband who I practically accused of hurting his wife.

Giving up on the books, I turn to the internet for help, using the laptop that has sat closed on my dining room table to hopefully help me find a solution. I'm not averse to technology and the internet – it's just I don't spend much time using it. Computers give me a headache and make my eyes blurry, which is why I much prefer a walk when I have time to kill, or to read a book when I'm looking for information, but I'll make an exception tonight.

Browsing the web, I enter all sorts of search terms from 'new ways to treat memory loss' to 'miracle cure for the brain', and then read all sorts of fascinating articles. Going deeper down the rabbit hole, I find all sorts of forums where partners or children of loved ones who are suffering memory loss – whether caused by an injury or a condition like Parkinson's or Alzheimer's – discuss their methods for coping, as well as anything they have tried that might have been a slight success. Someone says to take the patient back to their childhood home, while another suggests taking them to the school they attended as a youngster. One person in a forum about amnesia says that smelling salts caused his mother to have flashbacks to her youth, while another says that cold showers seemed to give his ailing father more good days with his memory than bad. But overall, there is no mention of any miracle cure, and of course there isn't. It's because one doesn't exist. If it did, a wealthy man like Adrian would surely pay every penny he has to give it to his wife.

However, one post does mention role-playing, not as a cure, but as a way to alleviate a sufferer's symptoms of memory loss, if only for a short while, or even allow them to remember things they had previously forgotten, and I find it interesting. I think of the times Scarlett has confused me with her daughter. While it initially troubled me – and Adrian would always correct her – I wonder what might happen if I was to play along with it? Suppose the next time it might happen, rather than explain I was not her daughter, I pretended that she was correct and I was her daughter. Presumably, it would at least cheer Scarlett up, but might it even unlock some of her memories and help with her overall condition? Possibly, and this post in this forum seems to think it could do, so I'll bear that in mind the next time it happens, jotting it down on the notes I have so that it's now part of the tools I have for the next time I go to work.

I suppose I've made progress of sorts here, but I know I've been on the internet for too long because my vision is a little blurry now and my forehead is starting to throb. But just before I close the laptop, I come across an account of a woman who made the hard decision to have her partner put into full-time care when his memory worsened. As I read, I wonder if Adrian has contemplated moving Scarlett into a facility where she could be monitored around the clock, because it could potentially be much safer than having her at home, especially if her confusion gets worse. But it's a tricky subject to broach with him, and I've already put my foot in it once today. But I note this down too, and figure I'll mention it to Pippa tomorrow, to get her opinion on whether or not Scarlett might eventually need more full-time care, somewhere other than her home.

That's enough internet for one night. But I find myself conducting one more search, though this one has little to do with being a better nurse and more about being nosey. I type the name 'Adrian Hoffman' into the search engine to see what comes up.

Disappointingly, it's very little. I was hoping to find some kind of presence on social media, or at least a few photos or articles relating to his medical career. But all the Adrian Hoffmans I find are not him. I search for 'Scarlett Hoffman' next, but it's a similar story. Not much to see there either.

Have they really managed to go so many years without popping up online somewhere? I would have thought there would be some digital footprint, especially given Adrian's job before he retired, and how successful he clearly was at it. But I suppose their generation wasn't as obsessed with documenting their lives as those that came after them, so it could be the case.

Or is there another reason there isn't much to be found about them?

A more sinister one?

Desperate for some respite from worrying about work and the complex configurations of the human brain, as well as the patient and the husband who mysteriously lack a digital footprint, I decide to head out for a walk. Part of me feels like staying in here behind locked doors, but another part is aware that I can't be afraid of unlocking my doors and going out, despite what happened last night. The police haven't been in touch yet to let me know they have caught the intruder, and I doubt they will make much progress there, but I can't hide away forever, just going to work and then going to bed. I should feel confident to walk the streets, especially as it seems to be the best way of clearing my head, so I am going out and I'm not going to worry about whether or not anybody might be following me or watching me.

I do triple-check that both my front and back doors are securely locked before I start walking, not wanting to come home to any nasty surprises. As I expected, I feel much better for being away from a computer screen and, as the fresh air works its magic on my mood, I am feeling more optimistic about life than I was half an hour ago. But that doesn't last long when I hear the scraping of a shoe on concrete behind me, and I spin around in the dark street.

I can't see anybody else out here with me, but I definitely heard someone, so I keep looking, my eyes scouring the shadows, searching the dark driveways, cars and sidewalks. Eventually, I give up and carry on.

'I'm not being followed,' I say under my breath, trying to convince myself of that. *And I definitely do not have a stalker like that policeman suggested.* But after turning onto the next street, I again hear what sounds like a footstep behind me, and despite being afraid, I decide to put this to the test.

I quicken my pace and round another street corner, darting into a front yard and hiding behind the wall so that I'm out of sight of any pedestrians who might pass by. I stay crouching there in the gloom while listening out to see if anybody passes and, ten seconds later, I hear footsteps approaching. I remain in my hiding place until I hear them pass before slowly standing up and looking over the wall. When I do, I see a man moving away from me. This is who must have been behind me, but is this person following me or not?

I decide to find out by walking behind him to see where he is going. He might have a genuine destination in mind, maybe heading home or to a bar and, if so, that is fine. But if he was following me then he'll surely stop and look around in a moment when he realises that he's lost me, and if he does that, I'll have caught him. Then all I'll need to do is make sure I get a proper description that I can pass on to the police.

As I follow this mysterious man, I'm aware that I'm taking a big risk, especially when there doesn't seem to be anyone else out on the street with us. What if he turns nasty? What if he tries to hurt me? Maybe this is a bad idea. Or maybe he's not even following me at all, and this is another figment of my imagination, an imagination that is increasingly running away with itself.

And then the man stops walking at the street corner and looks around, as if he's unsure which way to go next.

I freeze now, not just because carrying on would bring me closer to him, but because him stopping and being unsure about which way to go next is a very strong indicator that he was following me after all. Now that he's realised he's lost me, he seems uncertain about his next move, and that proves he was on my tail all along.

Then he turns around and stares in my direction. My breath catches in my throat.

I recognise him.

TWELVE

'You?' I ask, maintaining my distance from the man but still feeling the nerves rising inside of me.

The man realises he has been caught and doesn't do anything to close the distance between us, simply staring at me and presumably wondering what I am going to do now. The obvious answer is call the police, but aware of how useless they were before, I'm wary of that. That's why I try to figure this out for myself.

'Why are you following me?' I ask, stepping closer to the man. 'I know who you are! And I know you were in my house last night too!'

This man is familiar to me and, as I study his features, I only wish that I had been able to recollect them when the police officer asked me in the early hours of this morning. I couldn't then, but now I've seen him again I know this is definitely him – the same man I saw following me two nights ago – the one who forced me to run home and lock my door. But I'm not going to act afraid of him, not now that I have just gained the upper hand and, to prove it, I keep closing the distance between us. Part of me is simply trying to act brave though – I'm still terrified – and as I get nearer to him, I glance at a few of the windows of the houses on this street and hope that if anything bad happens here, one of these residents will see it and come out to help me.

'Wait,' the man says as I get nearer, but I don't slow down. He's the one in the wrong here, not me.

'Why are you stalking me?' I cry. 'Who the hell are you and what do you want?'

'Stop! Please, I'm not stalking you,' he tries lamely, but it's no good, he can't deny it, not when I just caught him trailing me.

'I'll call the police,' I say, but as expected it only makes him more fearful.

'No, please don't do that,' he begs me, his hands out in front.

'Give me one good reason not to!' I snap back. 'Why the hell should I let you get away with this?'

'I'm sorry.'

'Sorry for what? For trying to frighten me? For being a creep? For breaking and entering into my home?'

'What? I wasn't in your house!'

'You expect me to believe that? Why should I?'

'Because it's the truth!'

I have no idea how this man has the gall to stand here and say that wasn't him in my home last night, but he's trying it, despite all the evidence seeming to point at him.

'Who are you?' I ask him, although I'm not sure even putting a name to the face will make me feel any better about this.

'I'm nobody,' the man replies, which is a bizarre answer.

'What?'

'Forget about me. It doesn't matter. I'll leave you alone,' he says, and he turns to leave as if he actually means it.

But I'm not letting him get away that easily and rush

towards him. When I reach him, I grab his arm and expect him to try and pull away from me.

But he doesn't do that. He looks at me and shakes his head.

'I'm sorry. You're right. I was following you, but I won't do it again. I swear I wasn't in your house, though. Honestly, that wasn't me.'

I wasn't expecting the sudden change, nor did I think he would admit what I already suspected, although he's still denying being in my home.

'Tell me why you're following me,' I demand to know, needing a reason rather than just an admission.

'I don't know. I guess I'd seen you around, thought you were cute. I don't know. It's stupid. I'm sorry.'

None of that sounds convincing, but maybe this guy is some creepy weirdo who saw me out one day and liked the look of me. That still doesn't make what he is doing right, but at least I no longer seem to be under threat. At least I think that's the case, anyway.

I let go of the man's arm, but he doesn't run. He keeps looking at me, as if needing my permission to leave.

'You really weren't the one in my house last night?' I ask him one more time, and he shakes his head. I don't have to believe him, but something makes me want to, although he could easily be lying to avoid getting in trouble.

'If I ever see you again, I will call the police and I'll make sure they catch you,' I say, trying to sound as forceful as I can, though it seems I didn't need to make my final threat because this man is still apologetic.

'Okay, I'm sorry. Forgive me. You won't see me again,' he says. He turns and hurries away. I watch him go, crossing the street and disappearing around a corner.

That was bizarre, but I feel proud of myself for not only catching him but standing up to him too. However, I also feel a little troubled. If he wasn't the person in my home last night, who was it? I can't have two stalkers, that would be beyond bizarre, but what if that's the case?

I'm alone on this street and it's getting late, so I decide to get moving. But despite trying to convince myself that I handled that situation well just now, I realise that I really should go and report what happened to the police. My story of tonight, along with what happened in my house during the late hours of last night, will allow the officers to understand that something is going on and they should take it more seriously. Although I'm also aware that I told the man following me that I wouldn't go to the police. What if he's still watching me? If he is and he sees me entering a police station, he'll know I lied to him – and how might he react to that?

That's why I decide to head home, taking care to keep checking behind me as I do, making sure that man is really sticking to his word and is gone. There's no sign of him, and as I enter my house, I lock the door and then check the back is still locked too. Then I dial 911 and prepare to report what just happened. But as the operator answers, I pause – I think about what will happen next if I go ahead with this. A couple of police officers will most likely come to my house at some point to take a statement, or I'll be asked to report to my nearest station and make my statement there. Either way, it's going to be hours before this is done and, looking at the time, they are hours that I don't want to waste. I'm so exhausted after barely getting any sleep last night and then having such a busy day today. I crave my bed, rather than another awkward conversation with some cop who doesn't even take me seriously and mistakes my grogginess for an alcohol problem. That's why I hang up and decide to go to bed; even in my tired state, I expect that I'll still need a few pills to help me get rest tonight. I'm worrying that whoever came here last night might try and come back again.

. . .

I get in bed and lie under my comforter, listening out for over an hour before I assume that I'm safe, and pop a couple of pills. Then I settle down and try to sleep, saying a silent prayer that I won't be woken up by anything untoward and, fortunately, I am not. However, that doesn't mean my night passes entirely incident free – even though I'm asleep, my troubles continue when I have a very bad dream…

It's one in which I see Scarlett lying in her bed. While I'm with her in my nurse's uniform, it's as if she can't see me and I'm unable to communicate with her. I realise that I'm practically useless when someone else enters the bedroom. It's Adrian, and he is walking towards his wife on the bed, stepping right past me as if I'm not there, with a rigid look of determination on his face. I try to speak or reach out and stop him, because I have the sense that something is very wrong here, but I'm not able to move a muscle or make a sound, powerless to prevent what is about to happen.

All I can do is watch as Adrian picks up a pillow and brings it down over Scarlett's face, holding it there despite her wriggling and screaming for her life. She keeps fighting, but he keeps suffocating her, and all the while all I am able to do is listen to her muffled screams.

That's until I eventually hear my own screams, but by then, I have woken up and am alone in my bedroom, with nothing but the memory of the frightening nightmare rattling around in my head.

That was another case of my imagination running riot.

Unless it was something important emerging from my subconscious.

Something to tell me that Adrian is still not to be trusted.

THIRTEEN

I wasn't able to fall back to sleep after my disturbing nightmare, not even after taking another sleeping tablet, which is why, as I hear knocking at my front door, I cover my head with my pillow and wish the person making the noise would go away. But no sooner have I done that than it reminds me of the awful dream I had and, more specifically, of Scarlett with her head smothered by a pillow that her husband was wielding. So I quickly pull my head back out into fresh air and gulp in a few mouthfuls of precious oxygen.

The knocking persists, so I have to accept that I've regressed to being woken up again by an adult who is making a better job of life than I am. I wearily drag my tired body down the stairs and open the door to find that adult, the woman who looks in a far better state than I am at this time of the morning.

'Darcy? Are you okay? What's happened?'

I take one look at Pippa in her uniform and tears immediately fill my eyes, to the point where the name on her badge quickly becomes blurry and I wish I hadn't opened the door at all.

'Darcy! Come here! It's okay.'

Pippa takes me in a hug, and I initially try to pull back so I can pretend like everything is fine. It's not. So I quickly give in and start sobbing on her shoulder. She continues to try and comfort me as she leads me back into my house and sits me down on the sofa. I finally get a grip on my emotions and the tears cease.

'I'm sorry,' I say as I wipe my eyes with a tissue. 'I'm just so tired.'

'Is that all it is?' Pippa asks me, a grave look of concern on her face, and I decide to be honest with her.

'No,' I say, shaking my head and, as I do, a tear escapes my eye and runs down my left cheek. 'Somebody's been following me. I caught them last night, but I let them go.'

'What?' Pippa cries, aghast. 'Who is it? Have they hurt you?'

'No, I'm okay. They haven't touched me. I don't know who they are or what they wanted, but I told them to stay away from me and I think they will.'

'You think? How can you be sure? Have you spoken to the police about this?'

I shake my head. Pippa wants to know why, so I carry on being truthful, a little unsure as to why I am oversharing all this information with her, but aware that it might be easier to get these things off my chest.

'Because I already spoke to them a couple of days ago when someone broke into my house.'

'Someone broke into your house?'

Pippa still looks worried, as well she might be, because this must all be troubling to hear, but I try to downplay it.

'It's all right. I'm all right. Nothing was taken. I wasn't hurt. It was a shock, that's all. I spoke to the police, but they didn't seem interested or like they could help me. It was a waste of time.'

Pippa looks around the room, almost as if she is trying to do what the police should have done and solve the mystery of the intruder, but of course she can't.

'Are the police doing anything?' she asks me, and I shrug.

'I don't think so. I overheard them talking. They think I was drunk or hungover or whatever and probably making things up.'

'Are you sure? They haven't come back since?'

'No.'

Pippa shakes her head before taking out her phone.

'What are you doing?' I ask her, using my tissue again.

'I'm calling work and telling them you won't be in today,' Pippa replies.

'What? No, we have to go. Scarlett needs us.'

'I can cover for you. Or someone else can go instead of us if you need me here. You can't be working in this state.'

'I'm fine,' I try, but it's a difficult argument to make with tearstained eyes and a snotty tissue in my hand.

'Just give me a minute,' Pippa says. She leaves the room. I beg her to leave it so we can go to work as normal, but she ignores me.

'Yeah, it's me,' I hear her say on the phone a moment later. 'Sorry, I'm just letting you know that Darcy won't be able to work today. Personal problems. I am with her now. I can go to the patient's house soon, but I'd prefer to stay with her and make sure she's okay, so is there anyone else you can send?'

I can't hear the other end of the conversation, and I'm hoping I'm not going to get in trouble for not being able to report for duty today. But Pippa is right, I am in no fit state to work, and when my colleague returns, she lets me know not to worry about work now.

'The boss understands. You don't have to work today,' Pippa says. 'I might have to, but we'll see, maybe someone can cover for me.'

'I'm okay, honestly,' I say. 'I don't want to ruin your day. I just need some sleep.'

I bury my head in my hands, trying not to cry again, but it's easier said than done in this state of exhaustion. Fighting fatigue has become normal for me, but I've had enough of it, and Pippa can clearly see that.

'I had no idea you were this bad,' she says sadly. 'If I did, I wouldn't have kept coming here to take you to work. I'd have got you some proper help.'

'It's not your fault,' I tell her, meaning it. 'I've tried to cover it up. And coffee helps, quite a lot actually.'

I laugh and it feels good to break through a bit of the tension that has been building in the room, and thankfully Pippa laughs too as she takes a seat beside me.

'How about I stay here while you go back to bed and try and get some sleep?' she suggests. 'I'll let you know if I have to leave to go to work, but for now I don't, so you go and get rest, okay?'

That sounds like a great idea, but I still feel bad.

'Are you sure?' I ask, but perhaps the answer to my question lies in the uniform Pippa is wearing.

'It's no good just looking after everyone else if we can't even look after each other, is it?' she says, and I smile, appreciating her warmth and kindness.

Taking the opportunity to go and get the sleep my frazzled brain requires, I go and lie down.

I must have drifted off at some point because, when I open my eyes again, I see that it's the middle of the afternoon.

Shocked that I slept for so long, and afraid that poor Pippa has been sat downstairs waiting for me to wake up all day, I rush downstairs. I find that she has gone. There is a note saying she had to go to work for a few hours, but she will be back to check on me shortly. In the meantime, she has left snacks in the kitchen for me and, sure enough, I see that she has.

Feeling grateful, not just for the snacks but for the fact that

I actually slept, I try to use this rare moment of clear thinking to decide what I am going to do next. Maybe I will go to the police and chase up what they are doing about the intruder. Maybe I will tell them about the stalker and give them his description so they can try and find him. But those are all potential solutions to short-term problems. As far as the long-term goes, I know I need to do something about that too, because it's clear that I can't carry on like this. Pippa has covered for me today, and has been helping me keep my job by coming here to collect me, but that's not fair on her, and I need to address the issue as to why I need that help in the first place. My lack of sleep – and increasing dependence on medication – is something that needs to be resolved. If that means making some drastic changes in my life then so be it. Maybe I need to quit nursing. Maybe I need to move house. Maybe I need a totally fresh start. At this point, nothing is off the table, and I have to believe that I'll do anything if it results in feeling better a few months from now.

It's late afternoon when Pippa returns to my house. She wants to know how I'm doing.

'I'm feeling better, thanks,' I say honestly. 'I got some sleep, and I needed it.'

'Good,' Pippa says. 'But you still look tired. Do you want to go back to sleep now, and I'll stay here for a while? I could clean up a little.'

'Wow, is it that bad?' I ask nervously, aware that my home is looking slightly cluttered. I had been hoping my friend hadn't noticed.

'Let's just say I'm as good with a feather duster as I am with my patients,' Pippa replies.

I laugh at that before realising that, in all the worrying about me, I haven't asked her how her day has gone, or more specifically how the woman is who I was supposed to be helping look after.

'How was Scarlett today?' I ask, hoping to hear good news.

'She was okay, actually,' Pippa replies, which makes me feel a little bit better about my absence. 'And Adrian understood when I explained to him that you weren't feeling well, so don't worry about them. You just concentrate on feeling better yourself.'

It's a relief to hear that Scarlett was okay today, as well as the fact that Adrian didn't mind me not reporting for duty, but it's still frustrating that I was forced into taking time off work. I see now that it was necessary though – I had hit a wall and needed that sleep I got this afternoon, though Pippa still seems to think I need more.

'Seriously, I'm happy to stay here while you go back to bed,' she tells me. 'I can make sure nobody else comes back if that's what you're worried about.'

'No, it's fine, I'm not worried,' I tell her. 'And that's not just me trying to be brave. I think I dealt with that guy, whoever he was.'

'You really have no idea who he was?'

'Nope. Hopefully I won't see him again either.'

Pippa offers to make me a drink, but I tell her that I can manage by myself now, insisting that she leaves so she can get on with her own life for the rest of the day. She certainly must have enough to deal with, what with her young child to look after.

'You get home to your son,' I say with a smile, because I figure that mentioning him will cheer her up. 'I bet he can't wait to see you.'

'He's certainly excitable,' Pippa replies. 'But which four-year-old isn't?'

'True,' I say with a laugh, but it's a false one in the moment. Even though I was aiming to cheer my colleague up, I suddenly feel a pang of sadness that I don't have somebody who loves me waiting for me when I get home at the end of a long day. Not only does she have her son, but she also has her husband. I consider asking her about him, but seeing as she's not been wearing her wedding ring to work, I decide against it at the last second, at the risk of making her feel worse.

'I'll see you tomorrow,' I say, leading her to the door. 'A good night's sleep and I'll be raring to go, I promise.'

Pippa isn't exactly convinced, and I hardly have past evidence to back up my bold claim, but she eventually leaves, allowing me some time to myself. At that point, my plan really is to go back to bed, but after I take a shower I realise that I'm wide awake. That long sleep I had earlier has worked wonders and now I feel the need to be productive, so I consider my options. I could do what Pippa offered to do and clean up around here, but that doesn't inspire me, so I wander my home for ideas. That's when I see the patient notes lying beside the laptop in my dining room, and I suddenly worry that Pippa would have seen these earlier. If she did, she'll know that I took them from her car – having them at home is very unprofessional of me. But she hasn't said anything to me about them, so maybe I've got away with it. Or maybe Pippa took pity on me and figured I had enough problems without getting angry at me about this today.

I don't know for sure, but I scoop up the notes and put them by the front door ready for the morning, planning on showing them to Pippa when she picks me up tomorrow, and admitting to what I did before explaining why I did it. Hopefully she'll understand. Being honest with her is the least she deserves after how she has looked after me today. But as I hold the notes, I notice a few of the things I have written on them recently – and one train of thought in particular is underlined in bold.

Adrian could be lying. What if he is? <u>Scarlett could be in danger</u>.

Staring at the words, I wonder how I could have been so stupid. I suspected Adrian, yet easily allowed myself to be manipulated by him showing me a few invoices in his office to prove how hard he had been working to help his stricken wife. But what if all of that was a smokescreen? What if he knows there is no way her memory will return and he's just paying for these things to make it look like he is the caring husband?

What if Scarlett is still in danger now?

I feel guilty for not being at her house today, and even though I know I'll be there tomorrow, that feels like a long time away if I am right about this. That's why I make a decision to do something tonight.

I grab my jacket and head out onto the street. When I get to the main road, I hail a passing taxi.

When I get inside it, I tell them where to go.

It's after hours, but I don't care.

I want to go and see my patient.

FOURTEEN

The sun is setting as my taxi driver navigates us to where I want to go. After giving him the address printed on the patient notes, my driver had let out a loud whistle.

'Fancy,' he had said once we had started moving. 'It's not often I get a millionaire passenger.'

'I'm not a millionaire,' I had told him, but he had laughed at that.

'Anybody who is going to that part of the city must have a dollar or two,' he had replied, going on to tell me about how he came from an area in the West Side, where life was much leaner for the residents than it was for those living in the huge houses in the more affluent areas in the North Side.

My cab driver continues to make small talk with me as he drives, but I've been too busy staring out of the window to make sure I don't miss the street I want. I know we're close now because the properties on either side of the road are sprawling and familiar, but I can't remember exactly which street Adrian and Scarlett's house is on. Then I see it, the American flag fluttering in the breeze high up on the flagpole, and I know that's the house at the bottom of their street.

'You can stop here,' I say to the driver, and he gently eases on the brake pedal. The sun has dropped below the horizon and complete darkness is now only a matter of minutes away. That suits me though because it'll make it less obvious that I'm here, and I know I shouldn't be as I pay the fare and get out of the cab.

I'm not entirely sure why I have bothered to make this trip rather than wait until the morning when Pippa could have driven me here. I felt an urge to check in on Scarlett and double-check that she is okay outside of work hours, although I'm not sure what I'm expecting to see as I walk towards Sherwood Crescent. I know Pippa would worry if she knew I was here, assuming that I was being unprofessional, but I see it as being extremely professional. I'm ensuring a patient under our care is actually okay outside of the hours when we see her. After all, anybody could pretend while they have company, but it's what goes on behind closed doors when nobody is watching that really counts.

I'm not sure what I'm expecting to catch Adrian doing, but I know I'm here to ensure his wife's safety, so as I creep onto their street I'm hoping that I'll see nothing untoward. The house has huge windows, and I'm confident that I'll see something. I imagine Scarlett will be in bed upstairs, but I might see Adrian moving around on the ground floor of the home, and if he's being the caring husband, he could be taking his wife a drink, some food or her meds. Or maybe he is in his study, sifting through more medical reports and desperately trying to find a cure for his wife. As sorry as that would be for him, it would be a reassuring thing for me to see and it would help to convince me that he is not a bad guy after all.

But what if I see something awful? What if I catch him doing something he shouldn't be doing?

What if he's hurting her?

There's a sinking feeling in my stomach as I see Adrian and

Scarlett's house in the darkness ahead, and I know it's not just because I technically shouldn't be here this late.

It's because I might just be about to prove my theory about Adrian.

I walk slowly up the street, glancing left and right as I go to see if any of the residents in the houses either side might be looking out and spotting the stranger lurking near their properties. But nobody is at their windows, though the curtains are open, and I can see into the homes, spotting decadent lounges with huge flatscreen TVs and big armchairs beside bookcases and fireplaces. I bet it's incredible here at Christmas when everyone has their trees in their front windows, as well as a few lights on the exterior of their houses. The fact everyone has their curtains open even after sunset makes me think about how safe this neighbourhood must be. This isn't like one of those areas where people hide away, closing their curtains, locking their doors and worrying that somebody is going to try and break in. Here, it's as if everyone is shielded by some invisible force that says nothing bad can happen because we're all rich and, therefore, we're all safe.

The exact opposite of my current situation then.

Adrian and Scarlett's house is no different in that all the curtains are open, and as I reach their driveway I duck down a little and quicken my pace, worrying that Adrian might spot me approaching. But there's no movement at any of the windows, and as I reach the front door I figure I'm almost at the point of no return. This is my last chance to turn around and go home and stop whatever this stupid game is that I'm playing. I could possibly lose my job for being here, creeping around a patient's property without permission, and I guess it looks like stalking. Maybe it is, though I like to think that there is a big difference between me and that man I caught following me before. I do not have a sinister motive; I'm here because I want to make sure that the patient is okay. So with that in mind, I carry on, passing the point of no return as I approach one of the windows and prepare to peep inside.

As I look through the glass, I see the lounge I recognise. There's the sofa that I sat on with Pippa on our first day here not so long ago, and there's the armchair that Adrian was seated in too. But the room is vacant now, so I move on to the next window to see if there's anything of interest there. This one gives me a glimpse into the study, and I see the desk covered in papers, but nobody is in here either.

As I move on to the third window, I wonder if Adrian is upstairs. He could be with his wife in her bedroom or maybe he's in another one, and, if so, I guess I won't be catching a glimpse of either of them. But then I reach the next window and, when I look inside, I see Adrian. He's in the kitchen and he's opening a bottle of red wine. My heart rate quickens as I watch him, that dangerous feeling of voyeurism: both exciting and frightening, but I can't look away. He's wearing a T-shirt and sweatpants, which makes me wonder if he has been working out or if he's just chosen to put on some very casual, comfortable attire for the evening. If he was exercising before, it seems the healthy regime is over because once he's opened the wine, he takes out a bowl from a drawer, filling it with tortilla chips and sneaking a bite of one for himself.

He then pours himself a glass of wine and takes the glass and the bowl out of the kitchen. I have lost sight of him now, and hurry back past the windows I've already peeped through to see where he might be going. He doesn't appear to be in the study. I reach the lounge window, and he's in there, taking a seat on the sofa. Once he's settled, he picks up the remote and turns the TV on.

Putting his feet up on the coffee table, he looks very relaxed as he nibbles on his snacks and sips his wine – and the longer I watch him, the worse I feel about spying. This is a man's private moment in his own house. I shouldn't be witness to this. Maybe he's simply unwinding after yet another stressful day. I've been doubting his honesty, but seeing how alone he is here makes me think he'd probably give anything for his wife to be better so she could be sat beside him, eating and drinking too. But there's no sign of her, so I guess she's in bed, possibly asleep, potentially confused, but as alone as her husband is right now.

Tears well up in my eyes, though not just for this bleak couple. It's for me. I realise that I'm as lonely as this man. Why else would I be spying on other people rather than enjoying my own life? How did it come to this? Surely I should be able to do better. I'm still young, I'm smart and I'm a good person. Yet here I am acting like a lunatic.

I'm also crying because I don't know what to do about it. Even if I tell Pippa, or anybody else, and even if I quit my job and try to change things, there's no guarantee I'll be any happier than I am in this exact moment. Maybe my life might get even worse. Maybe creeping around and spying on this couple is as good as things are ever going to get for me.

I'm just about to leave and make a very long and sorrowful journey home when I notice the door opening behind Adrian, and as he turns around to look, I see who is entering the room. I gasp.

It's Scarlett, but never as I have seen her. She has always looked so pale and weak, and never wearing anything other than a dressing gown. Now she looks totally different. She looks radiant, her hair shiny and looking freshly washed, while her face has colour to it and she's even wearing a touch of make-up. It's not only her physical features that have improved but her choice of clothing has too. As she reaches her husband on the sofa, I marvel at her smart blouse and jeans, attire that transforms this woman from the ailing patient I'm used to seeing into a beautiful and healthy-looking woman enjoying an evening at home.

I have no idea what sparked the transformation and wonder

if it could be that Scarlett is enjoying a lucid moment. One that has allowed her to get out of bed by herself, shower and freshen up and even join her partner downstairs to watch a TV show. But knowing her injuries and condition, I wouldn't have thought such a thing was possible. The more I watch, the less I see any signs at all that she is a woman who needs medical assistance. She looks perfectly normal, a vison of health in fact, and while I'm amazed to see Scarlett like this, one person who doesn't seem surprised by her behaviour is Adrian. He doesn't bat an eyelid as she takes a seat on the sofa beside him; he even offers her the bowl so she can have one of the snacks he has been enjoying himself. Scarlett accepts the invitation before snuggling into her husband's shoulder and, together, the pair of them relax and watch the TV, suddenly looking like the perfect couple without a single care in the world.

What the hell is going on here?

How is this possible?

Unless...

The reality of the situation dawns on me as I keep watching Scarlett, a woman who I thought depended on my assistance, laughing at the television, grabbing her husband's wine glass and taking a glug herself.

There's nothing wrong with this woman.

She is faking it.

Worse, this couple are faking it.

The only question is: *why?*

FIFTEEN

The first thing I want to do is bang on the window and let the people inside this house know that their game is up.

Isn't that what these liars deserve?

I'd love to see the smug smiles wiped off their faces as they realise I've caught them, that whatever sick game they are playing is up. I feel like doing it because I'm furious at them. How dare they occupy the time of two busy nurses and take them away from other more needy patients, depriving them of care so they can play out whatever weird fantasy they might have going on here? But I am hesitating to knock, and I guess it's because, despite what I've seen, I know I shouldn't be here, so I'd still prefer not to get caught trespassing.

That's why I leave Adrian and Scarlett as they are, intertwined on the sofa in a bubble of apparent contentment, though I'm not going to let them get away with this entirely. Taking out my phone, I open the video app and then start recording, capturing footage of the couple that I plan to show to Pippa as soon as I've got out of here. When I do, I imagine she'll be just as shocked as I am, and then together we can make a plan with our employer as to what we do about this fraudulent behaviour. Surely this is a crime, although Adrian must be paying for us to care for his wife, so it's very bizarre. Why would the pair of them concoct such a game and spend money on a lie? For fun? Is this how they get their kicks? I know rich people can sometimes be a little eccentric, mainly because they have the extra cash on hand to do more unique things, or the spare time to concoct unusual ideas in the first place, but this would be very strange.

Pretending to be ill and paying nurses to help?

I've never heard of anything like that before.

I check my phone's screen to make sure that it's still recording, and it is. Adrian and Scarlett are right in the centre of the camera, him quaffing wine, her scoffing snacks, the pair of them smiling and occasionally laughing at what they're seeing on the television. I record them for a couple of minutes before I decide that I have enough to show Pippa. Then I think about the quickest way out of here. I head back to the main road with the plan of trying to get a taxi from there. I walk away, leaving behind the big house that hides a very big secret. I almost hope I do have to return – I want to see the look on the faces of Scarlett and especially Adrian when they realise it was me who exposed their lies.

I leave their street, my head still spinning, the video saved securely on my phone. I look for a taxi, but I can't see any. I guess this isn't a part of the city where cabs randomly roam, so I have to search for a number on the internet to call. I find one and tell the operator where I am, reading the street sign ahead of me, only to be told it will be at least forty minutes before they can get a taxi out here for me.

'What?' I cry, frustrated that I appear to be stuck here for a while. I'm so far from home that walking is not an option, but it seems I don't have any choice. Unless...

I end the call and then look for Pippa's number. I'm not sure if she'll answer at this time; she could be busy. Or she might see that I'm ringing her and not want to be bothered with any more of my problems today, but I'm trying her anyway because she's the only one who will understand why I am where I am right now. Besides, if she does answer, it means I'll get to tell her what I saw quicker.

'Darcy?'

Pippa's voice instantly relaxes me, suggesting I'm starting to depend on her even more than I realised.

'Hey, Pippa! Thanks for answering!'

'What's going on? Are you okay?'

'Yeah, but I need a favour. Can you come and pick me up?'

'Where are you?'

I hesitate – this is the part where I have to give away my location and, when I do, surely Pippa will figure out that I shouldn't be here at this time of night. But I'm going to tell her about what happened anyway, so I might as well get it over with.

'I'm near Scarlett and Adrian's place,' I say, wondering what kind of reaction I'm about to get from the other end of the line.

'Excuse me?'

'I can explain! It's a long story, but if you can come and pick me up, I'll tell you everything.'

'What are you doing there?'

I guess I'm going to have to explain *before* she comes and picks me up.

'I went to their house,' I admit.

'Why?'

'I don't know. I just had a feeling like something weird was going on, so I wanted to check.'

'You shouldn't have done that! You could get in trouble!'

'I know, but I'm glad I did, because guess what I saw?'

Pippa goes quiet now, so I fill the silence.

'They're lying, Pippa! There's nothing wrong with Scarlett. I saw her and she looked perfectly healthy. She had showered and got changed and she even had make-up on. She was with Adrian on the sofa, and they were eating and drinking and were so happy together. She isn't ill. She's faking it! I don't know why, but she is!'

'You must be mistaken,' Pippa says, but I would have expected her to doubt this story, which is exactly why I took the time to record a video.

'I have the evidence,' I say triumphantly. 'I've got a video on my phone, and I'll show it to you, but can you come and pick me up? I'm stranded here and I can't get a cab.'

'You took a video? Oh my god, Darcy, I can't believe you did this!'

'What's wrong? I've caught them lying!'

'This is so unprofessional!'

This is not how I was expecting Pippa to react at all. She sounds mad at me, and now I'm doubting if she is going to come and get me. Glancing behind me, I check that I'm still alone out here and neither Adrian or Scarlett are approaching, but they're not, so I guess my secret is still safe. I'd prefer to get out of here sooner rather than later though.

'Please, can you come and get me and we can talk about this?' I beg and, thankfully, Pippa calms down a little bit.

'I can't believe this. Okay, I'll set off now, I should be with you in twenty minutes, tops.'

'Great, thank you!'

Pippa hangs up. I feel bad for interrupting her evening, especially with such crazy news. Now all I need to do is wait for her to arrive. I kill time by rewatching the video on my phone. I watch it several times, noticing different things each time, from the way that Adrian looks at his wife to the way she steals his wine or scoffs another snack. But one thing that absolutely does not change, despite all the repeated viewings of this video, is my opinion that Scarlett is faking her condition and Adrian has also been faking his concern.

It's twenty-two minutes till Pippa arrives, and it's a relief to see her car approaching me, because every minute that I've lingered out here has made me more anxious that I'm going to somehow get caught by the people I was just spying on. I frantically wave her down so she can't accidentally drive past. She eventually stops alongside me.

'Get in!' she cries, clearly nervous that we're both going to be caught here, so I quickly slide into the passenger seat and then we're on the move.

'Oh my god, what a night,' I say, but Pippa doesn't seem as excited about this as I am.

'This is so wrong,' she says. 'I can't believe you spied on them.'

'Aren't you glad I did? Now we're not going to waste any more time going to their house and helping them when they clearly don't need it. We can go and help real patients, not liars like them.'

I have the video to prove her wrong and I can't wait to show it to her once we've stopped driving. We make it back to my place and I already have my phone out ready to press play. But before I do, Pippa speaks.

'This isn't working,' she says.

'What do you mean?'

'I'm talking about this. Me helping you. Making sure you get to work. Covering for you today. Having to come out tonight to pick you up when I've got enough to deal with at home. I can't keep doing this.'

'I'm sorry,' I say, feeling bad for being so wrapped up in myself that it's forcing her to reconsider what she's been doing to help me. 'I'm really grateful for all you've been doing for me,

I really am. I know it's asking a lot of you. You're such a good friend. I don't deserve a friend like you.'

I mean that, and for a brief moment, I wonder how many friends Pippa has herself. I know she's busy with her family life, but what's her social circle like? Is it full? Or is she as lonely as I am?

Despite what I've just said to her about being a good friend, it hasn't done much to make Pippa any happier. Suddenly she's the one with tears in her eyes.

'What's wrong?' I ask, sad to see her so upset, but she shakes her head.

'I'm tired,' she admits. I get the sense there is much more, but before I can ask her what's going on in her life, she looks at my phone.

'Let's see it then,' she says, and I guess she's ready to watch the video.

As I press play, I'm hoping that the footage I have on here is at least going to make all of this worth it.

'See, she's fine,' I say, referring to Scarlett, who is clearly shown in the video behaving very differently to how she does when we're both with her.

Pippa keeps watching it without passing comment, and I suppose she's taking it all in before giving me her informed opinion on it. So I stay quiet and allow her the peace to watch it. When the video is ended, I look at her.

'What do you think?' I ask.

'It's strange, I'll give you that,' Pippa says, which is an understatement. 'We've certainly never seen her like that when we've been there.'

'Exactly! So it shows she's faking it. They're using us for some reason, though I have no idea why. A weird game? For fun? More money than sense? Are they trying to trap us? I don't know. Why do you think they are doing it?'

'I'm not sure it is a game,' Pippa says, surprising me.

'What do you mean?'

'The accident could be real. Scarlett's injuries could be real too. Maybe what you saw was her having a lucid moment.'

A lucid moment? Is Pippa serious?

'No, a lucid moment is just that, a moment. But I was there. I watched her with my own eyes. Maybe it's not coming across as well on camera, but I saw her, and she looked perfectly healthy. Like she had no head injury at all and certainly no memory loss. Like it was a normal husband and wife enjoying an evening in together. She wasn't a patient, and he wasn't the worried husband like he's been pretending to be. It's all an act.'

'It can't be,' Pippa says, shaking her head. 'There's no way. It just wouldn't make sense.'

'I know it doesn't make sense, but I'm telling you, she's faking it. So what do we do about it? Report it to work, right? Have them investigate?'

'What? No, we can't do that!'

'Why not?'

'Because we'd get in trouble! How are we going to explain that you were there filming them without their knowledge? You'll lose your job. I could lose mine too because you've made me a part of this now! We can't show anyone this video, no way!'

Pippa looks very distressed about it and is clearly worried about getting in trouble, but what else are we supposed to do?

'So what are you suggesting? We let them get away with this?'

'I'm not saying that at all,' Pippa tells me, running a hand over her tired face, and I notice her checking the clock on her dashboard. It's late, but I'm wired; I'm not thinking about sleep, though my colleague might be. 'What I'm saying is, we have to be careful. I don't know what's going on here, so how about instead of rushing into something that we don't understand and potentially getting into trouble, let's slow down and be sensible.'

I suppose that makes more sense, but we still don't have a plan to proceed.

'Okay, so what do we do?' I ask my colleague. 'Because there's no way I'm letting them get away with this. I want to know what they are doing, and I won't stop until I do.'

SIXTEEN

It was late when I got out of Pippa's car and went inside, and it was even later that I actually went to bed to try and get some sleep. There were a few reasons for that, the first being the conversation Pippa and I had to finish before we called it a night and she drove away.

'We go back to their house and we carry on as normal,' Pippa had said to me when giving me her plan, a plan that initially sounded ludicrous.

'How can we carry on as normal?' I had cried, and my colleague had urged me to let her finish.

'That's the best way we figure out what's going on with them,' she had said. 'We stay close to them. It's also the best way of not getting in trouble for this. We keep working there and we keep watching and, if necessary, we gather evidence the right way. Not with secret videos taken at nighttime when we shouldn't be there, you understand?'

That had sounded like a very patient, almost methodical approach. It was obviously very different to the approach I had taken thus far, but I could see that Pippa was serious. I could also see that she was worried about our jobs, so I had to put my eagerness for the truth to come out to one side when I answered her.

'I mean, it won't be easy, working there while knowing it's all nonsense,' I had said. 'But I guess you're right. We need to catch them in a better way, so we're protected at the end.'

Pippa had thanked me then, before reminding me of how late it was, and she had told me that she would pick me up at the usual time in the morning. I got out of her car and went inside. But the reason it was still a while before I got into bed was because I had sat at my table and made several more notes that I was going to use to help me navigate the next few interactions with the deceptive patient and her husband.

I wrote about how neither of them were to be trusted, which was a sharp change from me initially thinking that only Adrian was a potential liar. I had also written a note to remind myself to watch the video when I woke up in the morning, because I knew that seeing it again would steel me for the day ahead. It would ensure that I didn't become sidetracked or unmotivated in my ultimate quest to have this couple caught for what they were doing. It boggled my brain to think of how many doctors and nurses they had lied to, how many times Scarlett had sat with a medical professional and told them she had no memory of things and struggled to perform the most basic of tasks, only to transform into a different person when none of them were watching her. It also baffled me how Adrian could play his part in the charade too, playing the role of the poor but dutiful partner, desperate for answers, clinging to hope, when all along he knew it was just a game, that all the sympathy or help he was getting was for nothing.

I thought about all those invoices in his office and whether or not they were fakes, designed to throw me off the scent, or if they were real and he had bizarrely been spending money on things he didn't need to. That's why I made a note to try and have a proper snoop around in his office when I got the chance.

I barely sleep. Pippa is back at my door, a new day having dawned and the events of the previous night still very much on my mind, not just because I have mostly been awake, but because I went over the notes several times and rewatched the video before my colleague knocked on my door.

'How are we going to catch them out then?' I ask Pippa as I get in her car, the two of us in uniform and on our way, looking very much like everything is normal – except we both know it's not.

'I don't know,' she says, and I notice that my colleague looks even wearier than she did last night.

'Are you okay?' I ask her, noticing she hasn't started driving yet either.

'I'm just wondering if we should even go today,' Pippa replies.

'What do you mean?'

'Maybe it's not worth it.'

I'm confused.

'Wait, so you want to show that video to our boss? I'm happy to do that. Let's expose that couple right now.'

'No, that's not what I mean.'

'Then what do you mean?'

'I'm just thinking we should maybe leave them alone.'

'And let them get away with it? No way!'

'We don't know that we're letting them get away with it. Maybe it's not worth it. Maybe it's...'

Pippa's sentence trails off.

'What?' I ask, urging her to finish it.

'Maybe it's dangerous.'

I realise she is serious.

'What do you mean dangerous?' I ask.

'I'm saying, it might be safer if we don't go back there. Not after what happened last night. I mean, what if they saw you?

You might not think they did, but if they know you were there, we might be walking into a trap.'

I study Pippa and realise that she means it. She looks genuinely worried about this.

'They didn't see me,' I try and reassure her.

'Okay, but it still might not be safe. How about I call the office and tell them there's a problem? We can get a new patient. Maybe take the day off, get some sleep. I'm exhausted. Are you?'

I can't believe Pippa is suggesting that we don't go back to see Scarlett and Adrian.

'Don't you want to know why they're doing this?' I ask her.

'No, not really! People do weird things. I'd almost rather not know!'

'Well I'm going back there, with or without you,' I say, shrugging my shoulders. 'I want to get to the bottom of this.'

I go to get out of Pippa's car to prove my point, but she shoots out an arm to stop me.

'Wait! Okay, we'll go. I'm just saying, we should be careful, that's all.'

'And we will be,' I assure her. 'Now come on, let's go. The traffic will be getting bad soon.'

Pippa finally starts driving and we're on the way, though she's quiet and still looks tired.

'Is everything okay at home?' I ask her.

'The usual,' she replies, but there didn't seem to be much thought given to that answer, so I'm not sure if it was an honest one.

'You can talk to me,' I say. 'We're friends, right?'

Pippa looks at me and smiles. 'Yeah, we are.'

'You've been helping me, so let me help you,' I go on, smiling. 'What's happening? What is it?'

'It's my son,' Pippa admits.

'What's wrong?'

'He's been playing up at preschool. Troublemaking. And he's not sleeping well at night.'

That explains why she looks so tired, and now I feel awful that she's been dealing with my stuff in between her problems.

'I'm sorry.'

'It's not your fault.'

'No, but I should have asked sooner.'

'It's okay, seriously,' Pippa says, forcing a smile on her face, but I have a feeling she is good at facing the day regardless of how she feels inside. That's a strength that I seem to lack, but I'm hoping to work on it.

'Maybe we can suggest some new tests for Scarlett,' I suggest, figuring it might be better to change the subject. 'They'll be resistant to anything like that if she's faking, surely?'

'Maybe, but I'm guessing, if they've kept up the act for this long, they can fool us with those.'

Pippa is probably right, but I'm determined to put this couple under pressure as soon as we see them, and I'm restless as we make the rest of the journey there. Finally, the house comes into view, and it's a contrast seeing it bathed in sunlight, as opposed to being under the cover of darkness only ten or so hours earlier.

'Remember, don't say anything that can get us into trouble,' Pippa reminds me as we leave her car and walk to the door, and I promise again that I won't. I knock loudly, wondering how Adrian and Scarlett will be getting into character now that they know we're here.

They must think we're so stupid.

But we'll see about that.

SEVENTEEN

It's all still here – the acting, the fakery, the lies. Adrian is continuing to play the worried partner while Scarlett is maintaining her position as the poorly patient, and if I hadn't been here last night I wouldn't necessarily know anything was amiss. But I was and I do, so I'm operating today with my eyes fully open, and that's why I'm constantly doing things to try and make this couple uncomfortable.

I probed Adrian on how things had been overnight with his wife when he answered the door to us. He said Scarlett mostly slept, but I kept probing, wanting to know if she had got out of bed, if she had eaten anything, if it had been hard or easy, if he had enjoyed any time to relax or if he'd been busy with his wife the whole time. Pippa kept giving me a look that said 'stop it' but I had ignored that as I'd followed Adrian upstairs while listening to him pretend like everything was still the same around here. It certainly looked like it was when we entered the bedroom and I saw Scarlett sitting up in her bed, her dressing gown on and her face lacking any make-up. If I didn't have that video on my phone, I would seriously have had to stop for a second and question whether or not I had really seen what I had last night. But I do have that video, and I watched it before coming here this morning, so it is still very fresh in my mind, and that's why I was less gentle with Scarlett as Pippa and I began our daily checks. I wasn't as careful wrapping the blood pressure strap around her arm, nor was I as patient when checking her pupils or her tongue. She probably thought I was being abrupt or even rude, but I didn't care because I was done playing silly games. I wish Pippa was done with it too, but she was still making the effort to go through the motions, despite what I'd told her about this couple. So either she really was worried about losing her job or she found it easy to go through life not rocking the boat.

'I think you're stronger than you think you are,' I say to Scarlett when we've finished with the checks. 'How about you try and get out of bed on your own?'

Scarlett looks nervously at Adrian, as she should.

'Come on, don't be shy. Just swing those legs out from under the comforter and put your feet on the floor. You can do it. I know you can. I believe in you.'

'Maybe that's not a good idea. I think my wife is tired today,' Adrian tries, but I was prepared for him to try and stall.

'No, I think she's okay. What do you say, Scarlett? Can you get out of bed all by yourself? I have a feeling that you can.'

Scarlett still seems reluctant, but I expedite the whole process by taking her arm and gently tugging her to get her moving.

'Darcy,' Pippa says warily, but I ignore my colleague.

'Come on now, let's get moving. You can do it,' I say breezily. As if by magic, Scarlett gets up and out of bed, looking far better than she did a moment ago.

'Let's go outside again,' I suggest, feeling a little brazen. 'Or how about we go down to the lounge and watch TV? We could get some snacks. Would you like that?'

I'm pushing my luck, but I can't help it, and as neither Scarlett nor Adrian are saying anything, I'm guessing they still haven't figured out that I'm toying with them. Pippa speaks up before I can lead the patient out of the room.

'How about you take a break?' she suggests, and I realise she is talking to me.

'No, I don't need one,' I insist.

'It wasn't a suggestion,' Pippa replies firmly.

When I look at her, I see that she's frowning. It gives me pause for thought, and because I desperately don't want to do anything to upset the woman who has helped me so much, I realise I should maybe take things easy for a minute.

'Fine,' I say, letting go of Scarlett's arm. 'I'll take a break.'

I walk out of the bedroom, figuring that, if nothing else, this will give me the opportunity to have a snoop around downstairs and see if there's anything else I can find to help me prove these people are lying.

My first port of call is the study but, when I get there, I see that all the papers on the desk have been put away. The desk is clear, barring a laptop, so I guess Adrian had a clean-up in here. That's annoying, but I figure the papers can't have gone far, so I try a couple of drawers on the desk, only to find they are all locked.

Why the sudden need to do such a thing?

'Is everything okay?'

I spin around at the sound of Adrian's voice and see him standing in the doorway. Thankfully, I had already removed my hand from the drawer handle, so I don't think he's caught me trying to open it, but he has caught me in his study. A place I don't really have a good reason to be in. I should apologise, but then I remember that he's the one with something to hide, so I decide not to.

'Looks like you cleaned up in here,' I say, gesturing to the desk. 'This place was full of papers the last time I was in here.'

'Yeah, it was long overdue,' Adrian replies, his eyes not moving to where the desk in question is, but remaining firmly fixed on me. 'It looks better, don't you think?'

I guess it does. Or does it just look better from Adrian's point of view, because there is now less evidence lying around that might expose his deceit?

I really want to confront him over what I saw last night and let him know that he's not fooling me. But I'm wary that Pippa is still upstairs, and she could get in trouble, so I hold off. It's just long enough for Adrian to speak again.

'I'm glad we've got this little chance to talk,' he says, stepping into the room now, and I feel the doorway shrinking as his frame completely blocks it.

'You are?' I ask a little nervously as I glance at the window, which would be my only other possible escape route here should I need it. Surely he won't hurt me, will he?

'Yes, because I've been meaning to ask you something,' he says, and then it looks like he's going to close the door behind him.

Am I trapped in here with him now?

Fortunately, he doesn't close the door fully, although it's still barely ajar, when he takes another step towards me.

'I've been thinking that Scarlett needs more assistance,' he says, surprising me.

'She needs more?'

'Okay, maybe it's not her. Maybe it's both of us.'

'I don't know what you mean,' I say, feeling very confused.

'How would you feel about helping us out more around here?' Adrian goes on. 'I mean by doing more hours. You're the perfect nurse and my wife enjoys your company, so what do you say?'

'More hours?'

Is Adrian really doubling down on this lie?

'Yeah, like the evenings,' he goes on. 'They can be quite tough. It's the end of the day, I get tired. There is the option, if you would be happy to do so, of you staying overnight here and helping. What do you say to that?'

Overnight?

'Erm, I guess I'd have to check with work,' I say, figuring that's a good enough answer to get me out of this for now, but Adrian already seemed to expect me to say that.

'They might not like it. You already work long enough hours as it is, and besides, I'd feel bad if you were doing more for us on a nurse's wage. I imagine you don't get paid nearly enough for the good work you do. So how about I pay you separately for this extra work?'

'You want to pay me to stay overnight here?'

'Would that be something you might be interested in?'

The prospect of extra cash is something I guess everybody would be interested in, and this man certainly has much more of it than I do. But is it worth what I have to do to get it?

As if reading my mind again, Adrian speaks up before I can reply.

'It actually wouldn't be that much more work. I mean, Scarlett sleeps for most of the night. It would be helping me with her at bedtime. Possibly watching the occasional movie with her in the evening. Giving me a night off. You'd get your own room, of course, and I'd provide meals. We can sort the finer details out later if you're interested, including your fee. So what do you say?'

I'm so surprised that I can't say anything at the moment.

'I could ask Pippa if you're not interested,' Adrian says, turning back to the door, and I surprise myself by quickly stopping him.

'No, it's okay,' I tell him. 'I think she's busy in the evenings with her family. But I'm not. I'll do it.'

'Excellent,' Adrian says, a wide grin spreading across his face. 'When would you like to start? Would this evening be too soon?'

EIGHTEEN

'This is not a good idea. I think you should reconsider.'

That's what Pippa said to me when I told her about Adrian's proposal while we had been having our lunch break, and I actually agreed with her.

I knew it sounded crazy and I should have said no to it.

So why did I say yes?

Firstly, the money played a part. I'm not hugely motivated by money, which might explain why I am a nurse and not some fancy lawyer working downtown in some towering office overlooking the Chicago River. But Adrian was clearly keen to give me some cash to work longer hours, and who am I to look a gift horse in the mouth? They say a fool and his money are easily parted, and Adrian might just be the biggest fool going if he is willing to pay me money to stay over at his house and help him care for a wife who doesn't need any help. Why shouldn't I take the money and improve my financial situation, especially if it helps improve my chances of one day getting out of my current home and living somewhere more like Adrian and Scarlett's place?

But I hadn't agreed to the idea simply for monetary reasons.

I had said yes because I'm genuinely curious as to what this couple are doing. Having observed them secretly and seen that Scarlett seems to not have a medical condition, I still want to know why they're playing this game. Are they both deluded, or is this really how rich people entertain themselves? I wouldn't know because I've never been rich.

I'd explained all of that to Pippa, but she had still been sceptical.

'It's not safe,' she had said in between bites of her tuna sandwich. 'I can't leave you here without knowing you're going to be okay.'

'I'll be fine,' I had replied confidently. 'They might be a lot of things, but they aren't dangerous. Maybe they have more money than sense. Whatever it is, they aren't stupid enough to try and hurt me. Not when you'd lead the police right here if I went missing.'

'Still, I'd feel much better knowing you weren't here overnight,' Pippa had gone on. 'Just go to Adrian and tell him you've changed your mind. He'll understand.'

'No, I won't. I need the extra money if it's being offered, and I want to find out more about them, so I'm doing it, and you can't talk me out of it,' I had said, although I'd been holding back a couple of sad reasons as to why I was willing to stay here in the evenings. It's because not only are my evenings incredibly lonely, there's also the fact that I've not been feeling safe at home recently. At least here I won't have to worry about any intruders in the night. But I hadn't specifically said those two reasons to Pippa – I didn't want her pitying me, although I'm sure she already does, just in secret.

Regardless of what my colleague thinks of me, I told her that I was going to take the offer of money for extra hours, so that is why, as she drops me off at home, she tells me to be careful.

'Ring me if anything weird happens tonight,' she says. 'I

don't care what time it is. And if you feel unsafe at any point, get out of the house.'

'Okay, Mom,' I reply with a laugh as I exit her vehicle and go into my house to get ready. I shower before putting my uniform back on and then pack an overnight bag, one with enough essentials in it to get me through until the morning. I don't know how many nights Adrian wants me to help out: this seems like a casual arrangement, at least for now anyway. But I'd be lying if I said the thought of extra money wasn't welcome as I put my bag by the door, looking outside to see if my taxi is here yet. Adrian said he'll pay all my cab fares to and from his place, which is great, but it's not just extra cash that will really help me. Looking around my fairly drab hallway, it's actually pleasant to have somewhere else to stay tonight. I'll surely have more peace of mind than here, listening out for any strange noises and tiptoeing around and worrying that I might get another unwelcome visitor. Most people wouldn't sleep better in a strange bed, but I'm not sleeping much here, so it's got to be worth a shot. If somebody does break in while I'm gone, at least I won't be in danger.

As I see my taxi driver and leave my house, I feel a little sad as I lock my front door, though it's not because I am having to go to work now at a time of day when most people are finishing. It's because I'm actually looking forward to it. How miserable is my life that I'd rather go to work than have an evening free to myself? Best not to dwell on that as I get into the taxi and we set off back to that extravagant home.

It's just after seven in the evening when Adrian opens his door and welcomes me for the second time today.

'Thanks again for this,' he says as I step inside. 'I see you've packed. Let me show you to your room so you can get yourself settled.'

He leads me upstairs. It feels weird to be here without Pippa nearby, but I better get used to it – it'll be the morning before my colleague is here again.

'So this is your room,' Adrian says as he opens a door and then steps aside so I can enter. When I do, I see a spacious cream-coloured room with a single bed covered in fine linen, two double wardrobes and an antique dressing table, as well as a view of the backyard from the window. 'Will this be okay?'

'This is a beautiful bedroom,' I say by way of positive response, and I mean it, because it really is a nice room, and I can't believe I'm getting paid to stay in it. It's much nicer than my bedroom at home, the one where my clothes litter the floor and the curtains are always shut because I can't be bothered to open them and look outside at my much smaller backyard.

'I'll leave you to unpack and then we can go and see Scarlett before bedtime,' Adrian says, and he walks away, leaving me standing by the bed with my luggage in hand.

I drop my bag onto the bed and unzip it, taking out a few items of clothing as well as my toiletries. It's weird, but I have those nervous butterflies one gets when they are trying to make themselves comfortable in someone else's home. No matter what I do to help settle myself here, I'm still in another person's house, so I guess there'll always be a part of me that's on edge. The only thing that could make me more comfortable here is time, but I'm not sure how long this arrangement might last. I guess Adrian would look to extend it if it seems to be helping both him and Scarlett, but that remains to be seen.

What also remains to be seen is whether or not I'll want to stay for very long if I discover more strange goings on here.

Once I've unpacked, I leave the bedroom and wonder if I should go downstairs and find Adrian or go and check on Scarlett. Then I remember that there's nothing wrong with her anyway, so I stop worrying about that and try to enjoy being here in this luxurious home. I go into the bathroom and wash my hands in the sink while checking my reflection in the huge mirror that lights up when I stand near it. I look tired, and I certainly feel it, and I wonder what time it will be when I get to go to bed tonight. I'm not sure how this is supposed to work, but as I leave the bathroom, Adrian is waiting for me outside Scarlett's room.

'Would you be okay to sit with her for a couple of hours?' he asks me.

'Of course,' I say, and we go into Scarlett's room.

As usual, she's in bed and looking weary, though it was only this time yesterday she was downstairs quaffing wine on the sofa, so I know this is all an act.

'Darcy is here,' Adrian says to his wife. 'Remember I said she was going to be helping in the evenings?'

Scarlett nods, and Adrian invites me to take a seat in the chair by his wife's bedside.

'Shall I make my checks first?' I ask, and Adrian almost seems surprised.

'Oh, right. Sure,' he says, so I go through the motions of checking Scarlett's pupils, blood pressure and heart rate.

'All good,' I say once I'm done, as if the results could be anything else. Adrian smiles. He turns the television on, stopping at a particular channel when Scarlett tells him to.

'Looks like you're watching this,' he says to me as another old movie plays on screen. As I take a seat, he says I can help myself to drinks and snacks downstairs whenever I want to. Then he leaves us alone, and I look at Scarlett, but her eyes are on the television.

'Are you okay with this?' I ask her now we have some privacy. 'I mean, me being here at night. I'm not taking away time between you and your husband, am I?'

'No,' Scarlett says, looking at me briefly before going back to the screen.

'Are you sure? I mean, I'm happy to help, but I've been

thinking that you might not need it anymore. You seem okay and I actually think you're recovering.'

I wonder how Scarlett will take that and whether or not she'll start acting again. I get my answer when she starts crying. But if she's acting, she's doing a damn good job of it. There are movie stars in Hollywood who couldn't turn on the tears this quickly.

'What's wrong?' I ask her, unsure whether to tell her to stop with the games or see where this is going.

'I'm so confused,' Scarlett admits as she wipes her eyes.

'About what?'

'Everything. About me. About my husband. My entire life.'

Even after what I saw last night, there is a part of me that suddenly thinks I have misread this situation and am wrong. What if there is something really wrong with Scarlett? So wrong that she can go from being perfectly normal like she was when I spied her last night to being like this, all needy and confused. If there is, no wonder it's baffling the doctors, because it's baffling me too.

'This was Adrian's idea,' she says, looking at me. 'To have you here at night.'

'Yes, he told me. So he could have a break,' I say, but Scarlett shakes her head.

'It's not for him. It's for me.'

'What do you mean?'

'He doesn't need a break,' Scarlett admits. 'But I do. I need things to go back to normal. But they can't. I don't think they ever will.'

'What are you talking about? You mean before the accident?'

Scarlett nods.

'The accident has ruined us,' she says. 'We keep pretending but it's futile. I can't do this anymore and neither can my husband.'

Scarlett really looks distressed and now I really don't know what to think. Is she ill or not? I guess there is something I could say to put it to the test.

'Have you considered going into a care home?' I ask tentatively. 'Maybe that will help?'

'No, it won't.'

'Why not?'

'Because it won't fix what the accident did.'

Scarlett looks towards the door and, sensing her nervousness, I wonder if my very first gut instinct about all of this was right. Is Adrian the threat here? If this is a game, is he coercing his wife to be a part of it? Or did he really hurt her and now she has to go along with whatever he wants next?

'Just forget it,' Scarlett says as she wipes her eyes, but I'm not prepared to let it go, though I have to as she speaks again.

'I'm tired,' she says sadly. 'I need to go to sleep. I think you should do the same.'

I try and get Scarlett to keep talking, but she's having none of it, so I see it would be best for her if I leave her room. But just before I do, she has one more thing to say to me. When I hear it, it sends a chill down my spine.

'There's a lock on your bedroom door,' she tells me. 'Make sure you use it before you go to sleep.'

NINETEEN

I stare at the key in the lock on the inside of my bedroom door and think about what Scarlett said to me.

Make sure you use it.

Even now, ten minutes after I heard her say those words, I still don't fully understand them. That's despite asking her to explain why she had told me to do such a thing.

'Just do as I say,' Scarlett had replied when I'd nervously wanted to know why I had to lock my door before bedtime.

'Is it to do with Adrian?' I'd enquired anxiously.

'Please, just do it,' was all Scarlett had said in return.

Scarlett had rolled over in her bed then and turned her back to me, signalling that our conversation was at an end. I knew she was tired and upset, but I still didn't have a valid explanation of why I had to lock my door. However, I left her room and came back to mine to try and figure it out. I've been attempting that ever since, but so far I still have no answers. My hand is on the key now, but I've not turned it. Should I? Or should I dismiss the idea?

I haven't said goodnight to Adrian yet. He's downstairs somewhere. Maybe I should go and find him – maybe I should tell him what his wife said to me. But is that a risky thing to do? What if she was telling me to lock my door because of him?

I'm having creepy thoughts of Adrian trying to sneak into my bedroom in the dead of night, the lights out and me lying defenceless in my bed as he approaches me to do god knows what. Is that the danger here? Is that why Adrian wants me in the house overnight? *To hurt me?*

I'm suddenly regretting not listening to Pippa and declining this 'job opportunity'. If I had then I'd be in my own house now rather than standing here, trying to decide whether to bolt myself into this unfamiliar bedroom. I think about what my colleague said to me earlier, how I could call her, whatever the time, if something felt wrong here. Well, something certainly feels wrong, but I'm not sure what good calling Pippa will do me. She'll tell me to leave, but can I even do that? Adrian would surely notice me trying to sneak out the door, and what happens then?

I could pretend like something has come up in my personal life and I really have to get home, but what are the chances of him believing that – and do I want to put them to the test?

The safest thing here seems to be doing exactly what Scarlett said.

So I do it.

Turning the key quickly, I lock the door and then stand staring at it for several seconds, as if I'm still not sure the lock is enough and Adrian is going to burst through it in moments, mocking my attempts at defence. But of course he doesn't do that. Nothing happens, nothing at all, and now I'm starting to feel foolish.

Then I hear footsteps in the hallway.

I hold my breath as I listen to them getting nearer. They come to a stop – *right on the other side of my door.*

It has to be Adrian.

But what does he want?

'Darcy? Are you okay?'

I hear the man of the house calling out to me, and I know I have to answer him or it will be very awkward. But I'm now nervous too.

This is ridiculous, I think. Ten minutes ago, I was happy enough to be here, thinking it was weird but also a very easy way to earn some extra money. But now I'm cowering in this room, fearful of the man who showed me into this room and told me to make myself at home.

It's bizarre.

It's also not helping me answer Adrian.

'Darcy? Are you in there?' I hear him ask, and I fear he is going to try the door handle next and discover that I locked it. Thankfully, he doesn't do that, at least not yet anyway, but he probably will if I keep ignoring him, so I have to say something.

'Hi! Yeah, I'm in here!' I call out, before thinking of a reason for my apparent reluctance to converse. 'I'm just getting dressed. Give me a moment. I'll be out in a minute.'

I guess that buys me some time, though it indicated to Adrian that I was willing to leave my room and maybe that was a bad idea. I can't stay in here forever, so I decide to make it seem like everything is normal and go along with my own charade now, getting changed out of my uniform into my pyjamas. I put my ear to the door to try and gauge if Adrian is still outside.

I can't hear anything, but he could still be there. That's why I take extra care when unlocking the door, turning the key ever so slowly so that he hopefully won't be able to hear that I locked it in the first place. It's only once the door is unlocked that I realise that my heart is pounding in my chest, and I guess it's because I'm vulnerable again now.

Opening the bedroom door, my paranoid brain has me imagining Adrian coiled like a spring on the other side of it, ready to attack. But he's not. He's not even here at all and, as I peer out, I'm wondering where he might be.

Is he in with Scarlett?

'Hi, Darcy.'

I spin around and see Adrian emerging from the bathroom, his toothbrush in hand.

'Are you okay?' he asks me. 'I thought you'd be with my wife.'

'Oh, erm, yes, I was, but she said she was tired and that I could go to bed. Is that okay?'

'That's quite predictable actually. I did warn you there might be a few quiet nights here. Don't worry, you'll still get paid though.'

'Thanks,' I say, but money is the last thing on my mind. I'm still thinking about Scarlett telling me to lock the door. Should I ask Adrian if it could have been a joke?

'I'm going to have an early night myself, so I'll see you in the morning,' he says, turning back to the bathroom. 'Don't worry about checking on Scarlett during the night. I'll come and get you if I need some help with her, but she usually sleeps quite well.'

Adrian disappears back into the bathroom, and I'm not sure whether to go into my room or run down the stairs and out the front door. This is my chance to tell him that I've changed my mind and don't want to sleep here, but I've not said anything. Until...

'Goodnight,' I call out to Adrian before closing my bedroom door. This time, I don't lock it straight away.

I tell myself that I'll feel better with it unlocked – then I'm not like some fearful woman hiding away. I sit down on the bed and try to focus on the task at hand, which is figuring out what this couple are really up to.

I reach into my suitcase and take out the one thing I didn't unpack earlier. It's Scarlett's notes, and I plan to read through them again before going to sleep. I also have a pen so I can add to them, and I make sure to reference the curious comment about using the lock on my door, as well as the fact that Scarlett got upset again when discussing her husband.

I hear Adrian's footsteps pass my room. A door closes. I guess he's settled for the night too. I check the time and see that it's only eight, which makes it a very early night, but I might as well try and get some sleep.

I get into bed and figure it'll take me a while to relax in this strange environment. It'll take me even longer as I realise I have forgotten to pack my sleeping pills.

'Oh no,' I say as I search my toiletries bag, but they're not in there. They must still be on my bedside table. How annoying. What if I can't get to sleep without them?

I have no choice but to try, but despite closing my eyes several times, they keep opening, and I find myself staring at the door.

It's unlocked.

Should I get up and turn the key, just to be safe?

I try to forget about it, but it's not easy. As I open my eyes for what must be the sixth time in five minutes, I see that I have a new message on my phone. It's from Pippa and she wants to know how things are going.

I type out a reply from beneath my comforter, but decide against mentioning the whole lock thing.

So far, so good. Quite easy. I've not done much. Feels a bit weird being here!

Pippa replies to tell me to be careful, and I assure her that I will before I put my phone down again and try to get to sleep. But how can I have said I'll be careful when I'm not?

That's why, after ten more minutes of tossing and turning, I get out of bed and do what I should have done already.

I lock the door again.

TWENTY

It's the dead of night, that time when the slightest noise can sound deafening, but I can't hear a single thing in this house. It's quiet, too quiet, and the silence is starting to unnerve me even more than if I actually heard something. In an unusual bed, and without my sleeping pills, I have been unable to drift off. As I pick up my phone and see that it's 3 a.m., I feel like giving up. I can't keep lying here and hoping something will change, because it's clearly not happening. I know that the sun will come up in a few hours and I'll be exhausted. Worse, I'll have spent an entire night here and still be no nearer to having any idea as to what is going on with these people.

The door is still locked, but I'm not sure why, because I haven't heard Adrian try to open it at any point since we all went to bed, which means Scarlett could have been messing with me. But if she's trying to scare me, it's not working anymore. I'm more curious than afraid, which is why I find myself getting out of bed and creeping to the door.

I turn the key and pray it doesn't make a sound as it catches in the lock. Thankfully, it doesn't. Then I open the door and peer out into the dark. A few slivers of moonlight seeping through the window at the top of the stairs allow me to see that all is quiet out here.

I can hear soft snores coming from one of the other rooms, though I'm not sure which one. But it does tell me that at least either Scarlett or Adrian is getting the kind of sleep I so desperately crave, and I have to assume the other one is too.

I have to assume that I'm not going to get caught.

Leaving the safety of my room, or at least what felt like safety when I was behind that locked door, I cautiously make my way to the stairs. The fact this is such a well-designed home means there are no creaky floorboards to worry about, and that helps me as I tentatively tread down the carpeted stairs until I'm in the hallway by the front door. But I'm not thinking about trying to get out of here.

My mind is firmly focused on getting answers.

I still think Adrian's study will be the best place for me to find those, so I creep in there, opening the door and seeing the desk through the gloom. I need light in here but wait until I have closed the study door behind me before I dare to turn it on. Once I have, I can see what I'm doing much easier and I rush to the desk to begin searching.

I try the drawers, hoping they might have been unlocked since the last time I was here, but they are still securely shut. Not to worry though, because I'm not giving up that easily and I should have more time to snoop around now Adrian is asleep.

I check the bookcase next and look inside a couple of textbooks on treating memory loss. This game, or whatever it is, really is detailed, and Adrian has gone to great lengths to make it look real. I see Post-It notes stuck to certain pages in some of these medical journals, highlighting particular pages in which the author has written something about brain injuries or coping mechanisms in dealing with patients. But as I pick up a third book, I notice something shiny lying on the shelf where the book once sat.

It's a key.

I wonder if it's for the desk, so I take it and try it in the lock and, just like that, the drawers can now be opened.

My heart is racing as I start to rummage through the first drawer, feeling like I'm now on the cusp of discovering what this strange couple are really all about. Initially, all I find are the papers that I saw on the desk before, the stacks of bills and invoices and medical documents, but at least I have time to look at a few of them properly to see if they really are forgeries.

The thing is, it doesn't look like they are, so this suggests Scarlett really is ill. But something tells me every doctor listed on these papers would be very interested to know how the patient could have been so coherent the other evening, especially when all the types of tests listed on here seem very intensive and intrusive.

I try the second drawer and I find something a bit more interesting than paperwork. It's a photo album. When I open it, I see that it is filled with images taken on what is clearly Adrian and Scarlett's wedding day. There are photographs of her in a white dress, looking beautiful and smiling in every single shot. There are also plenty of images of Adrian looking resplendent in a dark blue suit, his smile just as wide as his new wife's. They are younger here, fresher in the face and showing no signs of losing their looks of youth yet. It's almost hard to believe the couple currently sleeping upstairs are the same ones in these images here.

It's clear this was some kind of professional photoshoot – this album is all images of the happy couple in various poses, beside a car, on a balcony, next to a lake. I imagine how magnificent their wedding day must have been because, with all their money, surely no expense was spared, and I'm sure all the guests had a great time. But it feels very naughty of me to be prying at such a personal photo album, although I think I already crossed the line the moment I decided to sneak into here after lights out to see what I could find.

I go to put the album back but, just as I do, I hear something that causes every muscle in my body to go tense.

I can hear somebody coming downstairs.

I'm going to get caught in here. I'm going to get in trouble. Worst of all, I'm not safely in my bedroom, locked behind that door like Scarlett told me to be.

What is going to happen?

I stare at the study door and pray it doesn't open. I assume it's Adrian coming down the stairs, but he might just be going for a glass of water. With a bit of luck, he'll get what he needs from the kitchen and go back to bed without realising that I'm in here. Then I can sneak back to my room and this will all be okay.

But I turned the light on. Surely he'll see it from beneath the door. There's no way he's going to miss it in this otherwise dark house.

And then I see the door opening.

'Wait, I can explain!' I cry out, hoping to pre-empt all the anger that Adrian might have about finding me here in the middle of the night.

But when he sees me, he doesn't look angry, or even shocked. He says something I did not expect to hear.

'No, I'm the one who needs to explain something to you.'

TWENTY-ONE

'Why do you think you're here?' Adrian asks me as he fully enters the study I've been caught in, closing the door behind himself.

I am currently sitting behind his desk, and while I shouldn't be, I'm comforted by the fact that there is something between us, just in case things get dangerous for me in a moment's time.

'Why am I here?' I repeat, and he nods. 'To help you look after your wife.'

Adrian doesn't blink as he keeps staring at me.

'And how do you think that is going?'

I'm not sure what is going on. Is he mad at me for being in here? If so, he's not shouted at me yet. He seems to be wanting me to evaluate my performance as his wife's nurse, though I'm not sure if this is the time for it.

'It's going okay, I guess,' I reply, hedging my bets and offering a safe answer, just to see what he does next.

'Is it, or are you simply trying to be polite?'

'Erm.'

'Tell me what you really think.'

'About Scarlett?'

'About everything. Her. Me. This house. Our life. What is your opinion on it?'

'My opinion? Erm, I'm not sure what you want me to say.'

'I want you to say the truth,' Adrian replies calmly.

All I'm thinking is how I should have listened to Scarlett and stayed in my bedroom, but it's too late for that. Adrian seems to be wanting me to open up to him, though I don't know what I'm going to say. He says he wants the truth. But will he like it?

'I can leave,' I suggest, getting up from the chair, but Adrian raises his hand to tell me to stay where I am. So I do.

'No, it's okay. You don't have to go anywhere. You're not in any trouble, if that's what you're worried about.'

'I'm not?'

Adrian shakes his head.

'I honestly just want to know what you're thinking,' he says as he takes a couple of steps nearer to the desk. 'Tell me, Darcy. You can literally say anything here and I'll accept it.'

Anything? Like how I think he and his wife are fakers and this is all some strange game?

Okay, here goes nothing...

'I'm not sure Scarlett is really ill,' I reply nervously.

'You're not?'

'No, I think she's faking her symptoms. I think you both are.'

'Why do you think that?'

This is the tricky part – surely I can't be *too honest* and say that I was spying on them.

'Call it my professional opinion,' I say, which sounds vague, but also something a nurse could probably get away with saying.

'Okay, so what has led you to form this opinion?'

'Just my observations,' I reply, which is technically true. He doesn't need to know that one of those observations was through his lounge window when he didn't know I was out there.

'Give me details,' Adrian asks.

'Details? Okay, erm. I think your wife is capable of much more than it seems. I know she looks all pale and tired when she's in bed, but she's not bedridden. She can get up and move around.'

'Yes, she can. You know that. I told you that when you started coming here.'

'Yeah, but I think she can do it without assistance. I think she's perfectly capable of doing a lot of things herself, which makes me think that...'

'Makes you think what?'

'That either her injury isn't real or she's pretending it's worse than it is.'

'And why would she do that?'

'That's the part I've not figured out yet.'

Adrian nods, and he seems to be taking this quite well, considering I'm essentially calling his wife, and by extension him, a liar. So I wonder what he will say next. When it comes, it's the last thing I expect to hear.

'Would this opinion of yours be formed in any way by the fact that you were sneaking around outside this house the other night?' Adrian says, and I swear it feels like my heart stops beating for a second.

'What?' is all I can mumble.

'I know you were here,' Adrian continues, not smirking or doing anything to revel in his big reveal, simply telling me what he knows. 'I know you were spying on us, that you saw us through the lounge window. I guess you saw me and my wife watching television and you probably thought everything looked okay.'

I can't believe this.

'How did you know I was there?' I ask, still confident that I wasn't seen that evening.

'A big house like this needs security,' Adrian says, which

sounds obvious, but where's he going with this? 'And no good security system would be complete without cameras.'

Cameras?

I feel a sinking feeling in my stomach as I realise he must have cameras outside his home and he has seen me on them, sneaking around and peeping inside his windows. All that time, I thought I was in stealth mode, but my every movement was being recorded.

'When did you see me?' I ask him, feeling embarrassed as well as afraid.

'It wasn't until I went to bed last night. I always check the camera app at the end of the day to see if there was any movement in the recordings that shouldn't be there. It seemed that there was quite a lot of activity around last night, so I watched it back and there you were.'

'So why didn't you say anything?' I cry, still confused. 'Why have you pretended like you didn't know I was here?'

'There's a few reasons,' Adrian replies, still very calm, even in the presence of my jangling nerves. 'The main one being that you are a damn good nurse and they are hard to find, so I'd rather keep you around than get rid of you.'

'Or call the police?'

'Well, yes, that could be an option, but I'd rather not call them.'

'Why not? Why don't you want them here? What are you hiding?'

'Oh, so I'm the one hiding something now, am I?' Adrian says as he wanders over to the window and peers out, but it's dark out there.

'Yes, you are! Okay, so you caught me the other night, but I caught you too. Both of you! I saw Scarlett and she was eating chips, drinking wine and walking around like there was nothing wrong with her. So why do you need a nurse? What sick game are you playing here?'

The fact that Adrian caught me and didn't have me fired, or phone the police and have me arrested, has given me the confidence boost I need to go back on the offensive and turn this onto him.

'It's not what you think,' Adrian says, turning away from the window and looking at me.

'What is it then? Because from where I was standing, it seemed like Scarlett was perfectly healthy. Healthier than me, even!'

'I'd given her something.'

'What?'

'It's a little cocktail of drugs that gives her brief periods where she seems normal. I didn't tell you about it because I haven't told anyone about it.'

'What are you talking about? Drugs?'

'Pills. Meds. Painkillers. Sleeping pills. Various things the doctors have given her over the years that haven't worked by themselves, but when I tried them together they seemed to have had an effect on her memory and made her better, at least for a few hours.'

'You mix her meds?'

'Yes. I know I shouldn't.'

'It's dangerous!'

'I know it is, but I was desperate.'

'She could overdose!'

'I know what I'm doing,' Adrian replies, as if he's the medical professional in this room and not me; I'm still active, while he is retired.

'It's my wife. I'm not going to poison her,' he adds, clearly noticing I need further reassurance.

'What is this cocktail?' I want to know, but Adrian shakes his head.

'I can't tell you. You shouldn't know about it. I don't want you getting in trouble, so it's best if you forget about it.'

'Forget about it? How can I do that when I've seen what it does with my own eyes?'

'It doesn't always work. That was a lucky night. You saw Scarlett doing well and so it's understandable that you got confused, but believe me it's not usually like that.'

'So she really has memory loss?'

'Yes.'

'And she really slipped?'

'Excuse me?'

'I'm just checking.'

'That I didn't hurt her?'

I don't say anything to that, so my silence gives him his answer.

'I did not hurt my wife. I would never do such a thing. I love her.'

Adrian seems sincere and his response, along with the photos I just looked at in the wedding album, suggests he is telling the truth.

'Is this what all this is about?' he asks. 'Do you think I'm dangerous?'

This is probably a good time to mention the lock on my bedroom door and the fact that his wife suggested I use it. But I don't because, while we might be having a heart to heart here, I still can't fully trust this man, so I'll keep that back, just in case it would get me or Scarlett in trouble.

'No, you're not dangerous,' I say, but what else can I say when trapped alone in a room with him in the dead of night?

A silence lingers between us both, and the longer it goes on the less clear it is who's willing to break it.

'What do you want to do now?' Adrian asks finally, shattering the silence; my answer is an obvious one.

'I want to go home.'

Adrian accepts that but hesitates before he heads for the door. 'You will come back though, won't you?'

'I don't know.' It's the honest answer here. I walk past him to go upstairs to collect my things.

When I've got them, I go back downstairs, wondering if Scarlett has heard any of this, and I find Adrian by the front door with his car key in hand.

'Let me drive you home. It's raining.'

'No.'

'Why not?'

'Because I don't want you knowing where I live.'

'Darcy, please. You're our nurse, but I'd like us to be friends too.'

'Friends don't lie to each other.'

'Do friends sneak around outside each other's homes and spy on them?'

I have to admit that Adrian has me there.

'Come on, it'll be impossible to get a taxi at this time. Let me drive you. It's the quickest option so the pair of us hopefully get some sleep tonight.'

I would still prefer a taxi, but I know that Adrian is probably right, though there is one other problem.

'What about your wife?'

'What about her? She's asleep and I doubt she'll wake up before I'm back.'

That could either sound like an uncaring response or simply an honest one, but as usual with this man it's hard to tell. But he seems adamant, whichever way it is, so I give in and let him drive.

I get into his car, which is far more comfortable than any taxi I could have ordered. It doesn't have that strange scent that so many cabs have. In fact, it has a rather pleasant one and, as Adrian starts the engine, I find myself relaxing for some strange reason.

Maybe it's because a little truth has come out tonight, for both of us. Or maybe it's just because I'm so tired now that my brain is beyond the point of worrying.

I give Adrian the name of my neighbourhood, and he sets off in that direction, the rain bouncing off his windshield as he cruises through the quiet streets, getting me most of the way there before I have to direct him for the last few right and left turns.

'Get some rest,' Adrian tells me once I've told him which house to stop outside of. 'And I hope to see you tomorrow if you would still like to be our nurse.'

I don't say anything to that, choosing to get out of the car rather than make a commitment at this silly hour of the night. I rush inside, eager to get in and lock my door in case Adrian lingers outside. But he doesn't. He drives away as soon as he sees me go in, which is a relief, even though he now knows where I live – that unsettles me for some reason.

This should be the point where I can finally relax and go to bed, either getting some sleep or simply replaying events over in my head and trying to analyse them logically.

But something is wrong.

Looking around my home, I just know it.

Somebody has been here while I was out.

TWENTY-TWO

'So where were you this evening?' the cop asks me as I wait for his colleague to finish checking the house.

'I was out,' I reply, not really wanting to get into too much detail because it's complicated. There's enough for the police to figure out here without me mentioning that I was supposed to be staying overnight at a couple's home, a couple who are very mysterious and who might be paying me to be there just because they're rich enough to do such a thing.

'Out?'

'I was at work.'

'And where do you work?'

A deep sigh on my part.

'I'm a nurse. Look, what does it matter where I was? What matters is I got home and I could tell that somebody had been in my house.'

The officer is savvy enough to not speak for a couple of seconds, giving me the chance to calm down before he probes again.

'Right, you said on the call that there were footprints in your hallway.'

'Yes. Watermarks from wet shoes on the wooden floor, and they're not mine, so somebody has been in here and they might still be here now!'

'There's nobody else here,' says the voice in the doorway, and we turn to look at the second officer, who looks like he's just finished conducting his search. 'It's all clear. If someone was here, they're gone now.'

'*If* someone was here? Those are not my footprints in the hallway!'

'Okay, but are you absolutely sure? Because there's no sign of forced entry, just like there wasn't the last time you reported an incident of an intruder in your home.'

I get the insinuation. They think I'm confused or mistaken or making it up, like the last two cops who came here and failed to do anything about it.

'What do you want me to say? Someone has been in my house and yes, this is the second time it's happened, but I don't know who it is, how they're getting in or why they are coming here, so help me find out and keep me safe!'

That seems like a perfectly acceptable thing for a distressed citizen to ask of police officers, but it still doesn't get me anywhere.

'You are safe,' I'm told by the first officer as the second one goes to the window and looks out, as if the intruder is going to be out there waving back at them and making their job easier. 'We've checked your house and no one else is here, so there's nothing to worry about.'

'This is a waste of time,' I decide aloud. I've already had this conversation once before and it got me nowhere. 'If you aren't going to solve this, what are you doing here?'

'I didn't say that, I—'

'Forget it. Just get out of my house!'

I've had enough and now I want these cops gone. I'm prepared to drag them to the door if I have to.

'Just calm down, we're trying to help you,' one of them says, but I don't even know which one because I'm not looking at them. I'm at my front door and holding it open so they can get out.

They eventually leave as I refuse any more of their 'help', and I slam the door behind them. I look down at the footprints that caused me to call 911 in the first place. I suppose that if the weather had been dry outside then they wouldn't exist, but the recent rain has meant whoever came in here left a trail. While it's only faint now, I can see it. But whoever it was is gone, just like they were gone the last time. It has to be the same person. Is it that man I confronted? Is he still stalking me?

How the hell is he getting in?

I decide that I need to take matters into my own hands here – the police aren't much use and I know just what to do. Taking inspiration from Adrian and how he managed to 'catch' me sneaking around his house, I decide that I will purchase a couple of small cameras and set them up to record while I'm not here, one covering the exterior of my property and another one hidden within. That way, I'll find out who it is that's been sneaking into or around my home, and then I'll have the hard evidence I need to show to the police.

I guess I can buy a camera on the internet, so I stay up even later to place my order. With delivery times being so swift, I'm told that my camera will be with me later today. That's perfect, and I'll be here to take delivery because I've decided that I'm not going to Adrian and Scarlett's house, or at least not during the daytime. I'll message Pippa now and tell her that I need a day off. I certainly do because I've been up all night and there's no way I can work without getting at least a few hours' sleep. But that doesn't necessarily mean there's going to be no work at all for me later on today. I'm still thinking about going back to see Adrian and Scarlett this evening. Another night shift there might seem like the last thing in the world that I need, but it would provide me with an opportunity to be out of this house in the evening, which means my camera can capture anybody that comes here while I'm gone. There's surely more chance of someone trying while I'm not present.

I message Pippa to tell her not to bother coming to my door in the morning, and then I get into bed, popping a few pills and closing my eyes.

Mercifully, sleep takes me.

Little did I know, it was the last good thing that would happen to me for a very long time.

TWENTY-THREE

The first thing I do when I wake up is check on the status of the camera I ordered online. I see that it is already in transit and will be here mid-morning, so I'm very much looking forward to setting that up to see if it can help me catch whoever has been coming here. I feel less scared and more intrigued about who it is. Although I know that might all change if and when I actually see somebody on camera walking around in my house.

Checking the order on my phone, I also see that Pippa has replied to my message. I had told her I would not be going to work today. She has replied to let me know that another nurse can cover, but then she sent a second message asking me how last night was.

What should I say to her?

It was okay. I might go back tonight. I really think there's something strange going on there and I have to find out what it is. Can you keep covering for me at work?

I don't know how long it will take Pippa to reply to me, because she'll be working now, or if she'll even go along with my idea. It is asking a lot of her, but it's worth a shot. She hasn't replied by the time I go to take a shower, stumbling over my uniform on the floor, which I could have sworn I hung up in the wardrobe before bed, but I guess not. As I shower, I think about Pippa at Adrian and Scarlett's place, with a new nurse working alongside her. I wonder if anything unusual is happening there, anything that might be giving them cause for concern. If it is, I hope Pippa will tell me about it so I can add it to the long list of things that are troubling me about that couple.

Pippa has responded to my text by the time I return to my bedroom, and I smile when I read it.

Sure, I'll cover for you if I can, but I don't know for how long I can do it. I hope you're okay? You promise to tell me if you're not?

Pippa's being a great friend again and I hope she won't have to help me for much longer, but that remains to be seen.

Thank you and all is well, I promise.

I don't feel hungry so skip breakfast and wait for the delivery man at my door. When he arrives, I quickly take the parcel from him and unpack it. The cameras are tiny, as advertised, which means I should be able to easily hide them somewhere around here without anybody else noticing them. I plan to do just that, but first I link my phone to the pair of cameras, downloading the app so that it will show me live footage whenever I check it, as well as send me alerts when movement is detected within the cameras' range.

Once that's done, I set about finding a suitable hiding place for my sneaky devices.

I decide to position the first one in what I feel is the most obvious place, which is by the back door, where the intruder seemed to come in and out the last time. Finding a rain-proof spot beneath the canopy of the shed, I prop the device up so that it is pointing at the back of my house, covering the door, and therefore any movement that goes on around it.

Now to decide where my interior camera goes.

I consider putting this camera in the hallway – that's where the footprints were – and it is a very likely place for any intruder to move through. But there's not really anywhere I could conceal it well enough, so I decide that the kitchen is the best place. Ideally, I want a vantage point that covers the back door from this angle too. I find the perfect spot when I realise I can put the camera on a shelf in amongst some cookery books, the recording device peeping out from in between them, barely perceptible to the naked eye but very clearly showing me a view of my entire kitchen.

After checking the app and being satisfied with the positioning of the camera, I realise that the best way to truly put it to the test is for me to leave the house. If I want to find out who is coming here, and how they are getting in, I need to go out and give them another opportunity to intrude. So I put on my uniform and go outside.

I still have a few hours until my night shift will begin, so I take a walk, all the while keeping an eye out for that man or anybody else who might be following or watching me. But I don't notice anything untoward. By the time I'm in a cab to Winnetka, I am feeling surprisingly calm.

Pippa has already left by the time I get there, but that's okay. After making one last check on the camera app, I put my phone away and knock on the door.

'Thank you for coming back,' Adrian says when he sees me. As he steps aside, I think about how this is more about helping me than it is about helping him or his wife, but I obviously don't mention that. I do mention something that I've been thinking about since I left here though.

'I am going to go and see Scarlett. Could you give us some time alone, please?'

'Some time. How much?'

'A few hours.'

Adrian looks unsure for a moment, but agrees.

I go upstairs and enter the patient's bedroom. I find Scarlett lying in bed, and it looks like she is dozing until her eyes open. They narrow as she watches me taking a seat beside her.

'Who are you?' she asks me, frowning.

Does she really not remember or is she play-acting?

'I'm Darcy, one of your nurses. I've been here before. You remember me, don't you?'

Scarlett shakes her head.

'You're not a nurse.'

'Yes, I am.'

'How long have you been a nurse?'

'Oh, erm, quite a while now.'

'Do you like it?'

'Yes, I think so.'

Scarlett is still sceptical, even when I try to take her blood pressure, as if I'm the one acting. Then I ask her something related to what her husband told me last night.

'I believe your partner gives you medicine sometimes that makes you feel better,' I say, referencing the cocktail of pills that helped give her moments of lucidity. 'What is it exactly that you take?'

'I don't know,' Scarlett replies simply, though she isn't dismissing the notion of some magical medication that helps her, so maybe it is true.

'You don't have any idea? If you don't know what it is, why do you take it?'

'Because he tells me to take it.'

'And it works? You feel better for it?'

Scarlett stares at me vacantly, which isn't much of an answer, but I'm detecting sadness from her and my stomach churns again. I fear something awful is going on here. I just cannot for the life of me figure out what it is.

'How are you feeling?' Scarlett asks, and the question surprises me, because I'm supposed to be the one caring for her. Nobody ever asks the nurse if they're okay, do they?

'Me?'

'Yeah. How are you doing?'

'Erm, I'm all right, I guess,' I say, but Scarlett doesn't seem to buy it, probably because it's a feeble lie.

'Do you like us?' she asks me.

'Who?'

'Me and my husband.'

'Erm, yeah, I do,' I say, but it's another lie, and Scarlett seems remarkably good at picking up on those.

'Be honest. There is something, isn't there? Is it something about us? What is it?'

While this feels like an awkward conversation, it is the perfect chance to air my concerns with Scarlett instead of Adrian.

'I think there's something going on here. Something you're not telling me. I can't figure out what it is though.'

'What makes you think that?'

'Besides the weird feeling I get every time I come here? Oh, I don't know, maybe the fact that I saw you the other night and you looked absolutely fine, not like you do now. And when I asked Adrian about it, he gave me some story about some special mixture of pills, yet neither of you seem able to tell me what they are. It seems strange because, if it was true, you would surely take them all the time and tell others, to help them too. So you're lying, or at least one of you is. Are you lying to me, Scarlett?'

Scarlett looks like she wants to say no but doesn't, remaining still instead.

'Why are you lying?' I press on. 'What are you hiding? Or are you protecting something? Are you protecting your husband? Are you afraid of him? Is he hurting you?'

'I can't tell you,' is all Scarlett says, but that's enough to make the hairs on the back of my neck stand on end.

'What do you mean you can't tell me?'

'I just can't.'

'Why not? How bad can it be? If it's bad, I can help you. But you have to tell me or I'm going to leave here today and I'm never going to come back.'

Scarlett really looks like she wants to speak now, so I keep persisting.

'It's your husband, isn't it? Tell me what he does. Tell me why he's playing games with me. Tell me if you're in danger and I will get you away from him right now, I swear. I will help you. But you have to tell me. What is he doing?'

Scarlett looks like she's just about to speak but, before she can say any words, we are both thrown off by the loud beeping noise that suddenly starts emanating from somewhere in the bedroom. I look around, trying to figure out what it is, and then I realise it is coming from me, or more specifically my pants pocket.

Reaching into my pocket, I take out my phone: that's where the noise is coming from. But it's only when I look at the screen that I figure out why.

I'm getting an alert from the app that's linked to the cameras I set up at home.

Movement has been detected on both of them.

Outside my house.

And in.

'What is that?' Scarlett asks me, but I ignore her as I open the app and, with shaking hands, I see that there is someone inside my kitchen right now.

But that's not the most shocking part.

That would be who this person is.

I was talking to him in this very house not so long ago.

It's Adrian.

TWENTY-FOUR

I drop my phone and it bounces under Scarlett's bed, but I'm in no state to pick it up again quickly.

I'm too busy trying to breathe.

'What is it?' Scarlett asks me. She pulls back her comforter to get out of bed but I back away from her until I bump into the wall behind me.

'Darcy?' Scarlett says.

'Stay where you are!' I cry, my voice loud enough for her to know that I'm serious.

'What's going on? Why are you upset?' Scarlett wants to know, but I'm looking under the bed now at where I can see the light from my phone's screen shining up at the base of the bedframe.

'Why is your husband in my house?' I scream, my chest heaving as I continue to struggle to catch my breath.

'What?'

'Adrian! He's in my house! I've got a camera there and I just saw him. He's in my kitchen! What is he doing?'

'A camera?' Scarlett repeats, as if that's the strangest part about what I said, but it's nowhere near it.

'So it's him who's been in my house?' I ask, trying to make sense of it. 'How? Why? I don't understand.'

'Darcy, please, calm down. What are you talking about?' Scarlett tries one more time, but I reach down under the bed and grab my phone before rushing to the door.

When I look at my phone again, my kitchen looks empty and there's no sign of Adrian, but I know I saw him in there. If he's there then he can't be here, can he?

'Adrian!' I call out as I rush to the top of the stairs and look down, as if this is the test that will prove that my eyes weren't lying to me. If he is here then I must have been mistaken. But I'm sure I'm not and he isn't calling back to me to let me know that he's in the house somewhere.

I rush down the stairs and then fling the front door open. Looking outside, I check the driveway. Sure enough, Adrian's car is not parked outside, and of course it's not because he's at my place, or at least he was before I caught him on camera. Maybe he's on his way back now; he's probably hoping that I'll still be in his wife's bedroom when he returns, so I'll never know he was gone.

But I do know.

What I don't know is why he's in my house at all.

I desperately want to run from here, but where can I go to escape this couple? I clearly can't go home because, even if Adrian has left, that won't stop him coming back. But how can it be him who has been intruding all this time? He only found out where I lived last night when he took me home. But someone was in my house before that. Unless it has been him all along and he manufactured a way to get me to come to his house too.

Like faking his wife's illness so I could be her nurse.

I feel sick and my legs would have gone from underneath me if I wasn't gripping the doorframe now, and I don't know what to do, where to go or who can help me.

What about the police? I could call 911 and tell them what has happened, and they could come and save me and arrest Adrian. But what if they don't believe me? What if Adrian talks his way out of it? What if the cops make this whole thing worse?

I need to call someone else, someone who knows me, someone who will understand this all better.

Pippa.

She is the only person who knows where I am, the only person who knows that Adrian and Scarlett might be hiding something – I already told her that I didn't trust them.

If I call her, she will come – *won't she?*

I pull myself together enough to find her number on my phone, but there's no answer so I have little choice but to leave her a very panicked voicemail message that I pray she will listen to soon.

'Pippa! It's Darcy! You have to come and help me! Adrian is the one who's been breaking into my house! I don't know why, but it's him and he's there now. I'm at his house with Scarlett but I need to get out of here before he comes back. Can you come and get me? I'll be on the main road. Phone me when you're near! Please, I need your help!'

I end the call and figure I'll phone the police once I'm safely in Pippa's car and getting away from here. I can show them the footage of Adrian in my house and leave it to them. At least I'll be safe from whatever weird plan this couple have for me.

Now it's time to get out of here, so I go to run.

But then I feel an arm on my shoulder pulling me back inside.

I reach out for the doorframe, but I miss it, unable to prevent whoever it is from taking me back into the house. As I try to fight them off, I hear the front door slam shut behind me.

Spinning around, Scarlett is standing there, though not as I have seen her before. She looks strong and determined – even when I saw her that night when I was spying, she didn't look this healthy and composed.

I knew it. This proves it. She was faking her condition. There is absolutely nothing wrong with her.

But there is something wrong here.

Very wrong.

'What the hell is going on?' I cry, managing to free myself from this woman's grip, thinking about attacking her for all of one second, before I realise that might not be a smart move if she turns out to be stronger than me. Scarlett is older, so I might have the advantage of youth on my side if we grapple, but currently she has one much larger advantage on her side.

While I am losing my grip on reality, she is calm.

'Darcy, just stop,' Scarlett says, her hands out in front, trying to show me that she means me no harm. Yet she stopped me from leaving here, clearly because I'd caught Adrian doing something he shouldn't have been doing.

She must be in on whatever his plan is, but what the hell is it?

'What are you doing? What do you want with me?' I beg to know, unable to fathom any reason as to why this couple are tormenting me.

'Just try and calm down.'

'No, I will not try and calm down! Tell me what's going on!'

I glare at Scarlett, the front door only a few feet away, but I'm not lunging for the handle, nor am I racing to try and get out of the back door either. I have to know and, the way Scarlett looks now, I have a feeling she is on the verge of telling me. But she's not quite there yet, so I give her one more reminder.

'Why is your husband in my house?' I cry, thinking that there surely cannot be a good answer she can give me to that question, but I'll try anyway.

That's when Scarlett surprises me again.

'It's not your house,' she replies solemnly.

'What?' is all I can muster – that doesn't make any sense.

'It's not your house,' Scarlett repeats, shaking her head as she tells me this.

'Of course it's mine. Who else's would it be?'

Scarlett takes a deep breath as I hold mine.

'It's ours,' she says quietly.

TWENTY-FIVE

Of all the crazy things I've heard in my life, that has to win first prize.

Scarlett thinks she and her husband own the house I live in? *How can she be so warped?*

'What the hell are you talking about?' I ask, but Scarlett makes a move towards me. I give a knee-jerk reaction, which instinctively involves violence.

I strike Scarlett across her left cheek, and I lunge for the door and pull it open. Then I scramble outside and take off, running as fast as I can down the driveway, hearing Scarlett calling out to me as I go, but not looking back because I have to get away from her as quickly as I can.

She's deranged, and possibly dangerous, just like her husband, so I have to do whatever it takes to stay away from them until help is on the way. But I don't know if it is yet, because I have no idea if Pippa has heard my voicemail.

'Darcy! Get back here now!' Scarlett calls out to me, her voice surprisingly stern, as if she's still my employer and I have no right to go off-duty when I'm supposed to be at work. Stupidly, I look back at her to see exactly where she is and if she's chasing me, but I keep running – that's how I trip over something and go tumbling onto the lawn.

The grass is wet, despite it not having rained all day, and then I realise it must have been a sprinkler that tripped me up. It's dark out here, but I can see the lights at the house and Scarlett's silhouette in the doorway, trying to spot me.

Desperate to stay out of sight, I crawl to the bushes, crouching down behind them. Figuring I'm well-hidden for a moment, I take out my phone. But when I do, I see the screen is all cracked. Using my device is incredibly hard now because I can't see what I'm doing.

'No,' I say under my breath as I try to use my phone to make a call, or send a text message, or do anything that could help me, but it's no good.

With no way of calling Pippa or the police again, I have no choice but to keep running until I find somebody who can help me, and fortunately I shouldn't have too far to go. I need to get to a neighbour's house, and I can see the nearest property from here. It's another magnificent home, surrounded by tall trees and a lawn as landscaped as the one I just fell on, and I have to hope that whoever lives there is in tonight, ready to have their evening ruined.

Looking back at the house I escaped from, I feel my heart skip a beat when I see that Scarlett is no longer in the doorway.

Where is she?

I don't know, but I don't want to take my chances hiding here in her front lawn, so I dart out of my position and run across the street, careful to stick to the driveway this time rather than tread on the grass and risk another sprinkler hazard.

'Help!' I cry as I reach the front door and begin pounding on it. 'Help me! Open up!'

I look back over my shoulder, but I still can't see Scarlett anywhere, and it's extremely unnerving to be surrounded by shadows, any one of which could be helping her to hide. It's also unnerving to be the only one making any noise out here, but other than my cries for help the street is sinisterly silent.

'Open up! Please! I need help!' I cry out again as I hammer my fists onto the door, aware that I've given my position away to Scarlett, but praying that I can get inside here before she catches me.

And then I hear something wonderful.

It's the sound of the door unlocking.

'Thank you!' I say as I rush into the house, past the startled homeowner – a man in his forties wearing a green sweater and cream pants, who understandably looks stunned.

'Hey! What's going on?' he cries, but I'm already inside so I'm safe, or at least I would be if he would be so kind as to do one very important thing.

'Shut that door!' I tell him. 'And lock it! Quickly!'

'What?' the man mutters, clearly having no idea why I so desperately needed to get in here, but there'll be time to explain when that damn door is closed.

'Shut it!' I say, rushing forward and doing it for him, and once it's locked, I can breathe for a moment. But only a moment.

'Call the police,' I say. 'Tell them to come here and arrest that woman.'

'What woman?'

'Scarlett, your neighbour!' I cry. 'She's crazy. Her and her husband!'

The man is looking at me like I'm the crazy one and, right now, I suppose I do look ridiculous. An out of breath nurse in full uniform, turning up at a random house in the evening and yelling some troubling things. No wonder this poor man is looking at me like he's seeing a ghost. If things carry on like this, he's going to need a nurse himself to help him get over this shock.

'Is she out there? Can you see her?' I ask as I go to a window and peer out, but it's too dark and I can't see anything.

'I don't know what's going on, but you can't be here,' the man says behind me. 'Please, you need to go.'

'Go? But I'm in danger!'

'From Scarlett?'

'Yes! And her husband! He broke into my house, and Scarlett's been pretending to be ill so I'll be their nurse. But she's not ill, she's lying, just like he is.'

'What on earth is going on down here?'

We both turn to the stairs when we hear the female voice, and I see a woman in a dressing gown coming down the steps, looking very annoyed that her quiet night has been interrupted.

'What are you doing here?' she asks me when she sees me, and it looks like I'm going to have to tell my whole sorry story to this person too before we make any progress on getting the police here. But before I can do that, we all hear knocking at the front door.

'Don't open it! It's her!' I say as I move away from the door. 'It's Scarlett. Don't let her in!'

I have backed right up into a corner of the hallway, beside a coat stand and one side of the staircase, as if this is a good place to be in case Scarlett does get inside. But she won't, will she? Not unless...

'No,' I cry as I see the man going to unlock the door, and he stops to look back at me.

Another knock, quickly followed by another desperate plea from me to him to not make another move towards that door.

But he doesn't listen to me.

He answers the door.

And that's when I see Scarlett again.

'No!' I cry, fearful of what might happen now she has found me. I have no idea what she might do to keep their secret safe. If I make it out of here then I can hand over evidence to the police that will see the man she married arrested for home invasion – no wonder she has chased me here.

I thought I'd be safe with other people around.

But now I'm not so sure.

'I'm terribly sorry about this, but there has been a misunderstanding,' Scarlett says to her neighbours. But while she might be able to fool them, she can't fool me anymore.

'There is no misunderstanding! I know who you and your husband really are now. You're criminals!' I cry, as I wish I hadn't backed myself into this corner, but now it's too late.

'No, we're not,' Scarlett says as she steps inside and slowly walks towards me.

'Yes, you are!'

'Darcy, listen to me,' Scarlett says, getting closer still, and as the two neighbours simply stand by and do nothing, I realise I really am on my own here. 'We have lied to you but we're not criminals. We're...'

I want to run. I want to escape this house and this street and even this damn city. But I can't move and now Scarlett is right in front of me, totally blocking my escape route. That's when she says the words that take away the last bit of fight I had left in me.

'You were right,' Scarlett goes on sadly. 'I'm not really ill and you're not really our nurse. We didn't need one. What we needed was you, Darcy. We needed you because you're our daughter.'

TWENTY-SIX

I am speechless as I stare at the woman who has just told me that she's my mother. Of all the crazy things that have happened recently, this is easily the craziest. Yet why does Scarlett look so calm? Why does she look like she's told me a fact rather than an insane theory?

This makes no sense. I look to the other two people here with us to back me up. But Scarlett's neighbours aren't saying anything either. In fact, they look as calm as Scarlett does, which makes me think they are on her side and not mine.

'If you'll just sit down, I'll explain everything to you,' Scarlett says calmly as she takes another step towards me, but I can't allow her to get any nearer.

'Stay back!' I cry, and while Scarlett is startled, she does as I say.

'I understand this is upsetting,' she goes on, but I cut her off.

'It's not upsetting. It's just nonsense! I'm not your daughter! I'm your nurse! I'd never met you before I started working for you!'

Scarlett looks sad at that statement.

'That's just not true,' she says with tears in her eyes, and I notice that the woman on the stairs has tears in her eyes too, which seems very odd. *Why are they upset?*

'You and your husband have been faking this whole thing and, now I've caught you, you're trying to make up some weird story,' I say, shaking my head. 'But it won't work. I'm still going to the cops to tell them that Adrian was in my house. And my colleague, Pippa, is on her way here to help me, so you better let me go now, or you'll only be making things worse for yourself.'

'Darcy, listen to me,' Scarlett starts again. 'It's true. Adrian and I have been lying to you, but we've only been doing it because we hoped it might help you. We hoped it might help you remember who you are – who we are.'

'What's that supposed to mean?'

'You have memory loss. You were in an accident, and you can't remember anything from before it, which is why you can't remember us, our house or the fact that the house you're living in now was actually the one you grew up in as a child.'

This is getting more bizarre by the minute, and I keep shaking my head, but Scarlett keeps talking.

'You were in a car accident two years ago and, when you woke up, you had forgotten your life before it,' she goes on. 'We spent so long trying various ways to help your memory return, or even to improve, paying fortunes on various specialists, but nothing was working. You kept getting confused. We would tell you who we were and visit you, but it wasn't sticking. The type of brain injury you have means you haven't just forgotten what happened before the accident, but you struggle to store any long-term memories. That means you're prone to forgetting more recent things unless they are refreshed with you. Sometimes it only takes a couple of weeks for you to totally forget something. You kept forgetting us and we were getting desperate. The only thing you'd seemed to retain was your caring nature, which is obviously why you became a nurse, and a good one at that. So we came up with a plan that involved nursing to hopefully stir your memory back into life.'

A car accident? Memory loss? A plan? I still don't know what any of this has to do with me.

'It was your father's idea, Adrian,' Scarlett says, smiling for a moment, but I'm not doing anything to indicate that I'm softening here. 'He had read that role-playing could help someone with memory loss, so he came up with the idea that I would pose as a patient, and we would hire you to come to our house and work for us. He hoped that getting you to do what you used to do for a job, before your accident, and surrounded by people and places from your past, might spark something in your memory.'

'Doing what I used to do?'

'Yes. You are a nurse, Darcy. You have always been a nurse. You used to pretend to be one as a child, and then you became a proper one when you grew up. You love nursing and you were damn good at it. But you haven't been able to work since your accident, which is why we set all this up for you. It was supposed to help you, and I think it's definitely been good for you to use your nursing skills again. You really have retained them, and keeping a skill is not uncommon in memory loss patients, even when everything else seems lost. But I see that it hasn't worked in the bigger picture. You're still not remembering people or special memories from your past.'

It definitely hasn't worked, whatever *this* is, but I'm still refusing to believe it – it can't be true. None of it can be true.

'No,' I say, shaking my head so much that it's starting to ache. 'Why are you saying all this? Why are you telling me all these lies?'

'They're not lies,' the woman on the stairs says as she wipes her eyes. 'Scarlett is telling the truth. You are her daughter, and we know that because we have been your neighbours for over twenty years. We've lived next door to you and seen you grow up. I'm terribly sorry, but you were in an accident and your parents have been doing everything they can to try and help you since then.'

The woman is sobbing now, and her husband goes to comfort her, while Scarlett looks like she appreciates the input from her neighbour. But I don't appreciate any of this and I don't care how many people participate in this nonsense – I'm refusing to believe it because it simply isn't true.

With the man moving over to the staircase to tend to his wife, it has left an opening by the front door, and I realise that if I can force my way past Scarlett, I should be able to get out of here and away from these people before they can do anything else to me. That's why I decide to play a game of my own with the woman in front of me.

'It's true?' I say innocently. 'You're my mother?'

Scarlett looks relieved that she seems to be getting through to me now, and her stance noticeably softens, which is exactly what I wanted to happen. Now she'll be less prepared when I charge at her in a moment.

'Yes,' she says, nodding at me like I'm some child she is trying to teach something very basic to. 'I know it's hard, but you have to believe me. We've only been lying to you because we love you. And the only reason Adrian is in your house is because it's our house too. We still own it, even though we moved here many years ago. We thought that house would be a good place for you to live, to maybe stir up some old childhood memories. Adrian goes there when he can to make sure everything is okay. Because he cares about you. We both do.'

This gets crazier by the second, but I don't drop my act, pretending that I'm still taking this all in rather than waiting for the perfect moment to make my escape. That perfect moment presents itself when Scarlett turns to the couple on the stairs and asks them if they could get me a glass of water.

She's distracted.

This is my chance.

With lightning speed, I surge forward and barge past Scarlett. When I reach the front door I fling it open. Then I take off running – down the driveway and then down the street towards the main road, not looking back and not listening to any of the cries of Scarlett or the neighbours, begging me to stop and come back.

I keep running when I reach the main road, darting out across traffic and turning down another street, and I keep running for what feels like forever until I feel I am a safe distance away and can't be caught now.

As I lean forward with my hands on my knees and try to get my breath back, I realise I have no idea where I am, which is not going to help me if Pippa is coming to get me.

Pippa. I need to call her and tell her about these crazy developments, but as I check my pockets, I realise my phone is missing. *No, it must have fallen out while I was running.*

Without a phone, I can't call her or the police. Looking around, I see a bar across the street. They must have a phone I can use, so I head there once my heart rate has slowed a little and I've stopped sweating from the exertion of my sprint.

Entering the bar, I quickly realise that I'm the only female in here. The dozen or so male patrons drinking in this dimly lit establishment all look up from their drinks when they see me walking towards the bar. Even the bartender is eyeballing me as I approach him, clearly aware that a woman in a nurse's uniform, particularly one who looks distressed, is not his usual kind of customer, and certainly not one who looks distressed.

'Do you have a phone I can use?' I ask him as I try to ignore the attention that I'm getting around me, including from the two guys by the pool table, who have stopped playing and are just watching.

'I might do,' the bartender replies casually.

'Can I use it?'

'If you buy a drink.'

'Seriously?'

The bartender shrugs to prove he is happy enough for me to walk away if I'm not willing to hand over some cash.

'I don't have any money on me,' I say, aware that I left my purse back at Scarlett's house.

'I'll get it,' a voice to my left says, and I turn to see a man of a similar age to me sitting at the bar. He has a trimmed beard, and I spot a couple of tattoos on his arms that are poking out from a Chicago Bulls T-shirt. He's holding a glass of what looks like whiskey.

'What are you having?' he asks me with a smile, but I'm in no mood for some guy to try and hit on me by buying me a drink.

'I'm fine,' I say, and turn back to the bartender. 'Can I just get a glass of tap water?'

'I'm afraid it's going to have to be a real drink,' the bartender replies without skipping a beat. 'We're a bar so order some alcohol.'

'Get us a couple of JDs with ice,' the man on my side of the bar says casually, and the bartender is finally happy enough to get to work.

'I don't want it,' I tell the guy who ordered for me, but he just smiles, even though I was very abrupt with him.

'You look like you could use a drink,' he says simply, and invites me to sit down on the spare stool beside him, and while I'm still unsure, I feel bad for snapping at him, so I wait for the bartender to return with our drinks. When he does, placing a couple of glasses down in front of us, I get back to business.

'Now can I use your phone?'

'Who do you need to call?' the bartender wants to know.

'The police,' I say, but that is clearly the wrong answer because the bartender frowns.

'No cops here,' he says, wiping down the bar and wandering off to serve another customer.

I watch him walk away and realise this has all been a big waste of my time, but before I can turn and leave, the guy next to me slides my drink over.

'Here, take a sip. You'll feel better. I promise.'

I know I should go but, as I look down at the amber liquid and the two cubes of ice in the glass, it does look tempting. I can't remember the last time I had a proper drink. Maybe I need this. Maybe it will make me feel better.

I pick up the glass and glug the whole measure down and, as I finish, I hear a couple of guys behind me let out a cheer.

'Better?' the man next to me asks, and I have to agree that it is.

'Another one?' he suggests and, suddenly, leaving here and wandering the streets looking for a police officer to tell my sorry story to is less appealing than staying here and warming myself up with the safety blanket of alcohol.

'Sure,' I say as I take a seat at the bar. 'Why the hell not?'

TWENTY-SEVEN

I don't know where I am, or even who I am with, but I don't care because I've drunk enough to temporarily forget most of my troubles. The alcohol in my body is making me feel less anxious and stressed than I was when I entered that bar several hours ago.

Looking around, I see a coffee table covered in sports magazines and a TV that is playing music videos, but all I care about is getting another drink in my hand. My host is more than happy to accommodate me.

'Cheers,' he says as he takes a seat beside me and hands me a glass of vodka mixed with soda. I watched him mix it over by the drinks stand he has in the corner, the one just below the frame that contains a signed Michael Jordan photo. This man has his own drink too, and he clinks his glass against mine before taking a sip.

'What's your name again?' I ask him, and he laughs.

'Kelvin.'

'Got it.'

'Have you? I've told you three times already,' Kelvin says with a laugh.

'Sorry,' I reply, and take a sip of my drink. 'I guess I'm forgetful tonight.'

It seems like a silly, almost innocent thing to say, but no sooner have the words left my lips than I think about Scarlett again and the things that she told me before I ran away from her. But if none of them made any sense at the time, they are making less sense after drinking.

'I have to say, we don't get many women like you in that bar,' Kelvin says as I watch the latest music video playing on the TV. 'In fact, we don't get any women at all.'

'Is that why you bought me three drinks before inviting me back here? You wanted to seize the opportunity?'

'No, you just seemed like you needed cheering up,' Kelvin replies genuinely, and that answer makes me feel sad, because he's right.

'I guess I did.'

'Are you ready to tell me about it now?' he asks, reminding me that, as of yet, I have still not revealed to him why I'm so troubled this evening.

'It's a very long story,' I say with a sigh. 'Basically, I was working for this couple who've turned out to be crazy.'

'How crazy?'

'They think I'm their daughter.'

'Oh, wow. I wasn't expecting that.'

'You're not the only one,' I say, laughing, though it's only because the alternative is to cry.

'So you're not their daughter, I assume,' Kelvin says as he puts his drink on the table, and his arm brushes my leg.

'No, of course not. It's nonsense.'

'So why would they say it then?'

'I don't know. Why would they do any of the things they've done? All I know is that they've been proven to be liars, so they're obviously lying about this too.'

I take another glug of my drink.

'Okay, so who are your parents?' Kelvin asks, and the question catches me by surprise, even if it might be the most obvious thing to ask at this point in the conversation.

'My parents?'

'Yeah. Where are they? Are they in Chicago?'

'Erm,' I say, having to think about it, though surely I shouldn't because it can't be that hard to answer, can it?

'I'm sorry. I didn't mean to pry. You don't have to tell me,' Kelvin says quickly, and I feel bad for making him uncomfortable. But I feel worse because it's not a question of not wanting to tell him; it's more a fact that I can't.

For the life of me, I cannot think who my parents are. That frightens me enough to finish my drink and suggest to Kelvin that he makes me another one.

'Maybe we've both had enough,' he says.

'No, I'm fine.'

'Are you sure?'

He studies my face, and I can't lie. I'm not fine at all and I feel like if I can't distract myself with another drink, I'm going to cry. But if he won't get me another drink, maybe there is something else I can distract myself with.

I go in for a kiss, figuring it isn't the worst thing in the world to do. This guy is nice, probably far nicer than any of the other guys I could have got talking to in that bar, and he's looked after me up to this point. Besides, if it helps make me feel better, then why not?

'Wait,' Kelvin says, pulling back just before my lips can touch his.

'What is it? Don't you want to?' I ask, feeling foolish already.

'No, it's not that. It's just, I don't want you to feel like I'm taking advantage of you.'

'You're not.'

'Are you sure? You're upset. Maybe a little confused?'

'I'm not confused. I know who I am and what I want,' I say, which might be a lie, but maybe I can at least convince Kelvin even if I can't convince myself. 'And I want to kiss you.'

I try again and this time Kelvin does not pull away. Our lips meet and, just like the alcohol, the kiss is making me feel a little better about myself. But only a few seconds into it, and even with my eyes closed, I see the vision of me locking lips with another man.

It's a man I recognise, though it takes me a few seconds to figure out from where, and I have to break off from the kiss to do so.

'Is everything okay?' Kelvin asks me, presumably wondering if he's done something wrong. But he hasn't – whatever is wrong here has to do with me.

What was that flashback?

And who was that man I saw?

It takes me a couple more seconds before I figure it out.

It was the man who I caught following me a few days ago on the street.

I just had a flashback of kissing my stalker.

TWENTY-EIGHT

'I need to go,' I say, getting off the sofa and rushing to the door. In my haste, I bump into the coffee table and send my glass toppling over and rolling onto the floor, where it breaks into two pieces.

'I'm sorry,' I say, but I don't slow down. I need to get out of here and get some fresh air, figure out what that flashback was all about, and—

'Darcy, wait!'

Kelvin tries to slow me down, but I pull away from him and reach the door, bursting out of his apartment and into the corridor.

'What's wrong? Is it something I did?'

'No, it's not you!' I call back, hoping that will be enough to stop him coming after me.

'What is it then?' he asks as I reach the staircase and rush down the steps, taking them two at a time and almost falling, but I just about keep my balance.

'It's me!' is the last thing I scream at him. I exit the apartment complex and run off down the street, turning a corner and getting away before he can see which way I go and chase me.

I feel terrible for leaving Kelvin's apartment so abruptly, because the state I am in now is not his fault. But that flashback has me so confused and, on top of everything else that has already happened tonight, I'm starting to question absolutely everything about my life.

I need to get home. I'll feel better there, won't I?

I realise I won't because Adrian and Scarlett can find me there. Adrian might even still be at my place for all I know. But if I can't go there, where can I go?

It's the middle of the night and the streets are eerily quiet, apart from me, a confused woman in a nurse's uniform running around with no real sense of direction or purpose.

I quit running and sit down on a bench in a bus shelter and weep, my entire body trembling as various emotions pour out of me. Shock, frustration, anger, *fear*.

I feel like I'm losing my grip on reality. Rather than try and get up again and figure out where to go next, I keep my head buried in my hands as my sobbing continues.

I stay on the bench for what must be at least half an hour, but it's long enough to be spotted by somebody. I hear a car stop on the road in front of me. A door opens and a voice calls out to me.

'Ma'am. Are you okay?'

I look up and see a police officer standing beside his patrol car with another cop sitting behind the wheel.

There I was trying to call them earlier in the night, but now they have come to me.

'We received a call about a distressed woman in the area matching your description,' the officer tells me as he approaches slowly. I realise that Kelvin must have called 911 after I fled his apartment. He was worried about me, which is sweet, although it now means my very private moment in this bus shelter is finished.

'It's cold out here and not safe. Do you want to come with

us?' the officer asks me. 'We can take you to the station and you can tell us what's going on if you like?'

I am too exhausted to do anything else but agree, so I get up and follow the officer to the patrol car. Once I'm on the back seat, we set off to the nearest station.

I don't say a word, simply staring out of the window at the quiet homes and closed storefronts until we reach our destination and go inside. I'm taken into a private room where I take a seat at a table. Another officer hands me a cup of coffee and tells me to let him know if I need a blanket to warm up. The coffee helps somewhat, but only to the point of waking me up a little bit. I still feel terrible though, and I imagine I'll only feel worse when I have to try and explain what is going on to somebody in a minute. But I'm wrong – instead of me doing the explaining, that task falls to somebody else, and it's somebody I was not expecting to see as the door opens and they walk in.

'Pippa! What are you doing here?' I ask my colleague as she approaches the table, a grave look of concern on her face.

'Darcy! Oh, sweetheart, are you okay?' she asks me and takes me in for a hug. I squeeze her tightly, so pleased she's here. She's about the only person I trust, even though I'm amazed she was able to find me.

'What are you doing here?' I ask her. 'How did you know where I was?'

We separate and Pippa takes a seat in the vacant chair opposite me. She takes a deep breath.

'Scarlett reported you missing,' she tells me. 'She called the police and gave them your description and said you needed to be found because you were distressed. Then that guy you met tonight called Kelvin, was it? He gave your description too, and told the police you had just left his apartment and he was worried about you. Thankfully, the police were able to find you and bring you in here.'

I had no idea so many people had been actively looking for

me tonight, barring Scarlett and presumably Adrian, of course, but it seems like half of Chicago PD were on the case.

'But how did you know I was here?' I ask again, because she hasn't answered my question.

Pippa pauses before reaching across the table to take one of my hands.

'I'm here to help you,' she says, but that's still not an answer.

'How did you know where I was? I left you a voicemail, but how did you know to find me *here*?'

'Scarlett told me.'

'You went to her house?' I ask, wondering if I just missed her when I ran away. If so, that was unlucky on my part, but luck has been in short supply lately, so I'm hardly surprised.

'Yes,' Pippa replies.

'Did you hear what she had to say? The crazy lies she was spouting about me being her daughter! And did she tell you that Adrian was the one who had been breaking into my house?'

'No,' Pippa replies, shaking her head, but I'm not surprised.

'Of course not, because she doesn't want to get in trouble! But she said all those things to me, including that she'd been faking her memory loss! I wish I had recorded it all, but it's fine because I've got the record of Adrian on camera at my house so we can show that to the police. Plus, you'll back me up, right? You'll say they were crazy, and they must have manipulated things to get me to their home. You're a witness. You worked there. You listened to their lies too. You'll help me, won't you?'

'Yes, I'll help you, but you have to listen to me,' Pippa says calmly. 'There's something that you need to know.'

'What?' I cry, getting frustrated again.

'They're not lies.'

What Pippa said makes no sense. I go to take my hand back, but she keeps hold of it.

'Darcy, I'm telling you the truth here. I know it's hard to

believe, but Scarlett was right. She is your mother and Adrian is your father.'

This can't be happening. The one person I thought I could trust is siding with those lunatics.

'No,' I say, but Pippa keeps a tight grip on my hand so I can't get up from the table, and now she has tears in her eyes, just like Scarlett had when she was saying the same things earlier.

'It's true,' Pippa goes on. 'You're their daughter, and you were in an accident. Everything they did has been because they are trying to help you get some of your memories back, and everything I have done is to help with that too.'

'Everything you've done?'

'Yes,' Pippa says, a tear rolling down her cheek, but she can't wipe it because she's keeping hold of me. 'I'm sorry, but I lied to you too. I knew Scarlett was faking it and...'

Her sentence trails off.

'What?' I urge her to finish.

'I'm not just a nurse,' Pippa confesses.

'You're not?' I cry, stunned. 'Who are you then?'

Pippa finally lets go of my hand, but I don't get up because I need to hear this.

'I'm your sister,' she says, before finally wiping that runaway tear on her cheek.

TWENTY-NINE

The only reason that I've not run out of this room is because I have nowhere else to go or anyone else to run to. Not now Pippa has revealed herself to be a liar too.

'How can you be my sister?' I say, incredulous. 'How can you be making stuff up like those other people?'

'I'm not making anything up and, if you'll listen, I'll tell you the truth. All of it. Mom tried to tell you earlier, but you ran away, but if you listen to me, I'll tell you it all.'

'Mom? You mean Scarlett?'

Pippa nods, but I feel sick.

'You are a nurse, you were in a car accident one night and, when you woke up, you didn't remember anything, and that meant that you didn't remember us. We sat by your hospital bed every day, me, Mom and Dad, and we prayed for you to get better. But while you were able to leave hospital, your memory from before the crash has never returned.'

I don't recall any accident or even being in hospital, but before I can dispute this, Pippa explains why.

'It's called retrograde amnesia,' she explains. 'It means you can't recall things from your past, which is why your long-term memory is gone.'

It sure sounds like Pippa knows what she's talking about, and she is speaking with some confidence, but the person she's talking about can't be me. None of this is making sense.

'I don't expect you to understand,' Pippa says, reading my mind. 'You won't be able to remember it because you can barely remember anything from a fortnight ago, never mind your child-hood or your adult life before the crash, or the crash itself.'

'Nonsense!' I cry, but Pippa doesn't even flinch at the volume of my voice.

'Prove me wrong then,' she says. 'Tell me one thing about your childhood.'

I laugh, and try to think of something. But it's terrifying when not a single thought comes to mind.

'Now, try and remember what you were doing this time last month. Can you remember that?'

Last month? That should be easy enough.

'Last month, I...'

I can't recall a single thing I was doing last month. I can't even remember which month it actually is.

'I'm not making any of this up,' Pippa says sadly. 'This is the problem we have. We've spent the last two years trying to help you to remember us, but nothing has worked, because you can't retain long-term memories. You'll remember what happened today for the next few weeks, but the memory will gradually fade until it's gone, like wiping a slate clean. That's why we resorted to what we did. We had to try something to hopefully kickstart the part of your brain that isn't working anymore.'

Pippa wipes away another tear while I keep staring at her, allowing her to speak.

'It became clear that the more we tried to convince you of who we were, the more distressed and confused you became,' she goes on. 'Believe me, we tried everything for you. Mom and

Dad spent a fortune getting you the best rehab, the best specialists in Chicago and beyond, alternative therapy, natural remedies, trials. You name it, they tried it all. Dad's barely slept for two years searching for a cure to help you get your memory back. But nothing worked. Then we decided to give role-playing a go. It seemed silly to even think it might work, but sometimes the simplest ideas are the best and, by that point, it was the only thing we hadn't tried.'

Role-playing. There it is again, that same term that Scarlett used.

'We decided to create a scenario that the old you would have been used to. When you were working as a nurse before your accident, you used to go into other people's homes and care for them. You always worked in pairs, so I decided to pretend to be your colleague. Together, we went to Mom and Dad's. They were pretending to be no different to the couples you helped before your accident. We hoped that putting you in familiar situations might jog a memory, or spark something, plus it was a way to get you to spend time around us without us having to explain who we really were constantly and you getting upset.'

The horror of my reality is slowly starting to dawn on me as I listen to Pippa explaining it, but there is something I don't understand.

'But how come I didn't recognise you or remember any of you?' I ask. 'I mean, if I forgot you before the accident that's one thing, but if I spent time with you after it, why wouldn't I know your faces when you started this whole role-playing thing?'

'It's complicated,' Pippa says, but I bang my fist down on the table.

'Try me.'

Pippa is startled by my sudden burst of frustration, and she carries on.

'It's not that you can't make new memories since the accident, because you can,' she explains. 'But they fade over time, which can be as short as a few weeks. Short-term memory, no problem, barring a bit of confusion and brain fog, but storing things away and recalling them in the long-term is pretty much impossible for you without outside help. It's been two years since your accident, so there's been a lot of time for us to realise this. We did our best to keep reminding you of who you were, but understandably that came with its own challenges. When it was getting too much for you and our presence was upsetting you more than it was helping, we pulled back. We stayed away from you for a few weeks, or at least we stayed out of sight of you. So then enough time passed for you to forget us. That's when we came up with this plan to try the role-playing.'

'What do you mean you stayed out of sight?' I ask. 'What the hell does that mean?'

'We didn't just abandon you completely,' Pippa explains. 'We kept watch on you to make sure you were doing okay.'

'How?' I ask, but I have a feeling I might actually know the answer to this one.

'We would sneak into your house when you were asleep or when you were out,' Pippa admits. 'We'd check you were living okay, or at least living. Sometimes we'd clean up a little, although never so much as to tip you off that someone had been there.'

I think about all the times I've felt weird in my own home, the times I've felt the odd thing has been out of place or a general sense of uneasiness. It's because I hadn't been the only one occupying that space. It's also because I was presumably getting a vague sense of déjà vu.

'That's why Adrian was in the house?' I ask, and Pippa nods. 'It was him all along?'

'Not every time. Sometimes it was me. I was there the other night, while you were supposed to be staying over with Mom and Dad.'

The footprints in the hallway. *That was Pippa?*

'All this time I thought I was going mad,' I say, disgusted at what I'm hearing. 'Or I blamed it on not getting enough sleep, or drowsiness from the sleeping pills.'

'We're sorry, but we were just trying to get you back!' Pippa protests. 'We love you and we wanted you to remember us, so we stayed out of your sight long enough for you to forget, and then we put this plan into motion.'

'The house,' I say. 'The one I've been living in. Scarlett said it was my childhood home.'

'That's right,' Pippa confirms. 'We all lived there, all four of us. Me and you lived there when we were small until Mom and Dad moved us all to the house in Winnetka when we were teenagers. But they kept the first house as a rental. After your accident, they figured it was a good place for you to recover and get some independence, so you moved back there.'

I can't believe this. All this time I thought I was renting it, but it's really my parents' first home.

'We all lived in Winnetka?' I ask. 'In that big house?'

'Yes,' Pippa replies sadly, or maybe she's bored at having to tell me this again. 'I mean, we had both moved out years ago and were living our own lives, on our own career paths. I'm a nurse too.'

'You are?'

'Yes, though I work with children, whereas you always focused on adults. And you know what? Mom was a nurse too. That's how she met Dad. He eventually became the medical director of a hospital. They both retired early, but they were so proud when we both decided to become nurses too.'

I scratch my head, wondering how any of this can be my real life.

'If this was all role-play, what about the uniforms we had? The name badges? They seemed so real,' I say.

'We had them made,' Pippa tells me, an answer for seemingly anything I can throw at her. 'They looked like the real deal, but they were just for show.'

But that's not where my questions end.

'Wait, we have different surnames. They're the Hoffmans. My name badge says my surname is Miller.'

'Their surname is Miller too. We made up the surname Hoffman. It helped in case you ever tried to Google them. You wouldn't have found anything. We're all Millers. My surname is Simpson now, as I'm married, so my name badge didn't give anything away to you.'

This is crazy. It seems like they've thought of everything.

'But how could you pretend to be a nurse with me?' I cry. 'What about your real nursing job?'

'I've taken time off,' Pippa confesses. 'I had some days saved that I could take, just for a week or so to see if this would work.'

Now I feel even worse. Her vacation time from a demanding job looking after sick children has been role-playing with me?

'What about your family?'

'They're your family too,' Pippa says, smiling. 'I mean, things haven't exactly been easy between me and Karl lately, but that doesn't mean he doesn't want you to get better. And Campbell adores you. You're his auntie. I show him photos of you every day so he knows you so well, even though you've been like this for most of his life.'

Pippa takes out her phone and shows me a photo of myself holding a baby and smiling widely; it must be Campbell when he was born. That was before my accident, but there are a few photos of the two of us together since, though I'm not smiling in those.

'You had an apartment in the city,' Pippa goes on as she puts her phone away. 'But you had to give that up after your accident and you moved back into the house in Winnetka. You were there for over a year until it became too hard for everyone and we realised you needed your own space.'

I think about the first time I went to that house with Pippa, or at least what I thought was the first time. It was the first day we went to see Scarlett, the supposed patient, and I remember getting an odd feeling about the place then. I also recall feeling odd around Adrian, and a strange sense seemed to follow me around that house while I was there. Now I know it's because it wasn't the first time I'd been there.

'We were praying that something would trigger a memory,' Pippa goes on. 'We tried everything. The old movies Mom was watching when we went into her room, they were movies she had on the TV when we were kids. The photos, the different rooms, the backyard. Even Mom pretending to get confused and think you were her daughter. We were hoping something would spark a memory and you would remember a moment with us before your accident. But it didn't work and we're sorry. We're sorry we've caused you all this pain and confusion.'

Pippa genuinely looks remorseful as her tears start again.

'I just want my sister back,' she says, sobbing. 'And Mom and Dad just want their daughter back. We love you so much, but we don't know how to help you. I'm so sorry.'

Pippa puts her head in her hands, probably expecting that I'll either continue to dispute this story or, worse, walk out of here and carry on as if she means nothing to me.

But I don't do that because I can see how devastated she is about all of this – as scary as it is, I feel like I have no choice but to believe her. I also feel like I have to tell her that it might not all have been the waste of time that she thinks it is.

'I remembered something,' I confess. 'Not to do with you or Mom or Dad, but I think it was something before my accident.'

'You have?' Pippa asks, lifting her head up and looking hopeful.

'Yeah. A few hours ago. When I was at Kelvin's, the guy

from the bar. We kissed and I got a weird vision. A flashback or something.'

'Oh my god, this is amazing! What did you see?' Pippa asks.

'A guy. I was kissing him.'

'A guy? Do you know who he is?'

'Yes, I think so. But what if this is a memory from a few months ago or a few years ago, just after my accident?' I say fearfully. 'Maybe it's not from before.'

'No, it has to be,' Pippa says.

'How can you be so sure?'

'Because, my darling sister, you have not been with any guys in all that time. At least not until tonight, anyway. We've all been with you or watching you, so we know. If you've had a flashback to kissing some guy, then it must have been before the crash.'

Pippa looks overjoyed, but I have to temper her excitement somewhat.

'I don't know who this guy is,' I admit. 'I mean, I've seen him around, but I don't know his name or where he lives or anything.'

'That's okay,' Pippa tells me, a wide smile still on her face. 'We have to try and find him. He might hold the key to you getting your memory back.'

My sister, or at least the sister I have been reminded about, is thrilled and she says she has to go and call Mom and Dad right away. But as she does that, I have a sinking feeling in the pit of my stomach.

It's weird, but it's as if this isn't such good news after all.

It's as if I have the feeling that I'd be better off not remembering what happened before the accident.

Maybe I would be.

What if there is something in my past that would be better staying buried?

THIRTY

I'm sitting in a house that is allegedly the house I grew up in, at a dining table with people who are allegedly my family. But I'm having to take their word for it, at least until I get more information, which is why I'm remaining guarded and not getting as hopeful or optimistic as those I'm sitting with. We've spent time going through old family photos, though they might have been photos of another family for all I could recollect about them. I've also spent time listening to stories from my past, but it's hard to really engage with them when it feels like that's all they are – *stories*. It's as if everything I've been told about my past could have been written in a book or acted out in a movie, because that's how fictionalised it feels to me. But it hasn't stopped the people at this table from trying to convince me that I'm a part of this family. They even showed me my birth certificate, as if that was all the proof I needed of who I am and how they know me, but with a memory as foggy as mine, it might as well have been somebody else's name printed on there.

I still don't know myself, and I'm still wary of the people who claim to be my family.

The last time I saw Adrian, or 'Dad' as I'm expected to call him, he was caught on camera creeping around my kitchen, yet here he is now, sitting at the head of this table, finishing a sandwich he made in that same kitchen ten minutes ago. To his left is Scarlett, my 'mother', and the last time I saw her she was frenetically chasing me out of her neighbours' home after dropping the bombshell that I was her daughter. Now, here she is sipping a cup of coffee and looking at me with hope; but I keep avoiding eye contact with her and have only really spent time looking at the person across the table from her. That is Pippa, who is apparently my sister, and she has my laptop open in front of her and is busy typing away on the keyboard furiously, working with the determination of someone who has a big purpose in life.

She tells me that she does.

She tells me that she's going to help me get my memory back.

'Okay, so we need to find this guy, and what's the best way of finding anybody these days?' she asks us all.

'Social media?' Adrian suggests as he wipes a breadcrumb from the side of his mouth.

'Exactly! Well, kind of. We can use social media, but we can use other online platforms too. Local message boards. Forums. Advertising. We can harness the power of the internet to hopefully get somebody to come forward and say they are the guy who Darcy remembers kissing before her accident, or at least somebody might say they know who the guy is.'

'That's a good idea,' Scarlett says, looking at me again, which causes me to glance away.

'But we don't know his name,' I remind everyone, dampening the mood at the table slightly.

'You can describe him, and we can put that description online. Plus we can talk about you. Say who you are. A nurse who had an accident. We can put your photo up and this guy might see it and come forward. If you recognise him when he does, we'll know we've got our guy and then, hopefully, he can stir up a few more memories.'

'What if it doesn't work?' I ask, but Pippa doesn't seem in the mood for entertaining pessimistic thoughts.

'It's worth a try,' is all she says, and she starts typing again.

'Did you know of anybody I might have been dating?' I ask everyone, not just because it might jog their memory of who this mystery guy could be but because I'm putting them to the test. If they are my family like they say they are, surely they would have some knowledge of my love life prior to the accident, wouldn't they? But none of them seem to be able to offer up any ex-boyfriends or even casual male acquaintances of mine that match the description I gave them earlier of the guy in my flashback.

That description is written on a piece of paper that sits on the table beside Pippa, and she is referring to it as she types whatever she's putting online right now.

'You don't remember me having any boyfriends?' I ask them. 'Isn't that weird?'

'None that match that description,' Adrian says. 'Short dark hair, six feet tall, blue eyes, smartly dressed. I don't remember anybody like that.'

'Neither do I,' Scarlett says.

'I don't remember you having much of a love life at all,' Pippa remarks with a laugh before adding, 'Sorry, sis.'

It's strange to hear her refer to me as 'sis', but strange has become the norm lately.

I didn't have a love life? That sounds very bleak. Something must have been going on if I can recall kissing that guy, although nobody around this table seems to know anything about it.

'Okay, so I've just uploaded a post onto Facebook, and I'll update my other socials later,' Pippa says. 'Now I'm going to post on the *Chicago Tribune* public forum. Maybe I could even take out an ad in the newspaper itself. Do people still read the newspaper these days? It's worth a try, I guess.'

It sounds like she has it all figured out, but I'm sceptical.

'Even if this guy sees my photo and realises that he matches the description of the person we're looking for, how do we know he'll come forward?' I ask.

'We have to try, darling,' Scarlett says, looking at me sympathetically; but it's hard to warm to a woman I am still unsure about.

'I told you I saw him before,' I remind them.

'Yeah, you said you saw him twice,' Adrian says. 'You thought he was following you?'

'Yeah, but what I didn't tell you was that I told him to leave me alone. So what if he does that? What if he thinks he might get in trouble if he comes forward, so he stays away?'

'What if the world ends tomorrow?' Pippa asks sarcastically, looking up from the laptop. 'Look, I'm sorry, sis, but we have to try. You might not realise it fully, but this is the first bit of hope we've had to hang onto since your accident. Us three have been praying for you to remember something from before the crash, so now that you have, we're going to do everything we can to see what it might lead to. Who knows, this could be the start of you getting your memory back. Isn't that what you want?'

It sounds like there should be an obvious answer to that question, but my silence shows that I'm not so sure.

'You must have been close with this guy if you remember kissing him,' Adrian says. 'Have you considered that the reason he was following you around might be because he's still in love with you?'

That isn't something I had considered, but Pippa quickly warms to the suggestion.

'Yes! Maybe he's broken-hearted. Maybe you guys were madly in love before your accident, but now you don't remember him and he's wandering around Chicago like a lost soul, not sure what to do with himself, wondering if he'll ever be able to love again.'

Pippa is laying it on a little thick, but I get her point. This man, whoever the hell he is, might not have been some creepy stalker. He might have been someone who loves me and someone who I loved back, which makes me feel awful, considering I told him to stay away from me the last time I saw him.

'Okay, do whatever you've got to do,' I say, getting up from the table.

'Where are you going?' Scarlett asks me nervously, possibly wondering if I'm about to go and shut myself away in my bedroom again. But I'm not.

'I'm going to try and help,' I say, which surprises them, but in a good way. 'I told you I saw this guy when I was out walking. So I'll go out walking now and maybe I'll see him again.'

'I'll come with you,' Adrian suggests, but I dismiss him.

'No, I want to go by myself. I need some space,' I say, and everyone at the table looks like they know to heed such a request all too well.

I leave the house and it feels good to have some space from the three people who are trying to be nice but are suffocating me all the same. I'm still not at the point where I feel comfortable referring to them as my family yet, and I'm not sure if and when I'll be ready for that. I clearly struggled with them after my accident, to the point where they came up with such a drastic plan, and I guess I'm struggling with them again.

But as I walk, I'm aware that if I'm to stand any chance of gaining some semblance of my old life back, I can't cut them out of it, certainly not for any real length of time. Apparently, when I do that, I simply forget them and the whole process has to start all over again.

Forcing myself to forget about them for the time being, I

focus on my surroundings and, more specifically, the people around me as I walk these streets. It's a long shot, but I'm hoping to see that man again – if I can, and if I can catch him, he might be able to unlock more of my damaged memories. But despite walking for over an hour and going past the same places I saw him previously, I don't catch a glimpse of him.

However, I do see someone I know.

It's Pippa. I catch her following me even though she obviously thought she was being clever and staying out of sight. I guess she followed me as soon as I left, worried that I was going to run away again or get myself into danger. But that's not my plan, and I pretend I don't see her as I walk home, getting back to the house and telling Adrian and Scarlett that I'm going for a lie down upstairs.

I've barely been on the bed for five minutes when I hear Pippa creeping back inside.

I guess this is my life now. Always needing to be watched, constantly having to be handled with care. It's clear that it's not much of a life at all.

But then did I even have much of a life before my accident? Very little I've heard so far suggests that I did. It sounds like I just walked and had no love life or much of a social life to speak of. So with that in mind, what's the point of even trying to remember it?

Maybe I'm better off not even trying to recount the past.

If only I knew how true that really was.

THIRTY-ONE

A two-hour nap has done me the world of good, though as usual, the first thing I see when I wake up is my nurse's uniform lying on my bedroom floor. Any good feelings I have quickly fade. But at least there is no knocking at my front door to stir me off my mattress, as Pippa no longer has to come here and pretend to be my colleague. I don't have work to go to and I haven't for a long time, despite the pretence that others created.

As I lie in bed and think about those mornings when I would wake up groggy and unsure, I know now that it was simply because my brain was working overtime to piece together memories. All the times I sat in Pippa's car rereading the patient notes wasn't just because I was being conscientious, but because I was reminding myself, just like my uniform and my name badge and the photos in the hallway reminded me of who I was before the accident. It feels like everything since I had that crash has been staged, but that's not even the most frustrating thing.

The most frustrating thing is that I can't even remember the damn crash that has caused my life to be like this.

How bad must it have been? The car must have been a

wreck if it's done this damage to me. I guess I was lucky to survive. Pippa told me so, and Adrian looked very serious when I asked him about it. As for Scarlett, she simply refused to say a word about it and reached for a tissue whenever talk turned to that life-changing event. I did try to find out about it online, but there were only small news articles about it and none of them had photos of the car, so I couldn't gauge the extent of the damage from them. But at least I got the date of my accident – the date when my whole life changed so suddenly.

It was the twentieth of June 2022.

I force myself out of bed, but I don't leave my bedroom because I don't want everyone else in the house to know that I'm up. I want some time and space, but I also want to do some searching around and see if there is anything else that might jog my memory. There might be things that I've already looked at several times since my accident, but I have to try because I clearly never know when something might trigger a flashback.

I look in my wardrobe and while there's nothing but some of my old clothes – dresses, sweatshirts and pairs of jeans that I guess I used to wear all the time – I take each garment off its hanger and hold it, running my hands over the fabric and praying that it will spark a memory. But no such luck, and the same thing can be said when I pick up some of the shoes resting at the bottom of the wardrobe. I even try on a pair of heels, as if that will take me back to a time when I used to go out clubbing, but alas, it's all in vain and I feel stupid.

From where I'm sitting on the carpet, I take off the heels and throw them back into my wardrobe in frustration. I look under the bed. I see a box under here, so I pull it out and open it up, seeing that it's full of things that relate to my old life.

There are photos from my late teens or early twenties, possibly at university, partying with pals, drinking colourful cocktails, my arms raised on a dancefloor. I don't recognise any of the people, but most of all I don't recognise myself in these images.

I find some certificates next, paper records of my academic achievements, qualifications I gained towards my nursing degree, but again, I remember none of it, so it might as well be that somebody else sat these exams that I apparently passed so well.

I find more photos, ones of me working in a hospital, in full uniform, beside beds, tending to patients or smiling in a staff room along with other nurses. I guess I worked on wards before going to work for a private company, and I'm sure most of my on-the-job learning was done in these kinds of environments rather than in the affluent homes of rich patients.

I take time to study each and every face in these photos with me, praying that something comes to me, but nothing does. There is one face in particular that appears quite a lot beside me in several of these photos. It's another female nurse, her uniform matching mine. She has short, dark hair and looks pretty, even as she's mostly without make-up in these photos – we're at work and it looks like we had far more important things to be doing than beautifying ourselves. Of course, I have no recollection of who this woman is, but it's apparent that we were close.

A lost friend. Maybe a best friend. But she sure isn't around now, so I guess she's gone the way of almost everyone else from my past.

She's moved on and forgotten me as much as I've forgotten her.

Next up to come out of the box is a notebook and, as I open it, I realise it's a diary.

This might help, I think, feeling a rare wave of excitement as I figure that my past life must be documented here, so all I have to do is read it and it'll all come flooding back to me. But if that's the case and it's as simple as that, why hasn't that worked before? I get my answer when I start reading the first entry here, which is dated '13 May 2022'.

Tough shift today. I heard Lucy passed away and felt bad for not having seen her one last time. Losing a patient I cared for during the pandemic is awful. I know it was only a matter of time for poor Lucy, and she's not in pain anymore, but I still feel awful. Losing patients isn't actually the hardest part of the job. The hardest part is having to put on our uniforms and go and do it all again the next day, facing death again and again and again and trying to pretend like it's not affecting our mental health or even altering our personalities entirely. But there's not much time to grieve. There's always another patient, and my latest patient certainly takes all my attention now.

It's a sad piece of writing, clearly showing the effect that my job was having on me. As well as doing nothing to help me actually remember that time, it's managed to make me feel even worse. I guess this is why the diary is packed away in this box along with all this other stuff. It doesn't jog my memory – it makes me depressed.

Despite that, I turn the page and read the next entry.

I had the day off today, though I wish I hadn't as I had nothing to do. But I did get a card. He sent me one. It was on my doormat when I got back from a walk. He told me he loved me and couldn't wait to see me again. I guess it made me feel a little better about spending the day by myself, but only just. He says he loves me yet it's not enough to come see me properly. He's with her instead. But it's not his fault. She needs him. She needs him even more than I do.

I sit up a little straighter after reading this latest entry – it seems to be more revealing than the last one. I was clearly writing about somebody I cared about, maybe even somebody I loved. Is this the man I saw in my flashback?

I read the entry again, not in case I missed a name, I know there wasn't one mentioned, but because I'm hoping my brain does the one thing it's supposed to do and makes me remember who exactly this is that I'm referring to.

He told me he loved me.

He's with her instead.

She needs him even more than I do.

Damn it, why can't I remember what I'm writing about here? Why couldn't I have been more specific? Why couldn't I have used names and more descriptive details than this vague entry I have here? But the answer is obvious. When a person writes a diary, they are mainly pouring out their feelings, not reciting factual information, and I've been clear about how I felt at this exact moment in time, but haven't left any real breadcrumbs for me to use now – because why would I?

How was I to know I was going to lose my mind in the future?

I turn the page to the fifteenth of May.

Another lonnnnng day. But at least I got to see him. He apologised for not being with me yesterday. Said he'd make it up to me. I'd heard it all before, but then he said something else. Something I definitely hadn't heard before. Something that scared me. Something it might be too dangerous to write down here...

The entry ends there, which is of absolutely no use to me – it doesn't tell me what it was that scared me. What the hell could that have been?

The obvious answer is to read on, so I turn the page, but

when I do I see that is where the entries end, though it's not because I simply stopped writing.

The pages here have all been ripped out.

I frantically search the rest of the notebook for any more handwriting, but all the pages after this last date are missing, torn out so only the stumps of the paper in the spine remain.

Who has ripped these out? Did I do it? If so, why?

Or was it somebody else?

'Darcy?'

I look up and see Pippa peering around the bedroom door, and she sees me sitting on the floor, surrounded by mementos of my past.

'Are you okay?' she asks me, her eyes landing on the diary in my hands. 'I thought I heard something.'

I wonder if what she heard was me throwing my heels into the wardrobe a few minutes ago. Or has she come up here to check on me for another reason?

'Why is my diary missing so many pages?' I ask her, holding up the diary to show her exactly what I mean.

'I don't know,' Pippa replies.

I have to take her word for that, but is it true?

'You've been through all these things before, sis,' Pippa goes on as she enters the room and kneels down beside me. 'But it's never helped you recall anything.'

She tries to take the diary from me, but I keep it away from her.

'What's wrong?' Pippa asks, concern on her face.

'I don't know,' I say, but the fact I'm keeping the diary away from her might give away how I'm feeling inside.

'What's the matter? Do you think I'm lying to you?' Pippa asks. 'Do you think I'm making all of this up?'

'I don't know!' I say again, only this time louder and on the verge of tears.

'Don't be like this, sis. I'm just trying to help you,' Pippa says, and she puts a hand on my shoulder, but I shake it off.

'Stop calling me sis!'

'But that's who you are. You're my sister!'

This is all too much again and, as my tears flow, I don't know whether to throw the diary down, hit the bedframe or take out my frustration on the woman kneeling beside me.

'This is why we've had to be so careful with you and try to get you to remember things,' Pippa goes on. 'It always upsets you when you struggle.'

I want to get up and get out of this room, get some space and forget that this is my life and start all over again, but I feel so weak and helpless, and now Pippa is holding me, squeezing my hand and begging me to stop torturing myself.

'Don't push me away,' she begs me. 'Don't do this, please.'

And then it happens again, triggered by the last sentence out of Pippa's mouth. I get a flashback of a woman, young but weak, and she's holding my hand as I sit beside her bed in my uniform. She says exactly the same thing that Pippa's just said to me.

'Don't do this, please.'

Only in this case, I have a feeling the words mean something much worse.

It feels as if she's begging me for her life.

THIRTY-TWO

It was a frightening flashback, not only because it was so sudden and unexpected, but because it gave me the sense that something terrible was about to happen and I was involved.

Who was that woman I saw?

And what was she begging me not to do?

It was so troubling that I decide to keep it to myself and not tell Pippa. Instead, I tell her that I need some privacy and, thankfully, she does as I ask and leaves me alone again...

But she's barely been gone ten minutes when I hear her running back up the stairs, bursting into my room a moment later.

'I've had a message,' she says, a little out breath but a smile on her face. 'A response to the posts I put up online.'

'What?' I say, sitting up on the bed that I've hardly had a chance to relax on since Pippa left. 'Is it him? Or does someone know who he is?'

'No,' Pippa says disappointingly. 'It's from a woman who says she used to work with you at the hospital, and there's a reunion coming up next week. She recognised the photo of you online and says you should come, if you're feeling up to it.'

A reunion at the hospital?

'I know it's probably daunting to go to a party right now, but this could be a good thing,' Pippa says, taking a seat on the edge of my bed. 'Being around people you used to work with. It might jog your memory. It has to be worth a try, don't you think?'

It sounds like it might help, in theory at least, but Pippa is right. It is daunting, and I'm not sure how I'll handle it. I'm also not sure why getting together with some of the people I used to work with hasn't happened sooner.

'Who is this woman?' I ask. 'Has she visited me since my accident? Have any of the nurses visited me?'

Pippa loses a little of her exuberance then.

'It's been tricky,' is all she says.

'What does that mean?'

'Well, you'd left the hospital by the time of your accident. You'd started working for the private company, going into homes rather than working on wards.'

'So? I must have had friends there when I left, wouldn't I? Surely I kept in touch with them?'

Pippa looks like she's not sure how to break it to me.

'What is it?' I ask, figuring that anything she can tell me about my past has to be helpful.

'I've been over this with you several times since your accident,' she says, but that would be all well and good if I wasn't suffering from memory issues.

'I can't remember, so tell me again,' I say firmly.

'Okay,' Pippa says awkwardly. 'Well, you used to be quite a sociable person. You did have lots of friends. But...'

'But what?'

'You'd changed quite a bit in the months leading up to your accident. You'd become more withdrawn. Not just from friends, but from family too. You stopped replying to people's messages. You wouldn't pick up the phone when I called you. It was hard to speak to you, so I guess a lot of your friends lost touch and then either didn't know about the accident or didn't want to see you anyway after it.'

I think about what I've just heard and, once again, it's hard to know if it's really the truth or I'm being told another story that I'm supposed to believe.

'Why would I do that?' I ask. 'Why was I cutting people out?'

'I don't know,' Pippa replies. 'Dad thought it had something to do with work. The stress of your job. And Mom always feared what damage being around sickness and death so much was doing to you mentally.'

I think about the last diary entries I was able to read, and there were things in there that suggested I was struggling with my job, as well as struggling with some guy I was apparently in love with.

'Maybe this reunion is a bad idea,' Pippa says, interrupting my thoughts, but before she can leave the room again I stop her.

'No,' I say as she pauses and looks back. 'Reply to the message and tell them that I'll go.'

'Are you sure?' Pippa asks, looking concerned, but I get up off the bed and open my wardrobe again. I take out the heels I threw in there during my tantrum earlier.

'Yes,' I reply adamantly as I inspect the shoes for damage. 'It'll do me good to get out. I think I need it. And who knows what might come of it.'

Pippa doesn't look so sure anymore, but she leaves to go and do as I asked her, which is accept the invitation for the reunion.

I guess I'm going to a party, and I guess I'm going to see some people who used to know the old me.

Is it the right decision?

Let's find out.

THIRTY-THREE

'Are you sure about this?' Pippa asks me as we stare through the windshield of her car at the entrance to where the reunion is being held.

'Nope,' I reply simply. 'But maybe that's exactly why I need to do it.'

I keep staring at the doorway to this fairly plain venue, which is a restaurant and bar on the outskirts of the city, chosen presumably because it's a cheap place to hire for an evening for a reunion like this one.

I guess if you want to see how poorly paid nurses are, you just have to attend one of their parties.

We've been here for five minutes, parked across the street and watching several people go into the venue, but I haven't recognised any of them, though that may be because we're at a bit of a distance and it's dark. Or maybe it's because I'm never going to recognise any of them no matter how long I stare at them, and being here tonight is going to be more overwhelming than productive.

There's only one way to find out.

'Let's go,' I say, opening my passenger-side door and stepping out, the points of my heels digging into the blacktop of this parking lot, and the hem of my dress riding up a little. I pull it back once I'm standing. I readjust the handbag over my shoulder before setting off.

I'm a little unsteady on my heels – it's been a while since I wore shoes like this – and I'm not exactly feeling confident in my sequined dress either, but I've forced myself to make an effort with my appearance so that I turn up here looking good.

Maybe my dazzling appearance on the outside can cover up for the fact that I'm a mess on the inside.

I glance to my right and see Pippa walking beside me, here to offer support, or simply a familiar face in a sea of strange ones. She hasn't gone to quite as much effort with her look, opting for a blue blouse, leather jacket and jeans. Her flat footwear is far easier to walk in than mine.

'Just let me know if it gets too much for you and we can leave,' Pippa says as we reach the door, but I forge on, trying to enter with confidence, as if I can trick my mind into actually believing that I'm not wracked with nerves about being here.

As we step inside, I hear loud music and see several people standing at the bar, and the fluttering of the nerves in my stomach grows ever stronger – I know I'm supposed to walk right over to that bar and start mingling.

'Come on,' Pippa says, interlinking her arm with mine, and while I'm still being on guard around her, I appreciate her show of support. I also appreciate how comfortable she is at getting close to me. While I was wary of her at first when I was told she was my sibling, I'm starting to see more and more similarities between us that back up that link. She has a few freckles on her face like me, she fidgets with her hair like I do when I'm unsure about something, and then, of course, there is the nose scrunching that she does while concentrating, a trait of mine I first noticed in Pippa back when she was role-playing as Scarlett's nurse. I certainly appreciate the extra strength she is giving me now, as it enables me to keep my legs moving until I make it to where some of the other guests are assembled.

As a few of them turn to look at us, I once again draw a blank in terms of recognising them. But it becomes apparent that several of them recognise me immediately.

'Darcy! Oh my gosh, how are you doing?' a woman in a black dress asks me. Another woman next to her overhears my name and turns her head towards me too.

'Wow! It's so good to see you!' she cries. 'You look amazing!'

I glance nervously at Pippa, whose arm is still linked through mine, and I see her smile at me, clearly happy that some of these people seem pleased to see me. But are they pleased or are they just plain surprised? After all, it must be quite shocking to have an ex-colleague who was in a terrible accident turn up years later in a dress and heels, looking like nothing ever happened.

A few other women glance my way but don't seem as interested, so I presume I didn't work with them closely during my time at the hospital, or they simply aren't in any hurry to say hello again. But there are a few people who clearly know who I am and want to talk. I very quickly find myself in a circle that consists of six women, including Pippa, though I am very much the centre of attention.

'How are you feeling?'

'I meant to come and visit you.'

'I wondered what happened to you.'

'How long has it been now?'

Words are coming at me thick and fast, but the blur of faces, together with the loud music in here, is making me feel a little overwhelmed. I'm already looking beyond these women at the bartender, who is capable of making me something to take the edge off my anxiety. But just before I can do that, I'm tapped on the shoulder – when I turn around, I see a tall and friendly looking blonde woman with her arms open wide.

'Darcy! You came!' she cries. 'And you must be Pippa. Thank you for replying to my message!'

I realise this must be the nurse who made contact with us, and she seems delighted to see me, which I guess means we were close at one time.

'It's me, Cara,' she says, hopeful that I'll remember her, but it's not to be. She brushes over that disappointment with the confident ease of a woman of her stature. 'How have you been? I heard about the accident. I'm so sorry.'

'Thank you,' I say, still on edge around these people and still glad that Pippa is here alongside me.

'It's okay if you don't remember me,' Cara goes on. 'We worked together on Ward B at Chicago Memorial. It's a few years ago now. Where does time go?'

Ward B? Chicago Memorial? More insight into a past I can't recollect.

'It looks like a really good turnout tonight,' Cara says, looking around, and I notice a few more people arriving, more blank faces being painted onto this confusing canvas.

'Is Eden coming?' I hear someone ask, and Cara shakes her head.

'No, she declined the invite, but didn't say why,' Cara replies, looking back at me. 'Have you heard from her at all, Darcy?'

Cara seems to be expecting that I have, which makes me think I had some connection to this Eden person.

'Erm, no,' I say. 'Sorry, I can't remember her either.'

'You can't remember Eden?' Cara cries. 'Oh, what a shame. You two were like best friends!'

I had a best friend?

'Yeah, you guys were inseparable,' another nurse chips in.

I look to Pippa as if she might be able to shed some more light on who this mysterious best friend of mine is.

'You'll have seen her in the photos under your bed,' my sister tells me. 'The woman with the short, dark hair.'

I remember seeing lots of photos of me with a woman matching that description, and I remember because I've been looking at those photos every day for the past week. But, even so, I don't associate any feelings with her. I can't remember, which I suppose is the problem my family have had since my accident. They can get me to essentially 'revise' my past by telling me about it and showing me items from before, but it doesn't mean I mentally link them up to the person I am now.

'You must still hear from her though, right?' Cara asks me. 'You guys were practically joined at the hip.'

'No, I don't think so,' I say, shaking my head, and a sudden sadness comes over me as I learn once more of yet another thing I seem to have lost. If it's not bad enough forgetting my family and my career, forgetting a best friend feels pretty awful too.

'You weren't quite as close as you once were just before your accident,' Pippa tells me.

'Why not?'

'I'm not sure. We did ask you, but you never told us.'

That seems odd. I'd fallen out with my best friend before the crash? I wonder what caused that.

'Do you have a number for her?' I ask Cara, as well as the other nurses standing around, who are mostly listening to us talk but not engaging with us.

'Not her new one. I've lost touch with her too,' Cara admits. 'I think most of us have actually, as we no longer work at the same hospital.'

That's a shame, though more for me than them given my current plight, and I try to think of something else that might help me recall this person who I was apparently so close to before. But it's hard to think in here, because the music seems to be getting louder, or maybe it's just the volume of all the voices around me as more and more people arrive at this reunion and start chattering. That, mixed in with the noises coming from the bar as the bartenders make cocktails and hand over the alcohol that only makes the people drinking them get louder, and it's starting to feel deafening in here.

'I need to go,' I say to Pippa urgently, feeling like I could be on the verge of a panic attack.

'No problem,' she says, clearly realising that I'm struggling, and she takes my hand and leads me away.

'Are you leaving?' I hear Cara call after me, but I ignore her and allow Pippa to get me out of here as quickly as possible. But just before we make it to the door and the fresh air beyond it, a song comes on that sparks another memory.

I see myself on a crowded dancefloor, this same song playing, and she's there. The woman from the photos. My ex-best friend. Eden.

But we're not close with each other. In fact, it's quite the opposite.

It seems like we hate each other.

We're arguing.

But it ends when I storm off, though only after telling Eden that I never want to see her again.

'Are you okay?'

Pippa's question snaps me out of it, but my answer to her is a very concise one.

'We need to find Eden,' I say, turning back to the group at the bar. 'And those women are going to tell me where she is.'

THIRTY-FOUR

I get off the bus and make the short walk across the road to where all the ambulances are parked. I pass them, as well as a few paramedics rushing around, and then see several people sitting on benches or in wheelchairs, most of them wearing dressing gowns, and a few are talking on the phone. They are patients getting some fresh air, and I pass them all before walking through the sliding doors and entering the hospital.

Like many people who walk into a place like this, the first thing I'm greeted with inside is a huge board on the wall that shows all the various departments and which section of the hospital they are in. I see signs for the intensive care unit, radiology, paediatrics and a whole other host of departments that all sound very serious and scary, and whoever is here to visit one of these places is most likely nervous, either for themselves and their own health or for the health of a loved one they might be coming to visit. But I'm not here because I've got an appointment for a scan or to receive test results, nor am I here to support a patient who might need to see a friendly face during a difficult time.

I am here to find the nurse who apparently works here somewhere.

I am here to find my ex-best friend, Eden.

This is where I was told Eden was working now, and I was also told something else.

I used to work here too.

This is the hospital where I first worked once I had completed my training, and where I worked until I decided to take a job with a private nursing company. After having the flashback at the reunion last night, I had gone back to the bar to speak to Cara and told her I wanted to find Eden, and she told me that she would be here. She also told me that she works on Ward B, where I used to work, which helps because this is a huge place and I need to narrow my search down.

My eyes scan the sign for directions until I get an idea of which way I need to go, and then I set off down one of the myriad long, wide corridors, several bright fluorescent lights above my head guiding the way.

As I go, I see surgeons hurrying to the operating room, doctors consulting charts while on the move, and nurses grabbing coffee at a cafeteria during a well-earned break. I also see more patients being pushed in wheelchairs by hospital porters, some of them smiling, others looking like they have had enough of being here and putting up with the condition that has caused their stay in this place.

The strong smell of cleaning products stings my nostrils as I turn onto another corridor, every square inch of this place having been wiped down or mopped at some point recently to keep any germs and possible contaminations at bay. A place like this can cause sensory overload at any time, but for me, a woman who struggles with headaches, sleep deprivation and anxiety on a daily basis, it's very quickly proving to be too much. I pause before heading deeper into the bowels of the building. This might not be such a good idea. But the only thing that stops me from turning back is knowing that I won't get any answers if I leave now.

The only way to obtain any kind of truth about my past is to press on, so that's what I do, journeying deeper and deeper into this busy hospital.

I only stop when I see another large sign listing various departments, but I carry on once I see that I'm still going the right way. As I turn another corner, I see a female patient lying on a trolley in the corridor, two male porters standing beside her waiting for the elevator to arrive to take them to a different floor. As I pass, the woman on the trolley turns and looks at me, and I see a hollowness in her eyes, as if life is leaving her. She is scared but lacks the energy to really do too much about it.

The sight is unsettling, and I try to look away, but the woman maintains eye contact with me, and I find it hard to break. So much so that, as I'm busy looking at her, I end up walking right into somebody else.

'Oh, I'm sorry,' I hear a man say as the shock of the jolt snaps me out of my trance and I see a doctor looking at me to make sure I'm okay. But I'm not okay. My heart is starting to race again, and my breathing is getting shallower. Something about the way that woman on the trolley was looking at me spooked me, like she was seeing right through me.

I carry on, ignoring the doctor who calls after me, and after going through a set of double doors I find myself where I need to be.

Ward B.

Apparently I used to work here, but nothing feels familiar. Not the sight of the woman behind the desk ahead, or the doors to the various rooms to my right, or the thank-you cards on a noticeboard from families of patients who have spent time here and recovered. But I look familiar to somebody.

'Darcy?'

I turn around and see a female nurse coming out of a side room with a jug of water in her hands. She looks stunned to see me.

'Are you okay? What brings you here?' she asks me, putting the jug down and rushing over to me.

'I'm looking for Eden,' I say. 'Is she here?'

On the wall beside the noticeboard full of thank-you cards are photos of nurses, presumably who work here now. Is Eden's photo on there? I'm just about to check when this other nurse answers my question.

'Eden? No, she's not,' she says. 'Are you okay? Are you sure you should be here? I heard about your accident. Are you feeling all right?'

I ignore the nurse's concern and go to the wall of photos and search for Eden. I've just been told she's not here, but I got told this was where I could find her, so let's see who's telling the truth.

'Darcy?'

I ignore the nurse and keep looking – and then I see her, Eden, smiling as she sits beside the bed of a patient, the pair of them showing two fingers each on their right hands, peace signs supposed to make them look cool or funny or perhaps in protest or defiance at whatever medical condition they are both battling to treat.

So she does work here.

'I know she's here,' I say, turning to the nurse. 'And I have to see her. So tell me where she is or I'll just keep looking.'

The nurse looks unsure, so I go to move on, but then she stops me.

'She was here, but she's not anymore.'

'What? Where is she?'

'She just finished her shift.'

'How long ago?'

'Five minutes.'

'Where's the staff parking lot?' I ask, hoping I might catch her there. But the nurse seems hesitant to help me, and then she reveals why.

'I'm not sure it's such a good idea you trying to find her,' she says.

'Why not?'

'Didn't you two have a falling out before... well, before your accident?'

'I don't care about any of that,' I say adamantly. 'I just need to speak to her because she might be the only person who can help me get my memory back.'

The nurse looks sympathetic to my plight, but also remains wary, and I don't have time for this.

'Just tell me where she might be now! Please!' I beg.

'She'll be walking to her car. It'll be on Level D. But you won't be able to get there. It's for staff only, so you'd need a pass and—'

I cut the nurse off by quickly ripping the ID pass from around her neck and running back the way I came, through the double doors and out into the long corridor again. It was a totally irrational thing to do, but I acted out of a strong sense that Eden holds the key to me unlocking more memories, so I went ahead and did it, and now it's too late to turn back and apologise to the poor woman I just stole from.

'Hey! Give that back!' I hear the concerned nurse call after me, but I double down on my new plan and ignore her, I keep running until I reach the sign, trying to find Level D. When I see it, I sprint, the staff pass still in my hands and any thoughts about the way I behaved being pushed away out of desperation to find Eden before she leaves here. But in my haste, I must take a wrong turn, and by the time I find another sign, I cannot see Level D listed on here.

No.

Which way do I go now?

I look all around and see four corridors branching off in different directions, like I'm at the heart of a maze that I have no way of finding myself out of. Suddenly, the lights seem to be getting brighter, the corridors more crowded, the noises louder, not to mention that damn smell of cleaning products overwhelming me and making me feel sick.

Oh no.

It's happening.

I think I'm having a panic attack.

As if I can burn off this horrible feeling with exercise, I force myself to start running, but it's no good. I give up and lean against a wall, desperately trying to catch my breath, figuring that I have no choice but to give up. But then a janitor sees me and offers support.

'Are you okay?' he asks, possibly presuming I am a patient who needs assistance. But while I can't speak, he sees the staff pass in my hands and relaxes, and the sight of him calming seems to help me too. It helps me enough to catch my breath and then ask one question.

'I've got lost. Where is Level D?'

The janitor smiles and points the way.

'It's just down that corridor. Take the third door on the left.'

Feeling instantly better, now that I'm no longer running randomly through this hospital but have a definite way to go, I thank him before sprinting the way he told me to go.

I pass one door, then two, then see the third one, which has an electronic key pass beside it. Luckily I have the pass I need, so I swipe the stolen staff card in my possession and the door unlocks.

After flinging the door open, I find myself in an indoor parking lot with dozens of vehicles lined up neatly.

Is Eden still here somewhere, sitting in her car, preparing to leave?

Or has she already driven away?

I start checking all the cars, glancing through windshields and driver windows, but there are so many cars here and I might already be too late.

That's when I hear the sound of a car engine starting.

I look up and figure it came from the other side of this huge parking area, so I take off in the direction of it and, as I do, I see a blue vehicle leaving its space.

Realising I'm not going to make it in time, I quickly try and work out which way it's going so I can potentially cut the corner and get to the car as it's driving by me. As I see it turn left, I dart in the same direction, hoping to catch up before it reaches the exit, which I can see in the distance, but it's going to be close.

Then I see something that might help me.

There is a barrier at the exit, which means any vehicles leaving must have to stop there and presumably use their ID pass to get it to open. That gives me the chance I need to catch up. As I see the brake lights come on at the back of the car and it slows at the barrier, I know I'll make it.

I see a hand come out of the car and tap a keycard against a machine, and the barrier beeps and slowly starts to lift up. But it's not fast enough, and I reach the car on the passenger side and look through the window, trying to see who is driving. But the first person I see is sitting in the passenger seat, and when she sees me peering in, she almost jumps out of her skin.

It's Eden, in her uniform, and she looks like she's just seen a ghost.

Then she quickly reaches out to alert the person sitting next to her of my presence, and that's when I see who is behind the wheel.

It's the man I've seen following me. The same man I was kissing in my flashback.

As he turns to see me and we make eye contact, the barrier reaches its full height, open now and allowing exit.

But this car isn't moving.

It's as if time stands still for a moment.

Then the driver hits the gas pedal and speeds away.

THIRTY-FIVE

I saw them both. Together. Eden, my ex-best friend, and that guy I kissed. They were in the same car. They were close, not just in proximity but in the way Eden grabbed his arm when she saw me standing next to the car. It was as if she was warning him of my presence.

And how did he react to me being there?

He sped away.

Only a person with something to hide would speed away. Innocent people stay because they have nothing to run from.

But guilty people flee.

I tried to chase them, but I was no match for the speed of the car and it quickly disappeared, leaving me alone with all my questions unanswered, with several more having emerged since the shocking discovery that these two people know each other. But one good thing had come from my trip to the hospital, and that was gaining a new lead to work on in my search to discover the identity of this mystery man. It's a lead that I am desperately hoping will help me regain more memories and, therefore, more of a semblance of who I really am.

Having seen that he was driving, and presuming that it was

his car, I figured he must be an employee at the hospital too. He wouldn't have been able to get his car in that parking lot if he wasn't. He couldn't have just been using Eden's ID because, if he didn't work there, what was he doing all day while she was on shift? Just sitting in the car for several hours and waiting for her to return? No, surely not. That's senseless, not to mention unsecure, and surely a non-employee cannot get into that part of the hospital. I only got there because I stole an ID card, a card I left on a bench outside the hospital before I got the bus back home, so that it could be found and returned to its rightful owner.

No, if he was in that parking lot, he must work at the hospital too, and that means I have narrowed down a way to find out his name.

I'm home now, sitting in my bedroom on my laptop, a plate of pasta and a glass of water beside me, but the food Pippa made for me half an hour ago is currently untouched. I'm not hungry, or at least not for food. My only appetite is for finding this man's name, and that's what I'm trying to do as I search the hospital website for any photos of the mystery man. Annoyingly, there is no staff page showing all the employees at the hospital. I was hoping there might be a large database of photos showing the various surgeons, doctors and nurses, with their names and job title, but no such luck. I suppose there are simply too many employees there to list them all on a website, but that doesn't mean I won't be able to find him. It's going to take some time. I'm now scouring the internet for any photos connected to that hospital, of which there are many.

I see images in news articles about various charity fundraisers held at the hospital, with several staff members posing alongside patients as they celebrate receiving much needed funding from the local community. There are also articles about the hospital being expanded, new wards being built, or new equipment being installed that will help save more lives, and there are several staff members seen in these photos too.

But none of them are him.

I go through the old photos I have access to in the box under my bed again, but I can't see him in any of these either, as if he's deliberately eluding me by choosing not to be there. I only pause my search when I hear voices out in the hallway. I can hear Scarlett and Adrian talking quietly, and I'm not able to make out the words, but I presume they're talking about me. They've been hanging around here most days since the role-playing stopped and reality returned, presumably to make sure I'm okay. Thankfully, they go back to their other house at night. But Pippa stays overnight here once she's back from work – back from doing the type of job that I'm no longer deemed fit and able to do professionally. I told her not to stay here because she has a family who need her at home, but she has insisted, sleeping in one of the other bedrooms here, probably listening out after dark to make sure that I'm not going to run away. I definitely don't mind her being here as much as Adrian and Scarlett – I'd say I've warmed to her much faster than them, possibly because we're much closer in age or maybe because, sometimes, when I watch her, I do see bits of myself in her, which makes me think getting my memory back would be worth it one day so I could feel love again. But on the whole, I've mostly managed to avoid them all by staying in here and, as far as they know, I have eaten the pasta and have now gone to sleep. But not for the first time, they are wrong about me.

'Come on, give me something,' I say under my breath as I go back to scrolling through all the images my laptop's search engine has offered up, after entering yet another search term associated with the hospital.

I'm currently on page sixteen of the latest internet search results, which shows how far down this rabbit hole I'm going, but I'm not getting anywhere fast. There has to be a better way, or maybe there isn't. Maybe I'm just going to have to go back to that hospital tomorrow and try and spot him again, which carries risk, especially because the security guards there are surely on the lookout for me after the whole stolen ID card incident.

I push the laptop away in frustration and crawl onto my bed, taking one last look at the untouched pasta before closing my eyes and trying to get some rest. That's when I see her again. Not Eden, the nurse in the car so desperate to get away from me, but the patient, the one who was begging me for her life.

I'm sitting beside her bed again and she is looking at me helplessly. But I sense somebody else is with us too. There's somebody right behind me, but I'm not turning around. It's as if I can't, or maybe I'm too afraid to. But they are there. I can feel their presence.

There's something else here too. It's lying on the table beside the bed.

A syringe.

And then I see a man step alongside me.

It's him.

'Argh!' comes the noise from my mouth as I wake up from my bad dream. Once I realise where I am and that I'm safe, I scramble out of bed, almost knocking over the pasta as I rush to pick up my laptop again. I'm conducting another online search, but this one isn't to try and find that man. It's to try and figure out who that patient was – I have a feeling, if my ominous dream was anything to go by, that he's connected to her too.

Knowing the date of my accident, I start working backwards from there, searching for any notices online referring to the death of a female that matches the one I just saw in my dream. Without a name to go off, there's little I can type into my search engine other than *'Death Notices/Obituaries – Chicago – June 2022 – female, 30s.'*

I instantly get several links that could be of interest, so I start looking, clicking on the website of a funeral home that lists all the deceased people within that date range. Each name has a link that takes me to the tributes that were posted for that person by their loved ones, and there is an accompanying image with almost all of them. It's sad to see so many young faces of people who have passed away, all these women in their thirties, some of them succumbing to illness, some in car accidents and even a couple dying overseas while working abroad. But I don't see the woman from my dream, the one with the blonde hair and the green eyes, though I'm not going to give up. If that woman has died, I will find something about it online, surely.

And then I hit the jackpot.

It's the fifth link down on a funeral parlour website on the South Side.

It's her.

The photo matches the woman I've seen begging me for her life – and then I get a name to put to the face.

Melissa Murphy, 36, of Bridgeview, Chicago, passed away on June 5 2022, after a long and brave battle with illness. She was born on September 10 1985, at Chicago Royal, to parents Edward and Katherine Butler, and attended Bridgeview High School. After studying sales at MSU, she returned to Chicago and gained her realtor's license before embarking on a career selling real estate, progressing to...

I skip over the parts about her job – I want to find out if there's mention of any husband or boyfriend. Then I get it.

She met her husband, Laurence, in 2018, during a vacation in Cancun, and the pair married in early 2020. They enjoyed vacationing together, their favourite places being...

I break off from reading the notice because I have a new search to conduct now.

Laurence Murphy – Chicago Memorial Hospital

Instantly, I see the man I've been looking for. He's right here staring back at me from this screen, smiling widely as he poses for a photo, wearing a white coat. He's a neurosurgeon, which explains why he was at the hospital driving away with Eden. He's also a widower, which is of more interest to me, because he's clearly moved on from his late wife and he's done so with a woman I used to be close with.

My head is spinning as I try to connect the dots.

I was best friends with Eden. I kissed Laurence. I was at Melissa's bedside before she died.

But how did it get to this point where they won't talk to me?

Now I have his name – as well as the knowledge that both of them work at the hospital – I could find them there again, I suppose. But what would be better would be to find them somewhere else.

Somewhere like their home.

That way, there would be no other people around to get in the way of talking to them.

I search through anything I can find online for Laurence Murphy, wondering if I might stumble across an address, but barring a few articles about him receiving awards or contributing to research, there is nothing. So I go back and try the same for Melissa Murphy. I know from her obituary that she was a real estate agent – maybe I can find a thread to pull on there. But again, it seems like a dead end because all I get are a few photos of her standing outside various houses that she has helped sell, or in real estate offices surrounded by other sales people. Until I see something different.

Melissa Murphy Real Estate 101 – Tips for Aspiring Realtors

What's this?

I click the link and suddenly I'm watching a video in which Melissa is talking to camera, saying that she can help anybody who wants to get into real estate. All they have to do is sign up for her course on her website. I quickly follow the link to that website, where it is clear she was running some kind of side hustle alongside her day job, providing paid courses for aspiring real estate agents to subscribe to so they could gain tips and advice from somebody already in that industry.

So she had her own business.

The question is, where was it registered?

It could be her accountant's place, but don't some people use their home address for personal businesses? It's worth a shot, so I find where her business is registered with the US government and right there underneath '*Melissa Murphy Real Estate 101*' is an address.

Best of all, it doesn't sound like an accountant's office. It sounds like a residential address, and when I find it on Google Maps I see that's exactly what it is.

I now know where Melissa was living when she died.

The question is, does the man she was married to before her death still live there?

There's only one way to find out.

THIRTY-SIX

The street is dark and quiet as I try to match the image from my phone to the houses I am walking past. I've taken a taxi to the street where Melissa was living when she died in the hopes that Laurence might still be living here now, although I made sure it dropped me off a little further away so I have the chance to build up my confidence while walking to the right house – or the chance to chicken out if it gets too much for me at the last second. But I'm trying not to do that because it has taken a lot for me to find this lead, one that could give me more of an insight into my past, what with all the searching around online I've had to do, not to mention the incident at the hospital. It also took a lot for me just to sneak out of the house tonight without Pippa noticing I was going anywhere. I told her I was having an early night in the hope that she would go and do the same thing. It worked. I heard her coming upstairs not long after eight o'clock and closing her bedroom door. I waited until nine to make sure she wasn't still up and moving around before I crept out of my own room and down the stairs, glad to see the light was off under Pippa's door. With her asleep, I was able to sneak out of the house and get a taxi here.

I check the saved image from the street view on my phone and then look up – I think I have reached my destination. Double-checking, I am now certain I'm in the right place because this looks like the house. The black front door, the white blinds in the windows and the tall green tree in the front yard. This is it, Melissa's old home, but if I needed further confirmation that I was in the right place, I get it when I see the car parked in the driveway.

It's the same car I saw Laurence and Eden in, driving out of the hospital parking lot.

A surge of nervous energy pulsates through my body when I realise that Laurence must still live here and, if he's here, there's a good chance Eden is too. I've finally got them, the two people who were so desperate to evade me; the two people who seem to hold the key to me remembering what was going on in my life before my accident.

Now that I'm here and I know they are too, there's no way I'm going to chicken out.

I walk right up to the front door, take a deep breath and then I knock.

I have absolutely no idea what kind of reception I'm going to get when this door opens. Maybe it won't open at all, or perhaps it will be slammed back in my face once the occupants see who it is on the doorstep. But I won't give up easily, whatever happens, and finding this address is proof to those inside this house that's definitely the case.

I wait for twenty seconds and I impatiently knock again, but then I hear movement inside. It sounds like footsteps approaching, followed by a key turning. Then the door opens, and I come face to face with the woman who used to be my best friend, not that anyone else would know it with the way she looks at me when she sees me.

Eden's face visibly falls as I stare back at her, and I decide to wait for her to speak first, out of genuine curiosity as to what she might say.

'Darcy?' is the first word out of her mouth, though it's barely audible and is more of a hushed whisper, like all the air has just left her body.

At least she hasn't pretended not to know me or slammed the door. I guess that's a good start, so I finally open my mouth.

'Hi, Eden. I think we need to talk.'

Eden is still staring at me like I'm some creature straight out of a horror movie, but I suppose I have given her a shock.

'Can I come inside?' I ask.

She finally snaps out of it and looks past me, to see if anyone else is here, before asking me why.

'I've heard that we used to be close,' I say. 'I've been trying to find you. Now I have.'

'How?'

'I'm sorry?'

'How did you find me?'

'It's a long story, but we can talk about it all if you let me inside. I really hope we can go through everything. I think it will help a lot with my memory loss. Will you help me?'

Eden's expression suggests the only answer she wants to give is 'no', but either she's too shocked or too polite to tell me to get lost, so she steps aside.

'Thank you,' I say as I step in. As I look around the hallway, I see a photo on the wall. It features Laurence, smiling broadly, and he has company in the image, a woman beside him with her arm around him. But it's not the woman he used to be married to and who he shared this house with before her death. It's Eden, the woman who looks very nervous as she closes the door and turns to face me. I figured they were an item when I saw them sharing the same car at the hospital, but Eden answering the door to me here, as well as this photo, makes it ironclad.

They are a couple.

But when did they get together?

And at what point of this story does my kiss with Laurence come into it?

'Is he here?' I ask, gesturing at the photo of the smiling man, but Eden shakes her head.

'No, he's working.'

'Night shift?'

'Yeah.'

I nod, disappointed that Laurence is not home, but at least one of them is. I came here for answers, and it looks like Eden is going to have to be the one to provide them.

'Why are you really here?' she asks me as we continue to linger in the hallway rather than taking a seat somewhere more comfortable.

'I just told you. I'm trying to remember things from before the accident and this place, and you, had a lot to do with my life then. So I'm hoping you can fill in the blanks for me.'

'I'm not sure if I can,' Eden says.

But is that a fact or an opinion?

'You could start by telling me why we argued,' I suggest and, again, her face visibly drops.

'Argued?'

'Yeah, I had a flashback to us shouting at each other. I'm guessing whatever we were fighting about is why we stopped being best friends. I'm guessing it's why you didn't come visit me after my accident.'

'Look, Darcy. It was all a very long time ago and I've moved on since then.'

'I haven't,' I say plainly. 'I'm stuck and I'm scared I always will be. If you can tell me what was going on before my accident it might help.'

Eden still looks unsure and, as we're still lingering by the door, I fear she might change her mind and ask me to leave. That's why I suggest we go and take a seat.

'Wait, hang on,' Eden starts, playing for time, but I ignore her and walk further into the house. She quickly cuts in front of me, preventing me from opening a door.

'What's wrong?' I ask her, wondering why she doesn't want me to go any further.

'I just don't think this is a good idea,' she says, clearly stalling and looking very uncomfortable. 'I think you should leave, and I don't think you should come back here again.'

'Why would you say that?' I ask, but Eden has no good answer for that, which is why I push past her and open the door. I enter a large lounge with two sofas and a flatscreen television, and there's a big coffee table in the middle of the room, but for some reason I get déjà vu, and feel like this room didn't always look like this.

That coffee table looks odd. Out of place, almost. Like something else belongs there.

A bed.

I realise why I feel strange in here. It's because I have seen this room. I saw it in a flashback as well as in a dream. This is where Melissa was in bed, begging me for help while I held the syringe.

'I've been in here,' I say, turning back to see Eden standing in the doorway, looking very anxious. 'I worked here. As a nurse. I was caring for Melissa. She was in this room. Her bed was down here. She must have been too ill to go upstairs. She was right here where this coffee table is.'

'You're confused,' Eden says, but I know I'm not. I've spent an awfully long time confused, but I'm very clear on this now. This is a definite memory I have from before the accident, just like the memory of arguing with Eden. *And the memory of kissing Laurence.*

'Was I sleeping with him?' I ask Eden. 'Laurence, I mean. Melissa's husband. Was I sleeping with him while I was caring for her?'

'Darcy, please. You're going over very old things and you're confused. You were in a terrible accident. Your memory has gone. You're not sure what you're remembering.'

'I know I loved him!' I cry, raising my voice and startling Eden. 'I know I did. I can feel it. These flashbacks I've been having are enough to tell me that. But they tell me something else too. They tell me that something terrible was happening and it involves Melissa. I have to know what happened to her. I have to know how she died.'

'She had cancer. It was incurable.'

'But did the cancer kill her?'

'What?'

'Was it her illness or was it something I did?'

'Like what?'

'I don't know,' I say, picturing me sitting beside the patient with the needle poised, but afraid to say it out loud in case Eden isn't aware of such a thing happening and I could talk myself into trouble. But Eden is giving me the impression that she knows a lot more than she's letting on, so to try and spook her into telling me, I call her bluff.

'I'm going to go to the police and tell them about these flashbacks,' I say, gauging her reaction to that.

'The police? Why would you go to them?'

'Because maybe something I can say to them will spark a reaction. What if I did something bad? Or what if somebody else has done something bad? What if people are hiding things from me. People like you.'

'Darcy, you have to leave now,' Eden says urgently. 'Trust me, just go.'

'Or what? What are you afraid of?'

Eden glances to her left, and I realise she's looking at a photo of Laurence on a shelf.

'You're worried about him? Why? What's wrong?'

'Darcy, please. Just leave and never come back here,' Eden

tries one more time, but before I can ask her why she's so afraid of me still being here when Laurence gets back from work, I hear a floorboard creak in the hallway.

And somebody enters the room, somebody I was told was not home tonight.

'Hello, Darcy,' Laurence says with a disconcerting smile. 'It's been a while since we were both in this house together, hasn't it?'

THIRTY-SEVEN

'You said he was at work,' I remind Eden as Laurence loiters behind her in the doorway, blocking the only way in or out of this room. 'Why did you lie?'

'Because she was trying to get you to go away,' Laurence answers for her. 'She was trying to do you a favour. I guess she still has a little compassion for her old friend.'

I notice Laurence seems irritated at Eden for the warning she gave me, but it doesn't matter because I didn't heed it and now it's too late.

'Why don't you take a seat?' Laurence suggests as I stare at him behind Eden. Despite being so eager to come in here and get answers, I'm now regretting it because I can't see a way out.

'I'm fine to stand,' I tell him, figuring it's better to stay on my feet – where I might be able to move quicker if I need to – rather than sitting down and having him standing over me.

'Suit yourself. I have to admit, you've done well to find this place. I guess your memory isn't as bad as I heard it was. It has certainly improved since we last spoke on the street after you caught me following you.'

'Why were you following me?'

'Is that what you came here to ask?' Laurence asks, stepping into the room a little. As he does, Eden takes a step to the side to give him some space.

'Yes, amongst many other things,' I reply.

'Okay, well, if that's your first question for me then I suppose I better be a good host and answer it,' Laurence says. He calmly takes a seat on one of the sofas. 'Are you sure you don't want to sit?'

I can't believe how relaxed he's being. He's certainly calmer than Eden, who in contrast to him has a pained expression on her face that suggests she knows exactly why I should not be here. But I don't know why I might be in the wrong place and, seeing as it looks like it will be difficult to get out of here without Laurence stopping me, I have no choice but to find out what I've walked into. I'm also desperate to know. I've had enough of having questions and it's time for answers, which seems to be what Laurence is prepared to give me.

'I was following you because I have been keeping tabs on you,' Laurence says, casually brushing a speck of fluff off his jeans. 'I've been keeping tabs ever since your accident, and I was doing that to ascertain if your memory was returning. I didn't plan on you spotting me or confronting me, but even when you did, it didn't matter, because you clearly had no idea who I was.'

'But I do now,' I say sternly. 'I know exactly who you are. You're a neurosurgeon and you work at the same hospital where I once worked. I also know that you were married to Melissa before she died of cancer. And I know that I was here, in this room, caring for her before she died.'

'You seem to know a lot,' Laurence replies without skipping a beat. 'But you're wrong about one thing.'

'What's that?'

'You weren't caring for my wife. At least not at the end, anyway. By the time she died, you had changed your opinion of what it meant to be the perfect nurse, and you had certainly changed your opinion of my wife.'

I hate that I don't know exactly what he means but, even more so, I hate that it sounds like I'd be better off not finding out.

'You were both here,' Laurence goes on, filling the silence. 'You and Eden. You did work at that hospital, but you had left to work privately. But I knew you both and knew you were good nurses, so when my wife got sick and needed care at home, I contacted your employer and asked if they could send you two.'

I look at Eden, and she isn't saying anything to disagree with him. She hasn't said anything for a while now, not since Laurence entered the room and I realised she had been lying to me about him being out of the house.

'You were here almost every day for several weeks while Melissa was recuperating after her latest bout of chemo,' Laurence tells me. 'But she was so weak, and she'd been battling illness for a couple of years. By that point, I knew that it wasn't going to end well. I could have cared for her myself. Taken time off and spent every minute of the day with her, but I didn't. I couldn't. It was too much. So I hired you guys to help. And you certainly did that.'

I want to ask Laurence about the kiss I remember us having. I'm guessing, or maybe hoping, that the kiss occurred after his wife passed away. But did it?

'You remember me now, don't you?' Laurence asks before I can. 'I mean, I'm not just some weird guy you caught following you. I'm also not just someone you used to work for. I'm someone you were close to. You remember, don't you?'

I nod.

'Okay, so what do you remember?' the confidently calm man asks, and I am wondering what the basis is for his confidence. His good looks? *Or his seemingly total control of this unravelling situation?*

'We kissed,' I recall.

'Yes, we did,' he casually confirms. 'Several times, in fact.'

'We were dating?' I presume.

'You could say that.'

'After Melissa died?' I ask hopefully, but Laurence shakes his head.

'Not quite.'

Oh no. I was getting intimate with him while caring for his dying wife? What kind of a person does that make me?

Laurence must register the look of shock on my face, because he tries to say something to make me feel better.

'If it's any consolation, you felt terrible about it. You said it was wrong and we should stop. You also worried that I was only interested in you because I was heartbroken. But really the truth is that you loved me, and I was very fond of you too.'

He was fond of me? That doesn't sound like his feelings were quite as strong as mine, does it? It also sounds like my feelings for him were so strong that I put them ahead of the patient.

'Did your wife ever know about us?' I ask, terrified to hear his answer.

'That's hard to know for sure,' Laurence says, mysteriously. 'Let's just say she knew you weren't a typical nurse.'

That comment seems to amuse him, but I'm not smiling and neither is Eden.

'Did you know about me and Laurence?' I ask her, but she shakes her head.

'No. I mean, not until much later.'

'What happened later?' I ask tentatively.

'I think we've filled in the blanks a little too much for you now,' Laurence says, getting up from the sofa. He doesn't look like a guy who is going to shake my hand, wish me well and show me to the door. He looks like he is going to make sure I can never ask any more questions again.

That's why I make a snap decision.

I have to get out of here now, or something terrible is going to happen.

So I run for the door.

I see Eden flinch as I dart towards her, but I merely want to get past her so I can get out of this room. I've barely reached her when I feel a strong arm wrap itself around my waist and pull me backwards. Laurence has got me in a tight hold, pulling me into his body and not allowing me to squirm free.

'Get off me!' I shout, and I look to Eden to help, but she watches on helplessly as the man she shares this house with pushes me down onto the sofa.

But I am not going to give up. So I get back to my feet and go to run again. Before Laurence can grab me, I put both my arms out in front and push him strongly away. Then I barge past Eden, almost knocking her off her feet. Now I'm in the hallway and the front door is only a few yards away. I know it's unlocked because I didn't see Eden turn a key after I entered, so if I can just get to the handle then I can get outside. Then I will be away from this man and free to go to the police or go home or go anywhere that is safer than here. But despite managing to get the door open, I don't get to take one step outside – Laurence grabs my arm and pulls me back into the house. As he does that, a very frightening glimpse of my past flashes through my mind.

It's a memory of being right here, in this exact spot, and the same thing was happening to me then.

I was angry and upset and I was trying to leave this house, but Laurence was trying to stop me. I was screaming at him, but wasn't only begging him to let me go. I was telling him what I'd done.

I was telling him that I'd burned my uniform.

And I'm quitting nursing forever.

In my flashback, I remember managing to get away, and I see a vision of myself running to my car and getting inside, starting the engine and speeding away. I also remember crying and it's raining and it's dark and I'm struggling to see. Which is why I miss the turning in the road and veer off into a lamppost, crashing and hitting my head violently on the steering wheel.

My accident happened because I was upset about something that happened here in this house – with him.

But right now is different. Unlike then, I'm unable to make it out of the house and get away. Instead, Laurence's grip is too strong, and I'm dragged kicking and screaming back inside. The front door is slammed shut and I'm thrown to the ground.

Laurence is standing over me now.

He tells me he doesn't want to do this, but he has no choice.

Then everything goes black.

THIRTY-EIGHT

When I open my eyes, my head is throbbing. Instantly I try to put a hand to the sore spot on my skull to soothe it. But I can't, and that's when I realise my hands are tied behind my back.

Looking down, I see that I'm tied to a chair. I look around and see that I'm alone. It's dark, but I can just make out enough to see that I am in the lounge again, which tells me my desperate attempt to escape this house did not work.

Laurence dragged me back in here and hit me over the head, and now I find myself in this position. But where is he now? And where is Eden?

They can't leave me alone in here, and they can't assume they're going to get away with this.

Can they?

I'm about to try and call out to them when I hear voices. They're in another room, but if I listen carefully enough, I can just about make out what's being said.

'You need to get something from the hospital,' I hear Laurence saying. 'You have access to the drugs. I'll stay here and watch her until you get back. Then we'll finish this once and for all.'

I realise he is talking Eden through the plan for me, but it's an awful one, at least from my perspective.

He wants Eden to get drugs from the hospital and bring them back here so he can finish this? No, this can't be happening. He's a surgeon and she's a nurse. They're supposed to look after people, not kill them. But that's exactly what it sounds like they're planning to do here, or at least he is. Thankfully, Eden seems unsure about his plan.

'We'll never get away with it,' she cries.

'Yes, we will. I promise,' Laurence counters. 'Just do as I say, and this will all go away. There's no need to let that woman ruin the life we have, is there? Is that what you want? I thought you were happy here.'

'I am happy,' Eden says. But that's no good to me – I need her on my side, not his.

'We need to do this. You understand that, right?' Laurence says, but now their voices lower and I can't hear anymore.

Maybe they are hugging or kissing or doing something to show their commitment to one another, but again, that is terrible for me. Unless I can drive a wedge between these two then it looks like this is going to end very badly. Laurence clearly doesn't want me to leave this house alive, so Eden is my best bet. We used to be best friends, and she warned me to leave here before he walked into the room, so maybe she still cares about me. Then again, she lied about Laurence being here at all, and she's got herself involved with a dangerous man, so who knows where her loyalties lie?

Everything has gone quiet, so I think about calling out to my captors to try and negotiate my release. But before I try that, I have another go at freeing myself from my restraints. I'm not sure what my hands are tied together with, but it's strong. No matter how hard I try, I cannot free my wrists to bring my hands out from behind myself. I'm stuck to this chair, and powerless to prevent whatever those two want to do to me, at least physically.

My only option seems to be my words and my intellect.

I'm tied up here because Laurence is afraid that I'm remembering too much about my past. But I don't know everything yet. Maybe if I downplay what I do know, Laurence might see that I'm not quite the threat he thinks I am.

'Hey! What's going on? Come in here and untie me!' I call out, hoping the door is going to open and flood this dark room with light. But everything is quiet. Are they deliberately ignoring me? Or are they trying to figure out what is best?

I don't want to give them too much thinking time because, from what I heard a moment ago, that thinking seems to be going down a very dark path. So I call out again and again until I finally make some progress.

The door opens and I squint my eyes as light from the hallway seeps into the room. I see a silhouette in the doorway. It's him, the man who just attacked me, and the only thing stopping me from being a free woman again. Then I see another shape behind him. It's her. Eden, his loyal lapdog, but I need to stop her being obedient to him – my life depends on it.

'What are you doing? Why have you tied me up?' I cry as I keep trying to free my hands. 'This is crazy! Let me go!'

'I'm afraid we can't do that,' Laurence says seriously as he steps into the room. My eyes adjust to the light and I see his blank face staring at me. It's actually more frightening to see how relaxed he is about this. At least if he was full of emotion then I think I might stand a chance. But he seems so composed, as if this is the crazy situation it should be.

'Just tell me why you're doing this?' I beg. 'I don't understand.'

'See, she doesn't remember,' Eden chips in, speaking to Laurence. 'We can let her go.'

'Don't be fooled,' he replies. 'She's either trying to trick us or maybe she's telling the truth, but we can't take the chance. I thought her memory was gone for good, but if it's slowly returning then we're screwed. She's getting flashbacks now, so I guess her luck has run out.'

'What do you mean, my luck?' I ask him, confused.

'Don't you see, Darcy?' Laurence says, kneeling in front of my chair. 'Your memory loss wasn't a bad thing. It wasn't rotten luck or a curse. It was actually the best thing that could have happened to you, because it gave you the chance to forget what you had done in the past. Maybe now you'll realise that was a gift, instead of desperately trying to remember every single detail of your life before the accident.'

'Accident? It wasn't an accident! I crashed because I was trying to get away from you!' I exclaim, recalling the flashback I had in the doorway earlier, though it probably won't help my cause to reveal I've remembered something else.

'That may be so, but you have to think why it was that you were so desperate to get away,' Laurence replies coolly. 'What made you drive so fast and crash your car? Because it wasn't just something I did, Darcy. It was something you did too.'

I think about that for a moment before asking the question I've been afraid to ask since I got here.

'Did we hurt Melissa?' I ask quietly.

Laurence stares at me and looks like he might be about to give me an answer, but Eden speaks again.

'I'm due at the hospital in twenty minutes,' she says, and that gets his attention.

'Then you better get going,' he suggests, leaving me and returning to her in the doorway. 'And remember what I said. I need you to do this for me, okay?'

Eden nods, which is not a good sign.

'Eden, wait! You don't have to do this!' I plead. 'Whatever he wants you to do, you don't have to go along with it. You have a choice. Don't let him force you into doing anything!'

'Shut up!' Laurence snarls, his head turning back to me, a look of pure venom on his face. 'Or I'll shut you up again, and this time you won't wake up.'

That's an effective warning and I'd probably do well to heed it, but I have one more thing to try before I stop talking.

'I just want to go home,' I say honestly. 'I don't care about remembering anything anymore and, even if I do, I won't tell anyone. I swear.'

Eden seems hopeful at that declaration, but Laurence shakes his head.

'Nice try, but you're crazy if you think I can take that risk,' he tells me and turns back to Eden.

'Go to work and get us what we need. I'll stay here and watch her and, when you get home, we'll finish this once and for all.'

He pulls Eden towards him for a passionate kiss and, to my dismay, she kisses him back, not arguing with him or offering another option, but going along with exactly what he said, because she's clearly under his spell.

I fear I was under his spell once before, and it led to me doing something awful.

Now it appears that Eden is going down the same path.

What did I do for this man? Or rather, *what did he make me do?*

As I watch her put on her jacket over her uniform, Laurence follows her out of the room, closing the door behind him and plunging me into darkness again.

It's scary, but there's also a comfort to be found in the dark.

I know the next time that door opens Eden will have returned with the drugs from the hospital, and Laurence will be ready to administer them.

When he does, I'm going to end up in the same place as Melissa.

THIRTY-NINE

I gave up calling out to Laurence a while ago as my throat was too dry, and my voice was becoming too hoarse. He's clearly not going to open this door until Eden gets back – to do so would mean he'd have to be less of a coward. He obviously plans to kill me by injecting some drug into me, and that must be a lot easier for him than killing me with his bare hands or a deadly weapon like a knife.

But just because I've stopped shouting, it doesn't mean I've given up. I am desperately pulling at my restraints and rocking myself back and forth in this chair, trying to gain enough momentum to change this awful position I find myself in.

Wriggling and writhing while straining every sinew in my body, I end up toppling the chair over so I'm now lying on the carpet, with my hands still tied behind my back and the chair still stuck to me. I let out a frustrated groan because it seems I've managed to make my bad position even worse. But just before I give up entirely, I see something that causes me to stop moving.

From my new position on the carpet, I can see underneath the sofa. With my eyes adjusted to the gloominess in here, I can make out what it is.

It's the cap off a syringe.

And I realise I was the one who caused it to roll under there, where it has lain undisturbed for all this time.

Once again I remember being in this room, beside the bed where Melissa lies, this makeshift hospital room the place where the ailing woman is receiving care. The patient is asleep and I'm standing next to her, looking down on her. I'm accompanied by Laurence. He is right beside me, and he's speaking.

'It will end her suffering. You'll be doing her a favour, and us too. We can be together then. We can move on with our lives. Be a proper couple. Isn't that what you want?'

I process Laurence's words and look down, seeing the syringe in my hand. I know what I need to do. I need to take the cap off and then inject Melissa with this needle, giving Laurence what he wants.

He's so persuasive. So in control. So calm. He makes me feel safe, safer than anyone ever has before. I've never felt like this about a man, and I've certainly never had a man feel this way about me. He loves me. He wants to be with me. He wants to start a family with me. It's not his fault his wife got sick, and it's not either of our faults that we fell in love while I was helping him care for her. He is right in what he's told me several times. Melissa is going to die at some point, whether it be today, or next month, or this time next year. She will lose her fight, it's inevitable, so what sense does it make to prolong her agony, and ours too? It would be different if there was a chance that she could make a recovery, but there isn't. She's living on borrowed time, time loaned to her only after countless months spent receiving treatment that has made her existence a misery. The best-case scenario for her is that she keeps getting more treatment and continues to feel worse until her body gives out.

Laurence has said the kindest thing we can do is to help her along and speed up the process.

I take the cap off the syringe then, but it falls before I can catch it. I watch it roll underneath the sofa. I guess it happened because my hands are shaking so much, but Laurence hasn't noticed – he's too busy staring at his sleeping wife.

'Do it,' he says, giving me a gentle nudge forward, so he's now standing right behind me, and I can feel his breath on the back of my neck.

I stare at the end of the needle, the sharp point that I am supposed to use to pierce through Melissa's skin, before I push down the plunger on the syringe and administer this drug into her bloodstream. It might seem reckless and like we'll never get away with it, but the medical knowledge that Laurence and I have tells us that all the chemo and radiation pills Melissa has been having will mask this drug so that it won't show on an autopsy. But there should be no need for an autopsy anyway, because Melissa is a terminal cancer patient receiving palliative care at home, so everybody who knows her, including all her doctors, expect her to die, and they already know what it is that killed her.

Or at least they think they do.

Melissa has been stubbornly clinging on to life, and who knows how long she might live for if I don't do this. Laurence doesn't want to wait to find out. His wife's illness has drained him almost as much as it has drained her, and he's reached the end of his capacity. He's also become involved with me, and he's told me how he could never have got through this difficult time without me. We kissed a few weeks ago, and we slept together at my place last week, before he told me that he loved me. I said the same thing back to him. We've not been physical here, not in this house with Melissa around, because I've refused to do that. Laurence has almost given in to his desires a few times. But I have also said no, not here, not where his dying wife is. She still needs my help and I respect her, despite what I've become involved in. I never thought I'd do something like this, or planned to. It just happened. *Love just happened.* Even though I feel guilty, I have done my best to care for Melissa and ease her pain, but Laurence has reminded me of one very important fact.

I can't fully be with him until she's gone.

And what I want more than anything in the world is to be with him.

'Do it,' Laurence says, repeating his instruction, and I bring the syringe up to Melissa's arm. But something happens when I do.

She opens her eyes.

I instantly see fear on her face as she spots the needle so close to her skin and me looking down on her. I turn to Laurence then, unsure what to do, but he just nods.

'Do it,' he urges me again, the clarity of his command never altering.

I reach out and lift up the sleeve of Melissa's T-shirt, exposing more bare skin for the needle to potentially enter. But as I do that, Melissa shifts in her bed and tries to move away. She is weak, or at least I thought she was, until she shoots out a hand to grip my arm.

She's surprisingly strong. It could be because she realises she is fighting for her life here, but she's hurting me, so I try to release her grip with my free hand. It's not easy though, she has hold of me like a vice, and I think she's drawing blood under my uniform. That's until I eventually manage to remove her hand and see that the blood belongs to her, her pale skin so thin, bruising and cutting so easily in her weakened post-chemo state, that she has left blood on my uniform.

She looks terrified, but there's nowhere for her to go, and now the needle is only inches away from her skin and this will all be over in just a moment.

'I can't do it,' I suddenly say, pulling away from the patient at the last second, horrified I even allowed things to get this far – because it is wrong, and I've been brainwashed into doing this. I turn back to the man who has done that brainwashing to see that he looks disappointed at the decision I've just come to. But he can't be surprised – he must know it goes against everything in my nature. I'm a nurse, it's my duty to preserve life, not end it, and I can't believe I've allowed myself to be so blinded by love that I almost made a terrible mistake. But unfortunately, to my horror, he doesn't allow the delay to stop him from ultimately getting what he wants.

He snatches the syringe from my hand and injects Melissa with it himself.

It happens so fast there's nothing I can do.

Then the pair of us watch the patient shed a tear before her eyes close again and she goes still.

Forever.

Now I'm panicking, torn between trying to help Melissa, even though I know it's already too late, or wanting to get away from Laurence, a man whose love for me has not stopped him from doing such a hateful act that has sickened me.

I don't know what to do.

I'm frozen in fear.

As the flashback ends and I look away from the syringe cap underneath the sofa, I am the one crying now. It's because I realise that Laurence was right. My accident and losing my memory was not a curse, but a gift. It was a gift because it allowed me to forget the part I played in Melissa's death. I didn't inject her myself, but I was present when it happened and, therefore, I was complicit in her demise.

I was a witness and a co-conspirator.

I participated in a murder.

But while that's what it could be labelled, I know the real truth. I'm a nurse, an everyday woman, not some evil, callous witch. I didn't want Melissa to die, and I didn't take her life. It was him, the man I loved and trusted, the man I made a critical mistake ever getting close to. If only I'd known the terrible course of events that would unfold, I never would have allowed myself to get close to him, and maybe Melissa would still be alive now. Perhaps she might not be, due to the severity of her illness, but that was for her body to decide, not another person. But I feel so guilty that her life was taken while she had some fight left in her, and I'll never forgive myself for being present when it was, even if Laurence did the dreadful deed, even though I had no chance to stop him.

I wish I could forget. I wish I could go back to before, when I naively thought I had been a good person. A loving daughter, sister, friend, nurse. Not this. Not what I know myself to be now.

An associate of a killer.

The agony of knowing the truth is as bad as the fear of what's going to happen to me when Eden gets back from work and gives Laurence what he asked for. I guess history is going to repeat itself.

I'm now going to be the one put to sleep by lethal injection.

I guess it could be called karma.

But I'm not the only one who deserves to pay for what I did.

Laurence has to pay too.

'We killed her!' I scream at the top of my voice, figuring there is no way he won't hear me, but I want him to come in here and face me now that I know the full truth.

Or so I thought.

When Laurence does enter the room, there is one more surprise in store for me, though I didn't know it as I turned to look up at him from my awkward position on the floor.

'I remember it all now, you sick son of a bitch,' I say with my voice dripping in disdain. 'You wanted me to kill her for you and, when I didn't do it, you killed her yourself!'

Laurence doesn't seem too bothered about what I've just said and, if anything, I've only reinforced his motivation to kill me before his secret gets out. But would it get out? If it did, I'd be in as much trouble as him.

'That's why I crashed that night, isn't it?' I say. 'Because I left here upset over what we'd done. I saw you kill that poor woman, and you told me it was so we could be together, but it was an awful thing to do, and I knew it, so I left you. You tried to stop me, but I got away.'

I try to convince myself that I was perhaps on the way to the police station to tell them what had happened with Melissa, and if I was, maybe I'm not such a bad person after all. But Laurence just laughs and shakes his head.

'You idiot,' he says with a chuckle. 'That's not the only reason you were angry at me.'

'What?'

'You were upset about what happened with Melissa, sure, but you were upset about something else. You were upset that I was seeing Eden behind your back, because you thought what we had was love. As if love could justify what we did together. I bet you wouldn't have left me if it hadn't been for me cheating on you. You still loved me, even after I killed my wife.'

I did? No, Laurence is lying to me, I can tell. His answers are lacking the confidence they had earlier. He's trying to manipulate me. There's no way I would have been able to love him after what he did. We were finished from that point on. We may have seen each other again, but never to be intimate.

That love died when Melissa did.

'You're despicable,' I hiss at him. 'You fooled Melissa and now you're trying to fool me. But I won't fall for it! I know who you are. I might not remember everything about myself, but I can see you for what you are! You're a coward!'

'Call me whatever you want to if it makes you feel better,' Laurence says with a smirk. 'Believe me, I've been called worse in my time. But it doesn't change the fact that you weren't just angry at me for killing Melissa. You were angry because you found out that I had been lying to you. You found out that I didn't love you at all. I'd been seeing somebody else behind your back. I'd been seeing Eden. That's why you ran out of here and that's why you got into that accident. You told me I had broken your heart.'

I don't know what to say. While I know now Laurence was with Eden, I hadn't realised it was *before* my accident. But I think of arguing with her, and I guess that's what it was about. So I crashed because I hated him, and her, though the damage was already done. After what happened to Melissa, it sounds like Laurence knew that too, and opted to go all in with Eden and cast me aside almost as easily as he had his wife.

Laurence sniggers, as if he's won somehow, and leaves, slamming the door behind him. All I can do is bury my face in the carpet and cry, because I'm going to die here, and nobody is ever going to know the real truth.

He is the villain, Melissa was his victim and now it looks like I'm going to join her.

Most harrowingly of all, it's probably for the best that nobody else will ever know.

FORTY

The sun has come up now, which means I'm no longer lying here in the dark. But the sunlight filtering in around the edges of the blinds over the window is not doing anything to lift my mood. I feel like I've lost all my energy and fight, and it's been this way ever since I realised I wasn't innocent in this whole sorry saga.

Thinking back over it all, from what my family did to try and jog my memory to all the various ways I've tried to uncover the past, I can only say that, given where I have ended up and what I have discovered, it was all a waste of time.

I can't help but feel I would have been better off dying in that car accident. I also feel like the world would be a better place if I had. But before my one-person pity party can continue any longer, I hear something that causes every muscle in my body to tense. It's the sound of a car parking outside, and I fear what it means. The sound of the key in the lock is the signal that my worst fears have come true, and as the front door opens and closes, I know it's true.

Eden is back from work.

I'm guessing she has what Laurence asked her to bring home.

That means this is going to be over soon.

For me, anyway.

Despite how I was feeling a moment ago – that death might actually be merciful for me – I quickly realise I cannot go this way. I can't die – then Laurence will get away with what he's done. Eden will get away with it too, and my family will be left with so many questions, like where did I go, what happened to me and why? Perhaps most importantly of all, if I die here this morning, Melissa will never get justice.

Laurence killed her, so he deserves to die too.

But he won't if he can kill me first.

I hear voices – Laurence and Eden discussing their next move from the other room, where Laurence has presumably sat all night keeping guard on the door behind which I am trapped, making sure I didn't break free. But I haven't been able to do so and, as they both enter the room to see me again, I look at them both meekly from the same position on the floor I've been in for the past several hours.

'Please, don't do this,' I say, which I'm aware is the exact opposite of what Laurence kept saying to me over and over again when we had his wife's life in our hands.

'Let's get you more comfortable,' Laurence says, ignoring my plea as he lifts me and the chair to an upright position, so I'm now sitting rather than lying on the floor.

As he does that, I see that Eden is doing something behind him.

She's filling a syringe.

'Eden, listen to me,' I urge her. 'You don't have to do this. I know he's persuasive and he's probably told you he loves you, but he's a liar, so don't let him talk you into this. You don't have to follow his orders. You don't have to kill me. Don't have my death on your conscience forever!'

Eden hesitates, which is a welcome sight, but what is not welcome is the sound of Laurence laughing. Why is that his reaction to what I just said?

'Oh, Darcy. You are funny,' he says, still sniggering. 'I'm not forcing Eden to do anything. She isn't going to be the one to kill you. I am.'

I watch as Laurence takes the syringe from Eden, realising that he is going to deliver the fatal injection. I guess his experience with Melissa has given him the confidence to do this himself, rather than pressuring Eden like he originally pressured me.

'No, wait! Don't do this!' I sob as I try to wriggle free, but Laurence casually approaches me, the needle glinting and the liquid inside the syringe ready to find a new home inside my body.

'You won't get away with this!' I cry as Laurence gets closer. 'Melissa was dying, so you could cover that up, but you can't do that with me! People will know I was murdered. People will know I was here!'

'Nobody knows you're here,' Laurence replies smugly. 'And no one will know you were murdered, because nobody is going to find your body.'

With that devastating fact delivered, Laurence prepares to administer the deadly dose. All I can do is turn away from the needle as it approaches my skin, closing my eyes tightly, praying that if this has to happen then it's at least painless for me.

'Stop! I've changed my mind about this!'

I open my eyes and see Eden holding Laurence's arm so he can't finish what he was about to do, but he just shakes her off. That's when she grabs a large medical award of some kind from the shelf and hits it against his head.

I watch as Laurence crumples to the floor by my feet. He rolls onto his back, dazed but still conscious. Eden looks at the weapon she just used, as do I, and we both notice the blood on the edge of it, the golden statuette now tainted with a dark crimson from Laurence's skull.

She just saved my life, though I know this isn't over yet.

'Help me!' I beg her and, finally, she listens to me and quickly unties my hands, as Laurence holds his head and groans.

'You idiot. What are you doing?' he asks Eden as he looks around on the floor for the syringe. But he can't see where he dropped it, which is great news – although I can't see it either.

'I've changed my mind. We can't do this,' Eden replies as I get up from the chair. 'I'm not a killer.'

'Neither am I. But he is,' I say, pointing at the man trying to get back to his feet.

'Run!' I desperately urge Eden, and I push her to the door and set off behind her, but as I try to get away Laurence reaches out and grabs one of my ankles, causing me to fall flat on my face. Now I'm the one dazed on the floor, but there's no time for a proper recovery. I have to get up again.

I try and scramble back to my feet, but Laurence keeps me down. I have no idea where Eden is, but I think she's going to have to come back and help me, if she hasn't already run out of the house and made her escape. But then I see the cap from the syringe under the sofa again, the one that I dropped there on that fateful night when Melissa died. But I also see something else lying beside it.

It's the syringe that Laurence just dropped.

With him refusing to let go and threatening to climb on top and overpower me completely, I reach out for it and, once I've got it, I put my thumb on top of the plunger as Laurence raises his fist above his head and prepares to strike me. But before he can, I drive the needle into his leg and inject the contents of the syringe into him, seeing the look of horror on his face as he realises what I have just done.

As the syringe is drained, the life slowly starts to drain out of my aggressor too. He falls off of me and onto the carpet beside me, where he lies on his back and stares up at the ceiling. But just as his eyes close and his heart stops beating, I make sure that I get up and stand over him, so that I'm the last thing he ever sees before he dies. Then I make sure I'll be the last thing he hears too.

'This is for Melissa,' I tell him, and he registers the fact that, eventually, he got his comeuppance for his wife's murder.

And then he's gone.

I leave the body and rush into the hallway, trying to find out where Eden is – we need to make a plan as to what happens next. But all I see is the open front door.

Has she gone?

I race outside and run into the street, looking both ways to try and find her, but I can't see her anywhere. Where did she go? And what the hell am I going to do now if I don't have her to help me here?

'Darcy!'

I turn around and expect to see Eden, but it's not her who just called my name.

It's somebody I did not expect to see here at all.

It's another nurse in uniform.

It's Pippa.

'Are you okay? What's happened?' she asks me as she reaches me. But while she's worried about me, I'm worried about how she found me here.

'How did you know I was here?' I ask her as she relaxes once she sees that I'm apparently unhurt.

'I got woken up at dawn by the smoke alarm. It was beeping because the batteries must have been flat. I got up and got dressed for work and figured it would have woken you up too, but when you didn't come out of your room, I thought I'd check on you. Then I saw you were gone.'

I hear what Pippa is saying, but I'm also looking around the street to see if I can spot Eden. But she's definitely gone. I also check to see if any of the people on this street might be at their windows looking out, but nobody is, which is good. Although some of them will surely be leaving for work soon, and I'd rather not be out here when they do.

'I didn't know where you were, but then I saw your laptop open, so I looked at it and there was a street view image of this address open on screen,' Pippa explains. 'So I came here, hoping to find you. What are you doing here? Why did you sneak out of the house to come here?'

It's a very long story and I don't even know where to begin, so I consider not telling Pippa what just happened so we can both get out of here and get as far away from that dead body as we can. That seems even more of a tempting idea because Pippa doesn't actually know about the body yet, so if we do leave, she never has to know. But can I do that? Can I just walk away and leave Laurence to be discovered in his house at some point in the future? If he is, what will happen then?

'What is it?' Pippa asks me, and I realise I've given myself away – she's caught me looking back at the open doorway of the house I ran from, and now she's going to see why I was just in there.

'Pippa, wait!' I cry, and I try to stop her going in, but she enters the house and I can't prevent her from seeing Laurence's body lying on the carpet beside the sofa. She also sees the syringe next to him, and when she looks back to me, she realises I had something to do with it.

'Oh my god, what have you done?' she asks me, horrified.

'I can explain!' I tell her and I guess I can, but it's a wild story and I don't know how Pippa will react to it all. I also don't know if her being here has just implicated her in this too. And most troublingly of all, I still have no idea where Eden is.

'Then start explaining,' Pippa urges me as she looks back down at the body before us. 'And do it quickly, because I'm five seconds away from calling the police.'

FORTY-ONE

'I need a fresh start. Somewhere away from here. I think it's for the best.'

I wait to see what Scarlett's and Adrian's reactions will be to what I've just said, and as I expected they're not happy about it.

'Away from here? You want to move?' Scarlett asks me, dismayed.

'Yes. I think it's what I need. For my mental health. You understand that, don't you?'

It's calculated of me to try and remind them that they should only want what's best for me. It makes it less likely they can argue with me, or worse, stop me from leaving entirely, because I have to go.

I really, really do.

'Where will you go?' Adrian asks, looking as abject as his wife.

'I'm not sure yet. I'm keeping my options open. But don't worry, I'll keep in touch. I'll write to you and let you know that I'm okay.'

'You'll write?' Scarlett repeats; she's shaking her head. 'Oh well, that's something I suppose. It's nice of you to write and let your parents know that you're still alive and not dead in a ditch somewhere.'

'Mom, please,' the voice from the kitchen doorway says, and I turn to see Pippa leaning against it, her arms folded and a serious look on her face.

'What? I have a right to be worried,' Scarlett insists. 'You can't go away. If you don't see us for a long time then you're going to forget about us. You know your memory issues. What if you forget us again and then we lose touch with you? We might never find you.'

'That won't happen,' I say, nodding at Pippa, and that's her cue to speak.

'I've given her photos of us as well as a written letter that she can read to remember us by. I've also given her our addresses so she can find her way back here if she forgets where she comes from.'

It seems bizarre for me to need such things, but this is the reality of living with brain damage like mine, where I can never be sure what information I'll recall and what I'll forget as time goes by. I don't want to forget my family, and I'll do my best not to. But, at the same time, I don't want any more flashbacks of a past that might haunt me, though it remains to be seen if I'll get any.

Pippa knows to support me in this discussion here, because she already knows about my plan to leave and start afresh elsewhere. In fact, we both came up with that plan together. It's just one of the many things that the pair of us have done recently, but not all of those things can be shared with our parents.

That's right. *Our parents*. I have accepted that Adrian and Scarlett are my parents now, just like I've accepted that Pippa is my sister. It was too hard punishing myself by being paranoid around them and refusing to believe them. It was also too punishing for them to have to look after a family member who was ungrateful and untrusting.

'Mom. Dad. I love you,' I say, reaching out across the table we're sat at and allowing each of them to take one of my hands, so we're all now connected to each other. 'I just feel like I need to do this. The old me, the person I was before my accident, is gone, and now I need to work on the new me. But I can't do that here. I need to go somewhere new and somewhere I can be alone for a little while as I figure things out. It will really help me. You'll see.'

I hope I'm being as convincing as I need to be, because I do need them to agree to this. I absolutely cannot afford to have them trying to stop me leaving, nor can I afford to have them offer to come with me.

That's because I'm not actually going to be wherever it is they think I am.

'You'll keep in touch?' Adrian clarifies. 'And don't just write. Call us. Text us as often as you can. Come visit. And let us come and visit you too.'

'Of course,' I say, lying, but at least this way I'm getting to have a proper goodbye with them. Really, I should already be on the road now or in the air, travelling many miles away from here, and I could have left yesterday without saying a word to either of them. But I want to do this right, at least for them, just in case I never do get to see either of them again.

And especially if they hear some startling things about me once I'm gone.

As we all stand, and I hug Mom and Dad separately and then the three of us embrace as a trio, Pippa remains by the doorway, at least until Adrian beckons to her to join us so we can have a proper family hug. She reluctantly does so, which Mom and Dad appreciate, but not half as much as I do – I know just how much strength it's taking for her to be here with us.

I also know how much strength it's taken for her to get through the last twenty-four hours, but we're almost there now, and then this will be over soon.

Well, kind of.

'Let's get going,' I say to Pippa, and she nods, but Mom and Dad look mortified.

'You're leaving now?' Mom cries. 'But you haven't even packed!'

'I've got a small bag ready to go,' I say, surprising her and Dad again. 'But I don't want to take too much. Like I said, I want this to be a fresh start for me, so I'm not taking too many things that remind me of the past.'

I hug each of them once more before I follow Pippa to the door where my small bag is waiting, and I wasn't lying when I said I'm not taking much. Just a few clothes, some toiletry items and an envelope full of cash that Pippa has kindly given to me, which will help me get set up wherever I decide to stop next.

'Let us know when you get there, wherever that is, and I can send you money,' Dad says, but I knew he'd make an offer like that, so I'm prepared for it.

'I want to be independent,' I tell him. 'So thank you, but I'll be okay.'

I pick up my bag as Pippa opens the door, but as we turn to leave Mom pulls me in for a hug one more time.

'Please come back soon,' she begs me. 'Or let us know where you are, and we'll come visit. We'll visit all the time.'

'Of course,' I say, which will hopefully be the last lie I have to say today, though it definitely won't be the last lie I ever tell, because my new life is going to be built on a bed of lies.

'Goodbye,' I say to Adrian and Scarlett, who hold each other in the doorway as I follow Pippa to her car. I get in and, as she drives us away, I wave at the couple who both wave back to me, sad looks on their faces, but I tell myself they're far happier now than they would be if they knew why I was really leaving.

Only the woman in the driver's seat beside me knows why I have to skip town, and as she drives on there is something I have to say to her, now that I've already said my piece to our parents.

'Thank you,' I say, looking at my sister while she keeps her eyes on the road.

'I'm your sister,' she replies quietly. 'Sisters look out for one another.'

But the fact she doesn't turn to look at me as she says that tells me how hard she has found the last twenty-four hours. I feel bad about that – while I've struggled too, I brought it all upon myself. But Pippa hasn't done anything to deserve what she has had to do. She certainly doesn't deserve the fact that, even if we get away with it, she's going to have to live with the knowledge of it until her dying day. Again, that's where I am a little luckier than her. If my memory continues to struggle to remember things from a long time ago, there is a chance that I might forget what we did.

But Pippa is most likely cursed to remember it forever.

That means she'll never forget where we buried Laurence's body last night.

I want to keep thanking Pippa for what she helped me do, but I have a feeling it will only make her feel even worse, so I stay quiet for the remainder of our journey to the bus station. But I'm thinking back over it all as I stare out at these Chicago streets that I'll soon be leaving behind for good.

I'm thinking about how, after I had explained to Pippa exactly who the dead guy was and why I had been forced to kill him, she didn't call the police like she had talked about doing, but instead looked at the situation practically and realised that I was in trouble. Sure, I had a story that I could tell the police if we called them, but what were the chances of them believing it, particularly when I would be referring to events that had happened before my accident? With a medical record showing that I had brain injuries and significant memory loss, what was to stop the cops from thinking I was talking nonsense, making things up or trying to hide an evil crime behind my complicated health history?

There was also the issue of Eden, the nurse who had fled the scene just before I killed Laurence, and a person who was very much a wildcard in terms of what her next move would be. Would she go to the police? Would she take my side? Or was she as scared as I was about getting in trouble? After all, she had stolen the drugs from the hospital. Those drugs had caused Laurence's death, so while she hadn't delivered the fatal injection, it couldn't have happened without her input. We didn't know where she was or what she might say or do, but we couldn't waste time waiting to find out.

We had to try and protect ourselves.

But it wasn't going to be easy.

After Pippa said she would help me, I figured that meant we were going to move the body. But it was daytime, and neither of us fancied being seen carrying a corpse to the back of her car, so we left Laurence's house – though, crucially, we made sure the front door was unlocked so we could return in darkness if we got the chance. We wanted to see if any police officers arrived, but none did. So once the sun had gone down, we returned to Laurence's house with plastic sheeting that we used to wrap his body in. We put it in Pippa's car and she drove it to a very isolated part of Lake Michigan. There, we disposed of the corpse, watching it sink beneath the surface of the vast lake, and drove back to the city, vowing to never again talk about what we'd done.

After that, I was the one who suggested leaving Chicago, and Pippa didn't object. So here I am, getting out of here, a free woman for now and, hopefully, it'll stay that way. As far as I know, Eden hasn't gone to the police, because nobody has been looking for me – and she might never do so. That means I can get away, start afresh, and maybe no one will ever come looking for me, at least no one with handcuffs anyway. The police might be looking for Eden one day if they find out she was dating Laurence, a man that will soon be listed as missing by his employers, sparking an investigation. But if she disappears like I'm doing, they might never find her either. I hope that is the case because, as much as she did wrong, she did save my life at the last moment. She certainly did a better job of doing that than I did of saving Melissa's.

But whatever happens to me and Eden in the future, I'm comforted by the thought that Pippa won't get in trouble for what she's done. That's because only I know she was at Laurence's place yesterday, and I won't tell a soul that fact, whether I remember it forever or not.

Her secret dies with me, whatever the state of my memory might be going forward.

'Thank you,' I say to my sister after she has parked around the corner from the bus station, in a place where the cameras at the station can't pick up her car and allow a police officer to one day notice it, if they're ever trawling through CCTV to find out where I went.

'Stay safe,' is all that Pippa seems to want to say to me before I leave; as I go, I give her a hug and tell her that I'll let her know where I go and that it'll be okay, wherever it is I end up.

The truth is, I don't know where I'm going yet, and as I leave Pippa's car and walk across the street to enter the station, I'm keeping my options well and truly open.

There is only one real criteria.

It has to be very far from here.

When I start my new life, I cannot have anyone knowing what my old one was like.

Maybe it won't be as difficult as it sounds.

After all, not even I can remember half of it.

A LETTER FROM DANIEL

Dear reader,

I want to say a huge thank you for choosing to read *The Perfect Nurse*. I hope you enjoyed following Darcy and Pippa's journey! If you did enjoy it and would like to keep up to date with all my latest Bookouture releases, including future books in this particular series, please sign up at the following link. When you sign up you will receive a free short story, *The Killer Wife*. Your email address will never be shared and you can unsubscribe at any time.

www.bookouture.com/daniel-hurst

I hope you loved this first book in *The Perfect Nurse* series and, if you did, I would be very grateful if you could write an honest review. I'd like to hear what you think!

You can also visit my website where you can download a free psychological thriller called *Just One Second* and join my personal weekly newsletter, where you can hear all about my future writing as well as my adventures with my wife, Harriet, and daughter, Penny!

Thank you,

Daniel

KEEP IN TOUCH WITH DANIEL

Get in touch with me directly at my email address daniel@danielhurstbooks.com. I reply to every message!

www.danielhurstbooks.com

 facebook.com/danielhurstbooks

 instagram.com/danielhurstbooks

ACKNOWLEDGEMENTS

Thank you to my editor, Natasha, for helping me shape this story, which has gone on to be one of my most enjoyable to write. Thank you also to the rest of the Bookouture team for all their hard work getting this story out into the world. Last but not least, to my wife, Harriet, for putting up with me discussing plot points with her while we juggled having a baby in the house!

PUBLISHING TEAM

Turning a manuscript into a book requires the efforts of many people. The publishing team at Bookouture would like to acknowledge everyone who contributed to this publication.

Audio
Alba Proko
Melissa Tran
Sinead O'Connor

Commercial
Lauren Morrissette
Hannah Richmond
Imogen Allport

Cover design
Lisa Horton

Data and analysis
Mark Alder
Mohamed Bussuri

Editorial
Natasha Harding
Lizzie Brien